The London Lover Series

BECOMING Us

Published by Stars Hollow Publishing
ISBN 978-0-9903252-6-0
Editing by Heather Banta www.linkedin.com/in/heatherbanta
Cover design by Amy Daws
Cover photography by Megan Daws
Author Photograph by Megan Daws
Cover models Rachel Lausen and Eric McLaughlin

Dedicated to my friends and family
for supporting me on this writing endeavor.
I couldn't do this without you.

CHAPTER ONE

Before starting college, I'd never considered myself much of a coffee drinker. It tasted like cigarette butts to me and burned my mouth. Ick. Why did people like that stuff? If I ever needed a kick-start, I'd grab a soda. That actually had a *good* taste.

My first year at *K-State*, that all changed. Coffee became my savior. I had no idea coffee's caffeine was so much stronger than soda's. And holy crap, school is hard. Managing classes, complete and utter freedom away from parents, and a budding new social life have proven to be more than I can handle. I quickly realized coffee was the only thing that gets me through tests, papers, midterms, finals, last minute cramming—you name it. Coffee is now a vital necessity of my day-to-day life.

I still remember ordering my first cup at the University Plaza dining center. I was a green-behind-the-gills freshman and had no clue what I was doing. I just knew that the shower I took that morning physically hurt my skin and I needed something—anything—to get through the day. I had a huge slug of classes and a raging hangover. I needed to find the will to live.

I walked up to the counter and repeated something I'd heard my dad say when he ordered coffee: "Black." I had no idea what it meant, but sure enough, the person behind the counter handed me a cup of hot steaming liquid. I must have fooled him.

I don't especially like the taste of plain black coffee, but I look at it like I look at beer. Beer tastes terrible, and those that try to tell me otherwise are simply lying to themselves. I drink beer for the sole purpose of getting a buzz or getting drunk. Definitely not for the taste.

The familiar ringing sound of the door at Chaz's resonates in my ears as I enter the convenience store. "Hey Alex," I say with a small wave, heading over to the huge coffee dispensers next to the fountain pop machines.

"What up, Finley?" he drawls in his southern accent, not even bothering to look up from his cellphone. "SHIT!"

"What?" I ask, stopping suddenly in front of the counter.

"I'm trying to get more power gems. Do you play *Bejeweled*, Finley?" he asks, pushing his beanie hat back and looking at me seriously.

I smile, "No, sorry, I don't," and continue walking toward the coffee.

"Pshh, loser," he scoffs, hunching back over his phone and turning his back on me.

I look back at him incredulously. "You're the one swearing over digital jewels at eight in the morning," I reply, laughing slightly.

I smile to myself at Alex's accent. There are quite a number of people at *K-State* from the more southern parts of Missouri and Kansas, and they most definitely have thicker accents, like Alex's. My hometown of Marshall is almost smack dab in the middle of Missouri, so it's a tossup whether or not people from my area have an accent. I don't have the drawl most of my classmates do, but certain words do seem to have a mind of their own on their way out of my mouth.

I push down the tab on the dark-roast blend and begin filling my mug, glancing around as I wait for the cup to fill. It's the summer before my senior year, so there are not nearly as many students around. I love Manhattan in the summer. Without the entire student population mulling around, it's quiet and peaceful.

Chaz's C-Store is only a two-minute walk from where my apartment building sits. My roommate Angela and I are both permanent fixtures here, which is why most of the counter clerks know us by name. I've been walking to Chaz's every morning for over a year now to get my daily cup of coffee. My morning wakeup routine isn't just the coffee. The refreshing morning walk to get my fix really starts my day off. I need the fresh air to wakeup. I crave it.

The bell of the door sounds again and my heartbeat increases instinctively. I know who it is before even looking. Not wanting to deny my body what it so badly wants, I look up and see one of the most gorgeous men in all existence. Jake LeShae. Jake LeShae, oy— just his name uttered in my head makes me weak in the knees.

Okay, so maybe I don't just walk to Chaz's for the coffee.

Jake walks toward me with his familiar saunter I've literally had wet dreams about. I never even knew wet dreams were a possibility before I laid eyes on Jake LeShae. He's a senior like me, and a point guard for *K-State's* basketball team. Biggest point guard I've ever seen. I played basketball in high school, and never saw a man his size dribble a ball the way he does.

He smiles at me, like he has everyday for the past three weeks. I smooth back my messy brown ponytail and my eyes glance up into his shortly buzzed, nearly black hair. His presence is overwhelming as his height looms over me. I love tall guys. Growing up, I was always the tall girl in class. I spent the majority of my pubescent years towering over all the boys in my small town class—and I hated it. I topped out just under six feet by my sophomore year. And honestly, nothing makes me feel less womanly than dating a guy shorter than me.

Standing next to Jake, I feel every bit the woman I am. He is panty-dropping tall and gorgeous. I bet he towers a good six inches over me.

I stop hands from messing with my ponytail, silently chastising myself for feeling self-conscious. I'm wearing a pair of black running shorts and a neon green racer-back tank. Thankfully, I had the foresight to put on a bra.

This silent game of flirting we've been playing for nearly a month now is the epitome of the word *bittersweet*. Bitter because we don't speak—sweet because I don't ever want it to stop.

The first day I ran into him, I counted myself lucky for laying eyes on him. Then for the next four days in a row, we both continually went in to Chaz's at the same exact time for our morning refreshments. I would have cried *stalker* if he was anyone else. But he was Jake LeShae: Basketball legend, sex on a stick, and downright offensively good looking. Can I just say his name again for good measure? *Jake LeShae.* Damn, that feels so good.

He always comes in and purchases a 32-ounce fountain drink— half *Sprite,* and half *Powerade.* Not that I'm paying attention or anything. I realized by week two that we were on the same summer schedule. It was way too frequent to be a coincidence. He brings his own cup in, just like I do. The fact we've never addressed our commonality is weird and exhilarating. There's that bittersweet feeling again. Every morning I anxiously wonder if today will be the day one of us speaks to the other. But part of me doesn't ever want to say anything to him. I don't want to ruin this silent and sexy cat and mouse game we've got going on.

The ice plops loudly into his thick plastic cup. He glances over at me as I snap the lid down on my coffee. His eyes drift down my body and squint ever so slightly. I feel myself squirm under his perusal. I bite my lip, feeling frustrated at myself for drinking black coffee—if I used cream and sugar, I'd have an excuse to stand here longer, breathing in his fresh shower scent. *God, he smells so good.*

He smiles at me and I smile back—like we always do. Every. Single. Day.

"Hey," Jake says, looking at me speculatively.

Holy shit! He just spoke to me!

"Hey," I reply, trying to stop my voice from squealing with excitement. I really need to calm the flutters screaming inside my abdomen right now. Keep cool, Finley. Keep cool.

"I've seen you in your window," he says, and quickly scowls and shakes his head. I see a red coloring creep up his olive skinned neck. "I mean, my window looks into your window." He frowns again, even further, and sets his cup down deliberately. "Jesus, I'm sorry. This is coming out so creepy." He looks at me apologetically.

"What are you saying?" I look at him in wide-eyed wonder. If any other person was saying this stuff, I would either be running for the hills or screaming in their face for being a disgusting pig. But this is Jake LaShae.

"You live at Wildwood, right?" he asks, composing himself.

"Yeah!" I reply, way too brightly.

"I just moved there at the beginning of summer. I'm Jake." His expression says he's assuming I know who he is.

"I know who you are," I blurt, before thinking. Jesus, Finley. You could have at least played it cool and acted like you didn't know him.

He smiles cockily at me.

"So, what about my window?" I ask.

"Oh, um," he says, and grasps his cup and snaps the lid in place. "I think my apartment is directly across the parking lot from yours. I've seen you in your window before. Not naked or anything!" he finishes, looking nervous again.

"Thank God," I reply, not knowing how to respond to that. He looks down toward my chest, briefly, but then back up at my face. "So, um, *Sprite* and *Powerade,* huh?" I bite my lip again, feeling so incredibly lame. I'm biting so hard I've picked an area of skin completely raw. But I can't help it. I'm desperate to keep talking to him and I need to change the subject from creepy window-peeping.

He shrugs and says, "Yeah, it's my coffee." He gestures his cup toward mine.

"Cool," I reply, tipping my cup toward him in response.

Cool? God, this is ridiculous. I'm better than this!

"Campus is pretty dead in the summer, huh?" he suggests.

"Yeah, peaceful. I sort of love it," I start to take a sip of my coffee, but stop suddenly, realizing I'll burn my mouth if I take a drink right now. There is nothing I hate worse than swollen taste buds. Okay, there probably are things I hate worse. Like Ebola. That would definitely be worse.

"I've never been this close to campus during the summer before. I always go back home and live with my parents."

"That's cool." If I don't stop saying *cool* right this damn second I'm going to punch myself in the face.

"I've been seeing you here almost every morning for a while now, so I thought it was time I said hey."

"Huh," I reply, and laugh awkwardly.

"I didn't catch your name," he says, leaning down slightly, like he's trying to hear me. I catch a whiff of strong, manly-scented cologne.

"Fin...ley. Finley, or Fin...either's fine."

"Finley. Cool name. So, what are you doing this summer that has you coming to the gas station every day?" he asks, shoving a straw into his cup.

"I work in one of the IT offices on campus. It's open year round for faculty and summer students. It's just a computer lab, pretty much."

"That's cool. I'm doing an internship at a sports chiropractic clinic."

"Sweet, are you studying to be a chiropractor?"

"No. My major is sports management, but I still have two more years of school left. I red-shirted as a freshman. I play basketball."

"Yeah, I've seen you at a few games."

"Cool, you go to a lot of games?" he asks with a small hint of arrogance.

"Um, yeah, well...no. Not really I guess. I went to one, once last year," I stammer, and set my coffee down to adjust my ponytail nervously. "See, I'm not much of a sports or fitness person, per se. I played basketball in high school but was terrible. I rode the bench a lot. The only bit of exercise I ever get is my morning walk here every day. Unless you count dancing at the bar."

He nods thoughtfully, so I continue. "So yeah, my roommate says I waste so much money getting coffee here every day, but the way I see it is that it's cheaper than a gym membership, so…" I trail off and he looks down, evidently deep in thought. "Anywho, I only went to that one game because they were giving out free t-shirts to anyone that sat in the student section," I pause. "Yaaay," I finish dumbly, balling my hand into a fist and pumping it above my head in semblance of a cheer.

Jake laughs, revealing stunning white and perfect teeth. The corners of his lips turn down as he attempts to compose himself.

"You're funny, huh?"

I shrug.

"But not much of a sports person," he adds. "What do you like?"

"Oh, you know, the usual things: parties, social gatherings, reading, and watching movies."

"What kind of movies? Chick flicks?" he asks, heading over to the counter.

I follow behind him. "No! I love comedies mostly. I mean, I don't hate the chick flicks. I am female after all." I set my mug down in front of Alex, who looks at me with a slight glare that confounds me.

"That's cool. We should hang sometime. Campus is so dead

right now and my roommate isn't here this summer, so I'm bored out of my mind over there." Jake hands over some cash and Alex gives him his change.

"Um, sure! Sounds good! Do you..."

"I know where you live, I'll stop by sometime," he says, casually walking backwards toward the exit. "Catch ya later, Finley," he says, pulling on his straw as he exits.

Damn, he looked so cool doing that. I scrunch my eyebrows trying to decipher what just happened. I look up and see Alex still glaring at me.

"What the hell, Alex?"

"It's just lame," he says, with a sneer.

"What's lame?" I ask, my voice rising in pitch.

"That you don't play *Bejeweled*. 'Cause it's awesome. You should see me play the lightning level one time. Or play in poker mode. It's magical. I guarantee you'd be hooked."

"Um, I think I'm good," I reply flatly. Man, this guy is really serious about his games.

"You'll never be good without *Bejeweled* in your life, *Finley*," he says, speaking my name more forcibly than necessary as he hands me my change.

I tuck it into my pocket and step away from the counter.

"You need to get a better hobby, Alex. That digital game is frying your brain."

"Your brain...is ruined...without...jewels!" he sneers, shaking his head.

I make a hasty exit. *Jesus. I think I might go de-friend Alex on Facebook. That just got really weird!*

I gingerly sip my coffee and mull over the conversation I just had with Jake. Was that a date he asked me on? Or just a friends thing? Did he seem flirty when we were chatting? Maybe he's just bored and being nice? He did mention not having any roommates or friends around this summer, so that's probably all. He just needs someone to kill time with. I better not read too much into this. It's probably nothing. It's probably not even going to happen.

***

CHAPTER TWO

"ANGELA!" I shout, animatedly bounding into our apartment. "Jake LeShae was at Chaz's again and he finally spoke to me! He basically told me he wants to marry me and take me on a surprise honeymoon, but he won't tell me where. He'll actually have to pack my suitcase because he refuses to even tell me what the weather will be like because he just loves surprising me that much. Can you believe it?" I finish, dramatically throwing my arms up into the air.

"What the hell is happening right now?" Angela asks behind the foggy glass shower door as I sit on the toilet lid and take a drink of my coffee.

Cringing at the slight burn, I reply, "Yeah! He spoke to me…finally!"

She cracks the shower door open and aggressively bats soap out of her eyes. "Repeat all that you said before because I couldn't even comprehend it."

"You mean, the part where he's going to plan our honeymoon and pack my bag for me because he refuses to tell me where we're going, and just loooooves surprising me?"

"Nope. Got it now. You're an idiot." She closes the shower door and I sigh in response.

"I said *basically*," I mumble into my coffee cup.

"Does *basically* mean he actually spoke to you, or is this all made up?"

"No! He really did speak to me!" I retort, pulling my legs up to my chest.

"Cool! What did he say? For real this time."

"He said we should watch a movie or something sometime."

"Like a date?" she asks.

"I don't know. I can't decide. Probably not. But what if it is? How cool would that be? I've been pining over Jake ever since I saw him play that one time."

"Not pining enough to go to any more games, apparently," she murmurs softly.

"I heard that! Don't act like you like sports either!"

"I do like sports!" she screeches.

"You do not! You just pretend because Luke likes to go to games." Luke is Angela's latest and greatest. Angela has a tendency to date the biggest douches. Luke is no exception.

"Oh screw you, Finley! You don't know that for sure. I actually really like sports. You don't know everything about me!"

"A, I love ya, but you hate sports. Just admit it. You'll feel so much better."

"I'll admit that as soon as you admit you like sushi!" she says, popping her head out the shower door again.

"For the last time, I don't like sushi! It's fishy-tasting, and raw, and terrible. I don't and won't ever understand why people like it."

Angela rolls her eyes and closes the shower door again. Damn, I love Angela, but I've been living with her for four years straight now, and we've really learned how to push each other's buttons. For whatever reason, she is relentless in her quest to get me to admit I like sushi. She gives me shit about it all the time. It's a ridiculous bit she has continued since freshman year.

As much as she drives me nuts, we both know we hit the jackpot with randomly paired roommates. A few of the other girls we befriended freshman year got paired with some real doozies. Angela and I had an insta-friendship, even though we were polar opposites.

Angela was raised in a hard-core political family in the heart of Kansas City. Her father ran for Kansas State Senator when she was in high school. He lost, but he continues working in politics as Chief of Staff for the Governor. They are loaded and live in a mansion near the Plaza. I've been there before and about died of shock when a legit butler opened the door to greet me.

It was very different from my up-bringing on a small acreage in Missouri. Honestly, I don't even know who my parents voted for in the last presidential election.

When I met Angela and her parents on moving day, she was prim, proper, and quiet. She was wearing khakis and a button-down blouse. The picture perfect politician's daughter. I worried my freshman year was going to be a total bore, but as soon as her mother and father kissed her goodbye, she closed our dorm room door, turned around, and said, "Kay, first we need someone to buy us booze, and then we need to befriend someone connected to the party network here. Start drinking water now. If we start hydrating, our hangovers won't be nearly as bad tomorrow."

I knew in that moment, my freshman year was going to be epic.

Angela says she was cheated a proper high school experience because of her father's political goals. She attended a private school and was only allowed to go to school-sanctioned events. She didn't have time for friends because her mother was always carting her from one school activity to the next. She said she was going to use college to make up for it. She still was anal at times and balked at a lot of the crazy dumb stuff that came out of my mouth. But eventually, the shock wore off and she started joining in on my particular brand of crazy.

"Well, you've effectively ruined my LaShae buzz. I'm going to go get ready for work," I grumble sullenly, annoyed that we went from talking about Jake LaShae to sushi.

"I love you and your delusions!" she shouts as I close the door behind me.

"Delusions my ass," I mumble.

I walk through the small dining area of our apartment and into my bedroom. Angela and I love the apartment layouts at Wildwood because our bedrooms are on opposite sides of each other when we walk in. Mine is on the left and Angela's is on the right. Smack in the middle is a grand area with a living room and a galley-style kitchen with a two-tier countertop.

We decorated it cutely for a couple of college students. A large black leather sofa sits in the center with its back facing the kitchen area. My picture frame collection has spilled out from my bedroom into the living room. Anywhere a picture frame fits, one sits. They are mostly filled with friends from high school and college, and some of my family, including my two nieces, Megan and McKinley. My sister Cadence is ten years older than I am. I was only eleven when she had her first child, so I grew up babysitting and am very attached to those two little girls.

Angela's parents gave us five red patent-leather barstools for the long breakfast bar area. Apparently, they were vintage and belonged to Angela's uncle, but her mother thought they were tacky. So, of course, we love them.

I close the door to my room and quickly grab my go-to summer clothes: A pair of denim shorts and my purple *K-State* faculty polo. I finish getting ready, taking a quick look in the mirror, and I'm pleased my aqua eyes seem perkier than earlier. Perhaps this is a Jake LaShae style glow? I tighten my long brown hair into my ponytail, and grab my purse and university lanyard, along with my college ID and keys, and head out the door.

"See you later, Angela!" I shout and hear a faint reply as the door slams behind me.

***

CHAPTER THREE

"You're late," says a voice from behind me as I unlock the lab.

I swerve around to glance at the same person who beats me to the lab every day.

"Sorry Parni," I mumble, and open the door. She storms past me with a huge backpack and a stack of books clasped tightly to her chest.

"Don't be sorry. Be on time," she bites at me with a thick Indian accent. She drops her backpack down to the floor next to the computer she uses everyday.

Of course, it has to be the desk closest to mine. I sigh, not even considering fighting back with her. It's not worth it. The girl is wound tighter than a drum. Parni is an exchange student from India currently working on her masters. And she has no problem reminding me of that every time I'm even one minute late. I don't know how hard getting a masters is, but school has never been that tense for me. Sure, I had moments, most of them during my freshman year. I was an idiot and let some counselor talk me into an 8 a.m. class Monday through Thursday, which almost killed me. I missed way more than I should have, and even if I did show up, I was barely conscious. I was too busy enjoying my newfound freedoms with Angela to care about school.

But I found Jesus, and He saved me. And by Jesus, I mean coffee. Black—*like my soul.*

I boot up my computer that sits on a semi-circular desk to the left of the entrance. Straight in front of me are six long rows of computers, and the opposite wall is floor-to-ceiling glass windows overlooking part of campus.

Working in a computer lab is about as dull as it sounds. But it pays, and it allows me to get some homework done when idiots aren't coming up to me asking why the printer isn't working. *Like I know a thing about computers?* I'm just a warm body here to ensure the lab doesn't catch on fire.

I scored this job last year. This particular computer lab is in the College of Business Administration building. I had only ever taken one class here that was a prerequisite for my marketing degree. My senior year, the majority of my classes will be in the communications and marketing building.

I unzip my purse and pull out a new book I got in the mail the other day by *Marian Keyes.* It's an old one called *Watermelon*, but I got it used for a penny on Amazon. Can't beat that!

Just when I start getting into the book, my phone vibrates from inside my purse. I grab it quickly, and glance at the text.

Olivia: Party at my pad on the Saturday before school starts. Be there or be ugly.

I shake my head.

Me: Ugly is my Go-To. What's behind Door Number 3?

Olivia: Huh?

Me: Angela and I will be there.

Olivia: Oh, Angela too?

Me: Yeah, why?

Olivia: I just thought she'd be busy with Luke.

Me: He'll probably come too. Is that a problem?

Olivia: Yea, whatev. It's fine. This party is going to be huge. It's the last one before the students return.

"Can you please silence your phone? That vibrating is really distracting!" Parni snaps.

I look up at her incredulously. "Are you joking?"

"Do I look like a person who jokes?" she asks, scrunching her nose up in disgust.

"Good point. I'll silence it for you right away!" I sing at her cheerily after quickly typing a final reply to Olivia. I silence my phone and put it back in my purse. Parni isn't even worth aggravating. Honestly, when she snaps at me, I just find it really funny.

I feel slightly annoyed with Olivia's obvious lack of enthusiasm for Angela coming with me to the party, but I don't care. Angela and I are a package deal. She can just get over it.

Back when Angela and I were freshmen, we quickly befriended Olivia because she was an in-the-know upper classman that helped us find all the great parties. She was a bit snotty, and selfish, and always had an arrogance about her. But we tolerated it because we appreciated her connections and when it got down to it, we could find fun with pretty much anyone. And, bonus, she was 21.

Olivia graduated last year, but continues to live in a house just off of campus with Jen and Phil. Jen and Phil have been going out forever and I like them well enough. They are seniors too, and usually pretty fun to party with. I remember being surprised when she said she was going to continue living there after graduation. I just assumed it would feel strange to continue going to college parties when you're not a student, but that didn't matter to Olivia.

I wonder if Jake will be at Olivia's. He's never shown up at any parties at her place before, but summers in Manhattan are different. So many students go home for the summer, so the few that stick around end up finding each other. I wonder if he'll stop by before then. Maybe I can invite him to the party. That would be a perfect setting to hang out casually, without looking like a lovesick teenager. I just have to figure out which apartment is his first, and then maybe I can stop by and invite him.

I glance up and see Parni glaring at me.

"What?" I ask, feeling a bit uncomfortable because I have no idea how long she's been staring at me.

She shakes her head. "Even your thoughts are loud and distracting." Her lips purse up toward her large sloped nose.

"You gotta get a life, Parni," I reply, cracking my book open again.

"No shit," I hear her quietly mumble.

Huh. Parni has a soul. Who knew?

CHAPTER FOUR

After a long eight hours at the lab, I trudge home, buzzing at the prospect that Jake could be stopping by this week and I might be able to invite him to Olivia's party.

I go bounding into my apartment, feeling euphoric. I stumble upon Angela in the throes of a Downward Dog yoga position. Her black hair is fanning wildly around her on the floor.

"What the hell are you doing?" I ask, fighting a tremor of judgment in my voice.

"Yoga," she replies back, calmly.

"Why?" I ask, and she glances at me from between her legs.

"Because it's supposed to be good for you!" she replies. She stands up, placing her foot against the inside of her opposite leg.

"Says who?" I ask.

"People, the internet…*Justin Bieber.*"

I rip my lanyard over my head dramatically. "If the Biebs says it's good for you, sign me up!" I say sarcastically and rush over and join her, pressing my palms against each other, attempting to balance on one foot directly across from her. She laughs and loses her pose.

"Be honest," I say, staring at her speculatively and dropping my foot to the ground. "Luke told you to do this, didn't he?"

"No. I mean, he mentioned it, yes. He says it helps relax your aura and that my aura needs a boost. But I would have tried it regardless," she argues defensively.

I shake my head. I can't help the look of disappointment I'm giving her. Luke grates on my nerves. He has mastered the art of passive-aggressiveness in a ridiculous zen package. Douche, with a capital D—and Angela just takes it.

"Just don't, alright?" she frowns at me.

"Whatever A, I just don't know how you find these guys that love to boss you around."

"This is yoga, Finley! It's not like he told me I'm fat!" She places her hands on her narrow hips. Angela is petite and short. The thought of her being fat is ridiculous. Her small frame just furthers the extreme differences between us. I'm tall and curvy with an ample booty, and she's compact and tiny with zero muscle. I call her my little spinner, but I'm really just attempting to hide my jealousy. Angela is the skinniest fat girl I know. She eats horribly, yet doesn't gain a pound. You'd look at her and think she exercises nonstop to keep up with that tiny frame, but that couldn't be further from the truth. This Yoga is the most exercise I've seen her do…ever.

She lowers down to her knees and stretches her arms straight in front of her onto the floor, dropping her head between her arms. I flop myself onto the couch in response.

"What has you in such a cheery mood?" she mumbles against the floor, clearly attempting to deflect our conversation.

"Olivia is having a party in a couple weeks!" I squeal like a shameless tween.

She looks up briefly with her brow furrowed and says, "And?"

"And I wanna invite Jake!" I flash my eyebrows at her shamelessly.

"Oh, that's a good idea!" she says, joining in my enthusiasm.

I nod my head. "It'll be the last one they have before school starts, so now I just have to run into him again!"

"Which apartment is his?" she asks.

I can literally see the wheels turning in her brain. She's hatching a plan for me. I love this attribute in Angela. She attacks all areas of her life with a well-formulated and completely fearless plan. I just wish she would apply the same great logic to her own romantic relationships.

"I'm not sure. He said his window looks into mine."

"Creeper," Angela says with a look of disgust.

"A."

"F."

I scowl at her. I dubbed 'A' as Angela's nickname freshman year. She tried to give me the nickname 'F,' but I put a quick halt to that when we went to a frat party and a big bruiser of a dude heard us using our nicknames with each other. He laughed in that dumb jock chortle that I thought was something invented for TV, but there really are idiots who sound like that in real life.

The dumb oaf chuckled at us while we were waiting to fill our keg cups. "I get it, she's the smart ugly one who gets A's, and you're the dumb pretty one who gets F's," chortle, chortle, grunt, grunt.

Before I even had a chance to fully absorb his stupidity, Angela released holy hell terror on him. She said, "Hey dick-face! I can always fix ugly, but you'll never be able to fix the superior complex brand of stupid you've inherited from whatever dumb-ass redneck, hillbilly-holler family you come from."

She then smacked his beer out of his hand and stormed off. I followed with my tail between my legs, ashamed that I said nothing. The look on that guy's face was utter shock and stupor. He looked as though he didn't even understand what she said. The worst part of the whole situation is that Angela is beautiful. Her shiny black hair and striking nearly black eyes are a stunning combination. Her face is sharp and angular and dotted with several beauty marks. It's one of those extraordinary faces that belong on a runway as a high-end couture model. It's unique. Only a moron would be blind to the true beauty she is.

"Don't call me F," I reply, pouting slightly.

She smiles in response. "Let's go look out your window." She grabs my hand to haul me off the couch.

We enter my bedroom and she frowns at the mess of clothes scattered everywhere. She pulls back my black curtains and we peer across the parking lot to the apartment windows on the opposite side. My heart jumps in my chest when I see Jake clear as day, walking toward his apartment—shirtless.

"Holy shit, that's him!" I screech. I close the curtain as he wipes his forehead with the balled-up t-shirt in his hand. I press my back to the window and throw my arms out to block Angela's view.

"I didn't get to see!" she says, and bats my arms away to open the curtains. I grab her and rip her away from the window.

"Don't! He'll see you! Oh my God, his body is ridiculous."

"What? I *have* to see now!" she squeals.

"No! Oh my God, I'll kill you!" I grab her again and shove her away from the window to block her path to the curtains.

"Didn't you say he looks at you through his window? What's so bad about looking at him through yours?" she says, looking at me incredulously.

"Stop making sense in this scenario. It makes me want to punch you."

"We are acting like teenagers, Fin," she points out while physically trying to pull me out of the way.

"Angela, I'm not kidding. Don't! Please!" I look at her seriously, feeling panicky.

"Jeez, you really like him, huh?" she says, as she turns to sit on my bed. I instantly breathe a sigh of relief and relax my defensive stance.

"I don't know. I just…we've been doing this silent flirting at Chaz's for weeks now, and then out of the blue, he talks to me. I don't want to do anything to screw it up." I walk over and sit next to her. "I gotta play this right."

She smiles and nods her head smugly at me.

"Don't give me that look, okay? I'm gonna give it a day or two and if he doesn't come to me, I'll consider seeking him out."

I want to invite him to Olivia's party, but all I can do right now is picture a future with this gorgeous man. We'd have beautiful, tall, brunette babies. I already have the perfect picture frame in mind for our first photo together. Jesus, I'm insane. I have to slow my thoughts—or I'm going to enter stalker status.

"Okay. I can accept that plan. I'll leave it alone for a day or two," she says, leaning back and getting comfortable on my bed.

"Don't get comfy, I have an assignment coming from Val, and you have yoga to get back to."

"Harhar," she replies, and saunters out of my room.

I change out of my purple polo and slip into a loose pair of cotton shorts and a cami. I'm physically forcing myself not to peek back out the window to get a better look at shirtless Jake. *Mustn't be a creeper. Mustn't be a creeper.*

To distract my thoughts, I get comfortable on my bed and crack open my laptop to see if Val has emailed my assignment yet. Val is the creative director for a marketing agency in Kansas City. I had an internship with the company last year and we really hit it off. She's been hiring me for freelance writing gigs ever since. The money is awesome and I enjoy the work. She's all but guaranteed me a position at her company when I graduate. My family is really proud of me. Kansas City will be the perfect place to head after graduation—a little close to home, yet still on my own. I'm already working in my field before even having my degree. That's pretty awesome if I do say so myself.

As I wait for Val's assignment to come in, my mind wanders back to thoughts of Jake. I should really try to prepare myself for disappointment. He might not stop by. He probably won't stop by. But then, there's always Chaz's tomorrow.

***

I have a horrible feeling when I wake the next day. I tossed and turned all night after Jake didn't stop by. I almost talked myself out of going to Chaz's today just because I really don't want to face the awkwardness. But Chaz's is *my* turf. Jake LaShae can stick it where the sun don't shine! I sure as hell won't let a *K-State* basketball god scare me outta the best part of my day.

I rake a brush through my long brown hair and slip into my bright neon tennis shoes and head out for my morning wakeup call. I glance over at Jake's window and all seems quiet, so I take a deep breath and continue on my familiar walk.

My heart jumps into my throat when my eyes collide with Jake's as I stroll into Chaz's. Jake smiles at me cockily. I can't stop myself from smiling back. He looks so hot dressed up in his slacks and button-down.

"Hey Finley," he says as I approach the counter with my coffee mug.

"Jake," I say, attempting to be cool but struggling because I can still smell the fresh soap scent from his recent shower. I instantly want to press my nose to his chest and inhale deeply.

"How's it going?"

"Good," I reply with a nod, glancing at him briefly. "Better after my coffee," I say, pressing the silver nozzle down and watching the steamy liquid drop into my cup.

He chuckles politely. "I was going to see what you're doing tonight," he says, smiling.

"I got nothing," I reply. Okay, maybe he's not blowing me off.

"Cool, I thought we could rent a movie. You want to?" he asks, shoving a straw into his cup.

I finish filling my cup and look over at him. Gosh, he's so beautiful. I mean, I've never seen a man so beautiful. His face is chiseled and strong. And his dark olive skin looks positively lickable.

Stop picturing him without his shirt on, Finley.

"That sounds wonder...uh...fun. Where at?"

Was I seriously just going to say wonderful?

"You wanna come to my place?"

Yes! Yes I'll marry you, Jake LaShae! *Contain yourself, Finley!* "Sure, I can do that. Which apartment number are you?" My internal voice is cheering at how cool I'm playing it here. Hearing him say he wants me to go to his place is seriously revving my engine.

"309," he says, and smiles cockily at me.

"What time?" I head up to the counter and he follows closely behind.

"What time do you get off?"

"Five," I answer and hand money over to Alex, who barely acknowledges our presence.

"Can you do 5:30? We can order food or something."

"That should be fine," I say, heading for the door.

He nods and briefly looks me up and down. "I'll see you later then."

"See you later," I say, bringing my coffee to my lips to take a sip before I turn and exit. *Shiiiiiit! My mouth! Way too hot! Way too hot!*

CHAPTER FIVE

The day at the lab drags on so incredibly slowly. Thankfully, I have a project to work on for Val, so that helps part of the day. The rest of the day, I spend obsessing over what I'll wear to a casual movie night with a University basketball dreamboat. Parni glares at me only eighty-three times today.

I don't want to look like I'm trying too hard, but I also don't want to show up in ratty yoga pants and a hoodie—my usual go-to. I end up stealing a neon blue tank from Angela's closet, and pair it with my shortest denim shorts. It looks casual, but still shows off my long legs.

When the clock finally clicks over to 5:30, I head over. Jake opens the door wearing a pair of loose gray breakaway pants and a tight black t-shirt. His body looks sculpted, yummy, and I just want to wrap my arms around him and squeeze.

"Hey," he says, and his eyes flash down to my legs. He steps back, letting me in the door.

"Hey," I reply, looking around his apartment. It's the exact same setup as mine and Angela's. They have a large brown sectional in their living room and no barstools at their high-top counter area. It's pretty bare. There's not a single photo or frame to be found anywhere.

"I hope you don't mind, but I picked up a movie. It's *Hot Tub Time Machine*. I figured we could pick it apart together. Have you seen it?" he asks, opening the fridge and grabbing two bottles of beer and handing me one.

I tear my eyes away from his backside and respond, "No, but I heard it's terrible."

"I know, but sometimes that's the fun of it right?" he smiles and twists the cap off his beer and then frowns, grabs my beer out of my hand, twists the cap off and hands it back to me.

"I'm up for whatever," I reply, taking a swig of the beer and hoping the alcohol will settle my nerves.

"Want to order Chinese, or pizza?" he asks, grabbing some takeout menus out of a kitchen drawer.

"Chinese," I answer, walking around his couch. I glance out the window that faces my apartment.

"Is this the window you creep on me through?" I ask, smiling saucily. It's a bold question and I know it, but to hell with it. It's my meager attempt at flirting.

He coughs and chokes slightly on his beer. He saunters over to look out the window next to me.

"Not creeping, just noticing, funny girl." He furrows his brows at me.

"Yeah, yeah. Tell that to a judge." I purse my lips to the side playfully.

"Oh, please," he answers with a sigh, throwing his arm over my shoulders and assaulting my senses with all that he is, and all that I want. I have to physically stop myself from turning my nose into him to get a deeper sniff. "It's so dead here in the summers. I've never been this close to campus in the summer."

I scrunch my lips off to the side. "So you say."

"Come on," he says, and slides his arm to my waist and guides me over to the kitchen. We make a few selections off the menu and he orders while I continue perusing his apartment. The bedroom door to his room is open and I glance in and see a big gym bag and a few basketballs spilled out on the floor.

"You're kind of a funny girl, aren't you?" he says, startling me as I peer into his doorway.

"Holy random, Batman!" I reply, not sure where that question came from.

"It just seems you like to joke. I've never really hung out with a girl that's funny before. You don't wear much makeup either, do you?"

I frown in response.

"I think it's sweet," he says, picking his beer up off the kitchen counter and making his way over to the couch. He settles down and I sit a couple cushions over.

"It's awesome that I don't wear much makeup?"

"Yeah. My ex used to just cake it on. It would always be on my pillow cases and stuff."

"Oh," I reply dumbly, now wishing I wouldn't have asked. The last thing I want to do is talk about exes!

"I do wear makeup sometimes, when I'm going out and stuff. So, not really when you see me. When you see me, I've just rolled out of bed pretty much."

He nods and smiles as he turns on the TV and starts flipping channels.

"What were you like in high school, Finley?" he asks, muting the TV and angling himself to face me. I squirm, slightly, feeling like I'm being interviewed for a job.

"I don't know. Kind of wild I guess—at least, when I wasn't in one of my relationships."

"You had a lot of boyfriends?" His eyebrows lift in curiosity.

"Um, I wouldn't say *a lot*—but enough. I'd always end up in a relationship and my friendships would fall to the wayside. It was kind of stupid actually. Then when I'd break it off with the guy, I'd go nuts with my friends again."

He smiles and glances down at my chest briefly before returning to my eyes. "Like how?"

I laugh. "Nothing too crazy. My best friend Leslie and I used to go to parties and stuff a lot. We'd always break curfew and get grounded." He grins at me. "She was a bad influence. Actually she lives overseas now. She did a semester as an exchange student in London last year and pretty much lives there off and on now. She has to leave the country every so often because of her work visa. I miss her like crazy."

"Interesting. Did you play sports?" he asks and looks at me seriously.

"Yeah, some," I reply and fidget under his suddenly serious gaze. "I played softball for a couple years in high school and basketball up until my senior year."

"Basketball, huh?" he asks, looking intrigued.

"I wasn't very good," I reply, feeling stupid for bringing it up. "I actually quit partway through my senior year."

"Why'd you quit?" he asks, scooting closer to me and taking another drink. The look in his eyes is so serious. It looks like he's weighing something seriously on my answer to this question.

I take a drink of my beer and wipe my mouth with the back of my hand before replying. "I guess I just wasn't that good. I loved playing, but didn't really have a lot of natural ability. I just wanted to party my senior year."

He nods thoughtfully, appearing to be contemplating something. "Do you feel like you tried really hard?"

I laugh awkwardly. "I guess. I mean, I went to open gym and played for fun in the off season. But I seriously hate exercise—I wish I was joking." He scowls slightly, and fixes his face to look pleasant again. "I think I took it seriously but it wasn't my life like it was for the other girls. I probably cared more about my friends than I did about the sport."

"I never had many friends," he says, taking a swig of his beer and looking down at his hands.

"Why not?"

"No time. My dad was my basketball coach and he drilled the sport into me as soon as I was able to walk. My oldest sister is in the WNBA actually."

"Really? Cool!"

He nods. "My older brother played college ball at a D1 college in Texas. Sports in my family is…" he pauses, and takes another drink.

I frown at the faraway look in his big dark eyes. This subject matter seems light in nature, but his face appears so serious. It's puzzling me.

"Let's talk about something else," he says abruptly. The silence growing between us feels charged and strange. I sigh with relief when there's a knock on the door and our food arrives, giving us something else to focus on.

Jake places the crates of Chinese on the coffee table and hands me a fork. I sit down on the floor to eat at the coffee table as he starts the movie. He sits on the couch and we continue eating while the opening previews play.

"You like previews or should I fast-forward them?" he asks, and I turn around to look at him as he takes a bite of an egg roll.

"Like! How else do I know what movies I want to see next?"

He smiles, satisfied with my answer, and we continue eating.

I lean back, rubbing my stomach appreciatively. Jake shifts over on the couch so his legs are surrounding me. I start to stand up but he gently pulls me so my back is resting on the couch between his legs. When his large hands begin rubbing my shoulders, I bite my lip hard, trying to quiet the crazy butterflies inside my belly.

"Does that feel good?" he asks in a low murmur. I can feel his warm breath on the top of my head.

"It does," I reply, closing my eyes and savoring the swift work his hands are making of my tense shoulders.

"Your hair is really shiny," he says, as he leans down and inhales deeply and continues massaging the tiny knots.

Holy shit, did he just smell my hair?

"Huh," I laugh, unsure how to respond.

"Come sit up here with me," he says, and helps me up. He sets a pillow on his lap, indicating he wants me to lie down. I am more than happy to oblige. As his fingers play with my hair, we continue watching the movie and I burst with anticipation for what may come next. I feel like such a child right now, but God, this man is so yummy, and these feelings of lust that I have for him are intense.

He laughs at several parts of the movie, and I laugh with him. We talk randomly throughout. It feels casual and fun. Sometimes he asks me a question and I have to ask him to repeat himself because I'm too distracted by my thoughts of where this is going. I've already determined I don't want to sleep with him right away. I've been burned by other guys and I do not want to go down that road again.

I've always had a tendency to gravitate toward athletes, in both high school and my early days of college. But it never worked out. I either got bored with them or I was a notch on their bedpost. I wouldn't call myself a slut, but I am definitely graduating college knowing that I've sowed my wild oats.

When the movie finishes, I sit up and stretch. Jake hops up and ejects the DVD.

"Well, we both have to work early tomorrow, so I suppose..." he trails off.

Um, okay? This feels strange. I'm not saying I want him to try to have sex with me, but this feels like a brush off. Last I checked, he was the one rubbing my shoulders and talking about my shiny hair.

"It was fun," I say, kindly smiling at him.

He smiles back, and walks me to the door. "Yeah, it was. Maybe tomorrow we can go shoot hoops at the gym. Would you be up for that?"

Shoot hoops, huh? Well, okay. That sounds promising. "Yeah, I could do that."

"Oh, let me get your number before you leave," he says, and strolls over to his kitchen counter and grabs his cellphone off the charger.

After punching my number into his phone, he smiles and pulls me into his arms. My head hits his wide chest in a tight hug. I inhale deeply, savoring the feeling of his firm muscles under his fitted t-shirt.

"Talk to you soon," he finishes and releases me.

I offer a dumb wave and turn to head across the parking lot back to my place. What happened there? Was that a date? An impromptu backrub sure feels like a date. But then the bear hug at the end of the night felt more like friend-zone material. I'm so confused.

My phone startles me as I reach my apartment. An unknown number is calling me. I click ignore. A second later as I enter my living room, my phone alerts me of a text message.

Unknown Caller: Answer your phone.

Frowning, I reply: Who is this?

Unknown Caller: Your personal masseur.

Me: What?

Unknown Caller: Finley, it's Jake.

I glance around for Angela and see her bedroom door closed, so she must have gone to bed early. I head into my room, close the door, and press send on the unknown number. I'm greeted with the beautiful sound of Jake laughing on the other end.

"I asked you for your number!" he says, still laughing softly.

"I just left your house! Excuse me for not realizing you'd be calling me mere moments after I left," I reply, unable to contain my happy smirk.

"Are you going to bed?" he asks, his voice suddenly sounding deeper and more intimate.

"I was planning on it."

"Good, let's talk each other to sleep."

"Talk each other to sleep?" I reply, my eyebrows raised.

"Yeah, I like talking to you."

I sigh, "Okay, Jake, let's talk."

Two hours later, we've discussed everything from our family pets to our favorite tennis shoes. My skimpy bra size even makes it into the conversation somehow. Okay, not skimpy, but my B-Cups could be a little bigger and I wouldn't complain.

The intimacy of our exchanges is surprising but exciting at the same time. I ask if I can call him back so I can brush my teeth, but he said he would brush his teeth at the same time. We set our phones down, brushed our teeth, and resumed our conversation in bed. I had to pee like a racehorse, but I sure as shit wasn't going that far with him yet.

We bid each other goodnight when I started yawning into the phone. He said to meet him in the weight room next to the gym after work tomorrow and we'd shoot hoops. Despite my yawning, it takes longer than usual to fall asleep. Damn, Jake LaShae makes me giddy as a schoolgirl. Is this really going to happen?

CHAPTER SIX

"You skank!" Angela's voice echoes in our bathroom as I'm showering for work.

"What?"

"I heard you talking on the phone at all hours of the night! I came out to pee and heard you! I know it wasn't Leslie because your phone plans do not cover international calls for over two hours."

"It wasn't two hours," I argue, clearly deflecting.

"Who was it? You were giggling like a loon!"

"It was Jake," I answer nonchalantly, just because I know this will piss Angela off—and that's just fun.

"Oh, '*It was Jake, she says casually.*' I thought you hung out with him last night? Why would you talk on the phone too?"

"I did, but he called me after I got home and we just kind of talked each other to sleep, I guess," I reply, rinsing the conditioner out of my hair. I feel silly telling her what we did. Saying it out loud makes it sound so lame!

"That's kind of strange when you live right across from each other. Why didn't you just keep hanging out if you were going to talk for two hours after?"

I frown, wondering the same thing myself. "I don't know. Jake's strange. I can't really get a read on him," I reply, and shut the water off. A towel lands on my head.

"Thanks," I mutter.

"Don't mention it. So, what? You think he's in to you?"

"I'm not really sure. There were moments when I thought it was going somewhere, but then he sort of changed direction. I have emotional whiplash!" I finish, wrapping the towel securely around my chest and exiting the shower. "There were times I felt like I was on a job interview."

"That's kind of strange. Maybe he's just quirky or something. Did you see him this morning?" she asks, perching on the top of the back of the toilet.

"Yep! Our morning routine is still intact."

"Well, did you make plans to see each other again?" she asks. Her dark brown eyes are wide and demanding, like she's growing tired of having to ask questions.

"We're shooting hoops at the gym after work," I answer, grabbing my comb out of the basket. I begin untangling my hair.

"Oooo, exercise. Are you scared?"

"No," I say, with a glare. "I played basketball in high school, A. Don't be a dick." She laughs in response. "Besides, it's not like he's going to make me do sprints or anything. I'm sure it'll be casual. God, if he wants to run, I'm out. No guy is worth that shit–hot or not!"

She rolls her eyes. "You'll be fine. Keep me posted!" she sings cheerily, exiting the bathroom.

I wish Jake would keep *me* posted on what the hell he wants from me.

***

Parni doesn't show up to the computer lab, so it makes for an incredibly relaxing day at work. I packed a K-State slouch bag with long basketball shorts, a tank top, and a sports bra. I'm anxious to see how my basketball skills, or lack thereof, held up since high school.

Just as I'm berating myself for not shaving my legs this morning, even though I just shaved them the night before, a familiar voice fills the nearly empty computer lab.

"Hungry?" I look up and see the famous Jake LaShae—well, famous in my dreams at least.

"Hey!" I smile brightly as he approaches.

"I come bearing food," he says, and sets a brown bag on my desk, and leans one butt cheek on the side. *Lucky desk!*

"That was nice," I say, smiling. I look inside the bag and smile at the familiar wrapping of *Wildcat Market.* Our favorite place to eat on campus was a part of our late-night conversation, and by the looks of it, he brought me my favorite BLT wrap. I look at him proudly.

"You're very trainable, aren't you?" I say, smirking.

"I was picking up lunch for myself and happened to remember you like those. No big deal," he says, and smiles sheepishly.

"Are you eating with me?" I ask, opening the wrap.

"Naw, I gotta go lift weights with the team in an hour. I prefer to eat after. But I'll watch you eat."

A tall blonde, who I recognize as one of *K-State's* volleyball players, walks into the computer lab. She comes in all the time, but I don't know her name. She never talks to me—she barely even looks at me.

She and Jake lock eyes and exchange an uncomfortable look. She pauses midway, looks around briefly, and then leaves. Jake's expression and demeanor turn steely.

I raise my eyebrows and can't help but ask, "Who was that?"

"An ex," he says, easily. "It didn't end well."

"Care to elaborate?" I ask, taking a bite of my wrap.

"We split up. She wanted different things, I guess. We were together almost two years. She's an icy bitch," he says, and grabs the paper bag and begins slowly tearing pieces off of it. His physical demeanor is casual, but I can tell he's everything but.

"So, it was serious, huh? What's her name?" I ask, stopping myself from eating anymore because this conversation just got tense.

He laughs bitterly and answers, "Janelle. And yeah, I'd say so. I wanted to marry her. My family loved her. I thought she was it." He shakes his head.

Jake LaShae, scorned by a woman. Who knew?

"How long ago did you guys break up?"

"Just before summer," he replies, glaring at the doorway like she's still standing there.

I feel a sinking feeling in the pit of my stomach. It's only been a couple of months since he was with a woman he wanted to marry! And he's being so open and honest about all this like it's a casual conversation with a buddy. My mind is screaming the word *rebound!*

"Hey, do you want to share a book for Martin's class?" Jake asks, changing the subject. Last night in our two-hour phone call, we discovered we have a class together first semester. It's the Civic Duty class required of all seniors.

"Sure, sounds good," I say, and begin munching again, trying to get a read on his sudden mood change. He seems perfectly at ease again. It seems odd, but I'm just going to roll with it. Talking about exes isn't high up on my priority list either.

Jake hangs out for another hour and we chat about the rest of our fall schedule. When the time comes for Jake to head to the weight room, he gives me a quick ruffle of the hair and leaves.

A hair ruffle? Really?

CHAPTER SEVEN

"Hey!" Jake says, seeing me outside of the weight room as he exits with four of his teammates following close behind.

"Hey," I reply, rolling the waistband of my basketball shorts down. I have several pairs of these long baggy shorts left over from my high school days. They aren't the sexiest things in the world, but they are appropriate for the sport.

A dark-skinned guy, even taller than Jake, comes running out of the weight room, shoves Jake from behind and pulls him down into a headlock. "Is this her, you little pussy?" he asks, rubbing his knuckles into Jake's short dark hair.

"Shut up, Emmet. You're a douche."

He releases Jake from his grasp, laughing happily.

He approaches me next. "You Finley?"

My heartbeat picks up speed as his eyes, and the eyes of four other supposed teammates, all stare at me.

I tilt my head sideways provocatively, "Who's asking?"

"Oh, snap! You don't know me? I'm only the starting center for *K-State*, girl. C'mon now, stop messin', 'cause I know you know me," he says, then turns around and slaps the hand of one of his teammates behind him. They all chuckle in response.

I keep my face composed. "*Oh, snap* is right! I do know you!"

"Yeah, I figured," he replies, with a knowing smile.

"You're that guy that puked at the Sigma Ki frat party last year!"

His face falls as a loud, raucous laughter erupts from Jake and the rest of the guys.

"That was you, right?" I ask, looking sweet and innocent. His jaw drops even further in shock.

"She burned you, E-Dog! That's a burn!" a short, bald, black guy says, slapping E's back and crumpling over in laugher.

Jake breaks away from the pack and throws his arm around me protectively. He smells sweaty but sweet—and damn it all to hell, I like it!

"E-Dog, is it?" I say, with my face deadly serious. "Sorry, I don't actually know your name. I just know you as the guy that who puked in the kitchen at the SK Homecoming party. It was right by the food, wasn't it?"

E-Dog shakes his head slowly as the other guys continue cackling loudly around him. "Damn, girl. You really know how to hurt a brother's ego," he says, and begins walking slowly away from the pack.

"She makes my ego feel great!" Jake beams, and watches E and the rest of the guys make their way down the hallway toward the exit. They all continue slapping his back and laughing.

Deciding he's been teased enough, I shout over to him right before he exits. "Bye Emmet Bridgewater—leading conference and all time career scorer center from Omaha, Nebraska," I yell, and smile up at Jake. I look back just in time to see Emmet's surprised and happy expression shining down the hallway toward me. I don't like sports, but I'm not an idiot. I'm hanging out with Jake LaShae. I *Googled* the team. Emmet was all over the sports headlines last year.

"Girl, you're fresh," he nods cockily at me and walks out backwards. "I knew she knew me, y'all. I knew she knew me!" he says, playfully shoving his teammates.

"You're going to get my ass kicked," Jake says with a laugh, and pulls me by my hand into the gym.

***

Before I know it, we've been shooting hoops for almost two hours. A light sheen of sweat has formed all over me. This is definitely the most exercise I've had since high school, but honestly, if Jake is the bait, I'll follow. He, on the other hand, looks no worse for wear. He's obviously in much better shape than I am. Not to mention, he's already worked out once today.

My skills aren't stellar, but they aren't horrible either. I can tell I'm not impressing Jake because he spends a lot of his time attempting to correct my apparently horrible shooting form. I feel slightly annoyed because he's taking this all so seriously. I assume it has something to do with his father being a coach. Coaching probably just comes naturally to him.

Eventually, I'm able to joke around and he relaxes and has fun with me. By the end, I'm a little better, but still nowhere near impressive. I'm just glad he didn't suggest we run. *Shudder.* This is enough damn exercise for the week.

He offers to walk me back to Wildwood, even though he has a team meeting soon. As we approach my door, I decide to grow some balls and invite him to Olivia's.

"Do you know who Olivia Montgomery is?" I ask, lightly touching his arm, directing his attention to me and away from the group of people congregating outside one of the apartment buildings a ways down from mine.

"The name sounds familiar. She graduated, right?"

"Yeah, she lives with some seniors though. They are having a huge party the weekend before school starts…if you're interested in going. We could…" I let the sentence trail off because I'm too embarrassed to flat out ask him to the party with me. We're in college—we don't really do party dates.

He nods and looks at me thoughtfully. His eyes appear to hold a deeper meaning than he's willing to say out loud but he shakes his head briefly and replies, "How about I meet you there with my teammates? I think Emmet would get a kick out of you, funny girl."

A sick feeling rolls over me, but I grit my teeth and smile through it. "Sounds cool," I lie.

We get to my door and he gives me a brief hug goodbye. I rush inside and can't seem to close the door fast enough. Did I just get shoved into the friend zone? Was he insinuating I date Emmet—or just being friendly? The words *friends* and *Jake LaShae* together, taste like acid on my tongue.

CHAPTER EIGHT

The next couple weeks, Jake and I get closer and closer. He starts picking me up in the morning to walk over and get our drinks at Chaz's. We get together a lot in the evenings, always at his place because his roommate is gone until school starts. Mostly we just hang out and watch movies or TV. He is constantly trying to get me hooked on ESPN—it's not working. He even brings me lunch a couple times a week, and usually sits in the computer lab and eats with me, despite Parni's obvious and blatant frustration.

I find myself working harder on my appearance just to get him to notice me more—anything to ignite our apparent *friendship* into something more. There's still definite flirting going on, but nothing more so far.

What's killing me is that he's doing all the sweet things a boyfriend would do, except freaking kissing me! We're still doing our nightly chats. In fact, we've both developed a habit of falling asleep talking to each other. Thankfully, we have unlimited minutes—I've often woken in the middle of the night to Jake's soft snores through my phone line. It's nice. Amazing even. I just want him to physically be in my bed!

And his body language—ugh! He's so close, and intimate, and comfortable with me. Touching me seems natural to him and I swoon every time. The scent he emits is like a drug I can't get enough of. I start to wonder if the only obstacle is the volleyball-player ex. Would I be considered a rebound if it's been less than three months since he broke off their two-year relationship? Especially since it was someone he wanted to marry. Although, a rebound would have to involve some type of physical contact beyond bear hugs, head ruffles, and back rubs.

I find myself obsessing over it every single night, yet I still can't find the courage to make the first move. I don't want to be *that* girl. Call me old-fashioned, but I still want the guy to make the first move. I want a guy to grab me and kiss me and take what he wants! I want the moon!

Our intimacy doesn't go unnoticed by our friends. Angela's become extremely immature, and makes obnoxious sexual gestures every time I'm on the phone with him. When I finally do hang up to yell at her, she rattles on and on about how we're going to end up married with a bunch of tall basketball-playing babies. Even Jake's teammates pick on us every time we're around them. They've taken to calling me wifey—or ball and chain. It doesn't seem to bother him, so that gives me a glimmer of hope. I do my best to laugh it off with him, but on the inside I'm screaming for something to happen already!

With Olivia's party approaching, I've now dubbed it as my chance for a pivotal point in my relationship with Jake. It will be where things change between us. Liquid courage will definitely help me find the balls to tell him my feelings. I thought my feelings were completely obvious, but if that were the case, he would wise up and freaking kiss me or quit hanging out with me. The fear of rejection keeps me from speaking up. But I'm changing that at Olivia's party.

CHAPTER NINE

"What are you wearing to Oldie Oli's?" Angela says, bursting into my room, wrapped in a towel. She flings herself onto my bed and watches me put my makeup on, sitting on the floor in front of my mirrored closet door.

Oldie Oli is the nickname, Leslie, gave Olivia when she first met her. Leslie was my childhood best friend back in Marshall. She grew up on a dairy farm near my family's small acreage, and we got into all sorts of trouble together. Leslie was always my one friend who never held my boyfriend status against me. If I was deep into a relationship, she never complained about my absence. We always picked right back up where we left off. I always tried to make at least some time for her, no matter who I was dating.

Leslie went to college in Missouri before doing a semester as an exchange student in London. She shocked a lot of people in our small town when she dropped out of school and moved there permanently.

Leslie is like a wild, fun, and crazy storm that lights up a room. She has this amazingly thick, auburn hair. She's always saying the most outlandish things—I laugh constantly when I'm with her. We were freshman when she dubbed Oldie Oli as Olivia's nickname. She was visiting me at *K-State*, and the first time she met Olivia, she asked her if she was an alternative student. Apparently, Lez thought Olivia looked a lot older than the rest of us, but in reality, she's only two years older. That's Leslie though, she doesn't hold back. Olivia was none too impressed, so we do our best to avoid her every time Leslie visits.

"Speaking of Leslie, she's going to come visit next week!" I offer brightly turning back toward the mirror to continue my makeup application.

"Really? She's back from London?" Angela asks, looking equally excited. She and Leslie get along swimmingly.

"Yeah, she just got home. She's here for a few months trying to reconnect with her parents because there's been some family drama or something. She says she needs a break from them. She'll be here the first week school starts. It's just for a night I guess, and then she's going back to their farm."

"Awesome! There should be some sweet parties going on, I'd think. Or at the very least, the bars will be packed. That first week everyone comes back is always wild."

"I know. I'm pumped!" I can't wait to unload on Lez about all my Jake drama. We've always told each other everything. Whenever one of us is in a mood or a funk, we force the other to empty everything in our brain—even the cracks.

"I'm so sad school starts next week. Summer here was so nice, wasn't it?" Angela says, flipping onto her belly with her feet swinging behind her.

"Yeah, it was. I'm just hoping this Jake thing takes a turn in the right direction tonight. I can't stand this uncertainty!" I'm approaching my senior year—I'm way too old for this high school bull crap.

"You have nothing to worry about. I've never seen a man as gorgeous as Jake, and a girl as beautiful as you, not be into each other."

"I hope you're right," I say with a sigh.

Gosh, I've really never been this nervous about a boy before. In high school, boyfriends came relatively easy. College isn't the same though. I'm too busy partying with my friends and sowing my wild oats, so I think I just feel a little out of practice.

"I'm always right. Now, back to more important things." She hops off my bed and begins riffling through my open closet door. "What are you wearing? Luke is going to be here soon to pick us up."

"Yippy skippy," I say flatly, turning my unimpressed gaze on her.

"Don't start, Finley. Please. I don't want to get into this shit right now. Let's talk clothes. That's way more fun."

I shake my head and bite my lip. Angela is a big girl—she can make her own decisions. After four years of living together, we've just become so engrained in each other's lives, we can't help but judge, comment, and referee life choices. I'll respect her request for now, but eventually, she needs to see Luke for what he really is.

I end up wearing a pair of soft leather leggings and a fitted black tank top. It's casual, but sexy. I add a little grey eye shadow beneath my eyes to get that smoky effect and then throw on some long electric-blue dangly earrings. My brown hair falls loosely down my back in soft waves. Angela ends up in a pair of skillfully ripped skinny jeans and a colorful print tank top with spaghetti straps. The color looks awesome with her striking black hair. The weather in Manhattan is warm in August, but the evenings cool down some the closer we get to September.

Luke shows up just as I'm throwing on a pair of high-heeled strappy sling backs. We walk together to Olivia's house. I'm biting my lip, trying not to be completely aggravated by Luke and his judgmental tone. The first thing he did when Angela came out of her room to greet him was shield his eyes and say, "Whoa, who left crayons in the dryer?" I saw Angela's face fall just slightly before she laughed it off like she thought he was the funniest thing ever. He is such a prick. She looks gorgeous—it kills me to see her with a dick like Luke. Even his name makes me shudder now. He is the epitome of douche-baggery in his dark-framed hipster glasses with non-prescription lenses. I know because I asked. He wears them because he thinks they make him look cool. They don't.

"Hey, sluts!" Olivia's voice shouts down the sidewalk as we stroll up to her large three-story blue house.

"You better be talking about Luke, because he's the only slut I see!" I yell up. Luke cuts me a look, and Angela laughs awkwardly, tugging self-consciously at her top.

"I've already been pre-gaming without you, so you gals have some catching up to do! Hurry up!"

There's a medium-sized crowd as we walk in, and I know in another couple hours, it'll be packed. Olivia's house is a plain, barebones old college house with bald carpet, old furniture, and putrid peach cabinetry. Nothing special. But that's what makes it such a great place for parties. It's big, open, minimal, and there's little to no fear of damage.

We follow Olivia into the kitchen where there's a keg of beer on ice and several bottles of liquor on the countertop. She lines up three shot glasses, completely ignoring Luke's presence behind Angela. I'd feel sorry for him, if I didn't hate him so much.

"Drink up, bitches! To getting fucked and fucked up…in no particular order!" She tosses the shot glass back and downs it in one fail swoop. She hands one to me and throws her arm around my waist. I eye her cautiously and deduce that she is already drunk. Her blue eyes look red around the edges, and her medium length brown hair is straight, but mussed, like she'd been thrashing her head around. Olivia is a good foot shorter than I am, and extremely busty. Despite her often-vulgar mouth, she really is a pretty girl. Her body is short, stocky, and uber toned. She was apparently a pretty serious gymnast in high school, and it shows. Her quads are bigger than my ass, which is saying a lot.

I've downed three shots and three beers so far, and the party is bumping. Angela and Luke retreat into the living room, obviously having had their fill of Olivia. I stick to the kitchen and laugh and drink with Olivia, Jen, Phil, and a few familiar faces I've partied with the past few years.

I keep looking around, in hopes of seeing Jake's tall, lean presence looming in the doorway, but he's nowhere to be found. I obsessively check my phone, which eventually causes me to bump into some random guy who spills his beer all over the floor. I casually apologize, barely acknowledging his face because I'm consumed with thoughts of Jake. I decide to follow Olivia outside for some air.

We push through the crowd of people on the front porch and stand out on the front lawn sipping our beers and chatting. When I realize I'm looking constantly up and down the street for any sign of Jake, I become frustrated with this desperate side of myself. It's after midnight and he hasn't shown or texted. Screw this. I'm partying.

Olivia joins her roommates by the side of the house for a cigarette. I haven't smoked a cigarette since high school, but right now, anything bad sounds good. That, and I'm feeling pretty hammered, so what the hell.

Phil hands me a cigarette and I inhale deeply, coughing at the sharp burning sensation in my throat.

"Easy Finley, don't inhale so much," Olivia says, laughing at me with her cigarette tucked between her lips.

I take a smaller puff and the burn is less intense, so I'm able to stifle a cough. The cigarette has an instant woozy effect, taking my already alcohol-induced buzz to a whole new level. I lean my shoulder on the house and continue fuming internally at Jake and the bullshit he's been putting me through the past few weeks. Honestly. Girls and guys just can't be friends. It never works. Someone's feelings always get involved, and this time, it's mine. My feelings have been involved since day one.

Jake is full of mixed signals. Touching me all the time, and calling me constantly. I don't think I've ever even been this close to my previous boyfriends, for goodness sake. But yet he doesn't do anything more. He's never stuck his damn tongue down my throat, so what gives? I'm so tired of this. I'm tired of his mixed signals. Tonight was supposed to be my big night. I was going to reveal everything to him and try to take this to the next level. Now, he's a no-show. I wish I didn't want him so much.

But damn it, it's so hard for me not to want a future with him. An official date even! We get along so well and have a lot in common. What could be making him hold himself back from me? I'm not a sexy volleyball player ten, but he did say I have nice hair. So he's noticing me physically in some capacity. *God, I sound pathetic.*

My ankle slightly rolls, and I stumble backwards with my cigarette firmly locked between my lips. I'm caught by a pair of large hands.

"What the fuck?" Jake's deep voice says, with an edge to it.

I right myself and turn around and pull the cigarette out of my mouth. "Jake! You made it!" I put my arms out to hug him. Damn, I shouldn't be so happy to see him. I want to be stronger than this. Less needy. But he looks so pretty!

"What the fuck are you doing, Finley?" he asks, grabbing the wrist of my hand holding the cigarette. He holds it far away from him and pins me with a look of utter repulsion.

"Partying. What do you mean?" I pull my wrist out of his tight grasp and look back at Olivia and Jen self-consciously.

He shakes his head at me, disapprovingly. "That is disgusting," he says, pointing to the half-burned cigarette in my hand.

I shake my head, preparing to explain I don't normally smoke, but before I can get a word out, he turns and stalks off back to the front of the house. I look back at Olivia and she just shrugs her shoulders at me.

I quickly step my cigarette out, and totter after Jake toward the front door. There's a mass of people huddled on the porch.

"Jake!" I yell, pushing past the people that so easily cleared a path for Jake LaShae, but don't seem to give a shit about letting me through. "Just stop! Will you talk to me?" I ask, as I approach the front porch. Just as I reach him in the doorway, he turns around, points an icy glare at me, and slams the door in my face.

The front porch full of people goes deathly quiet. I hear one random girl's voice giggling over the silence and my blood begins to boil. What the fuck just happened? Is he really this pissed at me for smoking? Demanding to know the answer, I throw the door open and storm down the short hallway to find Jake in the kitchen with a red *Solo* cup in his hand. His jaw is hard and fixed, like it's taking all of his effort to control himself.

"Mind telling me what the hell that was about?" I ask, loudly enough to have the people in the kitchen stop and look at me. I don't even give a shit. I'm drunk, and that was embarrassing as hell being scolded in front of my friends and having a door slammed in my face. So screw it, let's add more humiliating drama to the night.

Emmet and a couple of his teammates are standing around the keg, looking into their cups awkwardly. Jake shakes his head, obviously refusing to reply. My eyes rove down his body and take quick inventory of his appearance. Sexy-ass torn jeans and a blue button-down. Dammit, why does he have to look so damn irresistible? And why is he scowling at me right now? We should be laughing and having a great time—not shooting daggers at each other! It's after midnight and he just now shows up and he's acting like a dick. *Oh, hell no!*

"Come on, Jake! What? Nothing to say? You get all pissy and slam a door in my face, but you got nothing?"

He turns his dark eyes on me and I swear they darken even further. "Smoking is disgusting," he says flatly, and takes another long drink from his cup.

I glare at him in response. I agree that smoking is disgusting. But shit! I'm in college for goodness' sake. I'm not a regular smoker—I just wanted to do something rebellious. I was in a mood and it seemed like a good idea at the time.

I bite my lip, hard, relishing in the scrape of my teeth on my tender skin. This friend-zone bullshit has my mind reeling. He's been jerking me around for weeks now, and suddenly he's going to show up to a party and play the role of protective, disgruntled boyfriend. Fuck that. I haven't felt relaxed since Jake and I started hanging out. *I've had enough.*

"What's it to you anyway?" I ask him dramatically, swiveling my head on my neck with attitude. I cross my arms across my chest and tap my foot provocatively, waiting for an answer.

"You're better than that, Finley," he says, and his eyes glance quickly down my body and lock on my eyes.

God, this could make me laugh! *I'm better than that?* I'm good enough to not smoke but not good enough for him to ask out on an official date? That's rich.

"You don't know what I am, Jake. You don't know everything about me. And moreover, I'm *not* your concern." I purse my lips and shake my head back and forth, attempting to control the anger and emotion quickly knotting in my throat. He just humiliated me outside and I'm already feeling fragile from his lack of interest in me.

"We're nothing, right? You're not my boyfriend. I'm not your girlfriend. I'm just a girl. A girl you want to be good ol' buddies with, right?" I reach over and playfully punch his shoulder like I've seen his teammates do time and time again. This is so not how I wanted to admit my feelings for him. I played out this night in my head so many different ways. But he had to go and be five hours late and yell at me in front of a crowd of people.

He looks at his shoulder where I hit him and sneers with disgust. His eyes look up and glare down into mine. I thought he looked angry before, but he *really* looks angry now.

He doesn't reply.

"Nothing to say, huh, Jake? Got nothing? Okay then!" I shove past him to the liquor counter. "Excuse me, bud!" I tap his shoulder until he moves. I then nod for Emmet to get out of the way. I quickly pour myself a shot and down it, savoring the burn down my throat.

"Stop acting like this, Finley. You're being fucking stupid," Jake says, coming to stand beside me as I pour another shot. I grip the bottle tightly, shivering as his hot breath beats down my neck. My heartbeat picks up with his close proximity. I look back at him, and his dark chocolate eyes are narrowed on me. He grabs the bottle out of my hand and pins me with a death stare. "I'm not kidding."

I laugh incredulously, turning to face him. "Don't you get it, Jake? You have no authority here," I say, gesturing wildly at myself. "We're friends. That's it. But you know what? I don't have any other friends that would freak out on me the way you just did." My wide eyes flicker back and forth between his eyes and his mouth. "God, I'm tired," I say, with a huff of laughter. I grab a different bottle of liquor and turn to leave. I see Angela standing in the doorway of the kitchen, next to Olivia, watching the scene unfold. Emmet and the guys quickly clear a path to let me through. They appear quiet and solemn, clearly uncomfortable with the spectacle Jake and I are putting on. If I wasn't so drunk right now, I'd be mortified.

For good measure, I flip Jake the bird over my shoulder without even looking back. It's immature and juvenile, but damn it all to hell—it feels good. With the bottle of vodka in one hand, I wrap my free hand around Angela's arm and pull her toward the front door with me.

"You okay?" she asks softly in my ear.

"Get me out of here before I lose it," I reply, hearing my voice quake.

She grabs the bottle from me and sets it on the foyer end table, and with that, we're walking down the dark sidewalk back to Wildwood.

***

CHAPTER TEN

"I made the biggest ass of myself last night, didn't I?" I ask in a scratchy voice, waking Angela from her deep slumber next to me.

Angela rolls from her stomach to her back, scrubbing her hands over her face. "I wouldn't say you made an ass of yourself. You just said it like it is." She clears her throat and continues, "He had it coming, Finley. I know I've been putting pressure on you and joking about this going somewhere. But the way he behaved last night was bullshit."

I sigh, deeply, and look around my room. After we got back to our apartment last night, I rushed into the bathroom and threw up the contents of my stomach while Angela held my hair and rubbed my back. I'd love to say I was strong and stoic, but I wasn't. I bawled like a baby. I don't think there's ever been a time in my life when I didn't cry when I puked—even when the puking wasn't alcohol-induced. It's like my gag reflex is connected to my tear ducts. But it doesn't take a genius to know this Jake drama is eating me alive.

I vaguely remember asking Angela to spend the night with me. She snuggled in close, letting me feel the direct contact of her body until I passed out. I needed the close comfort of someone who loved me. This torture with Jake has just become way too much for me to handle, and I needed to know there was someone out there who loved me.

"I've lost him, haven't I?" I croak out, feeling a slight sting in the corners of my eyes as tears blur my sight.

She sighs heavily. "Do you even want him anymore?" She looks at me thoughtfully with her dark eyes drooping from lack of sleep.

I turn to look away from her and tears slip down my temple into my hair.

"Ugh," she replies, knowing my silence is as big of an admission as she could have received.

I hate myself for still caring about him. I can't even stand to say the words out loud because I'm so ashamed. But damn it, I do.

She shakes her head and the look of disappointment is torture. "I don't know, Finley. I wish you'd just forget about him and move on, but I know as well as anyone, no one can tell you who to love."

"What do you think he'll act like when I see him again?" I ask, rolling onto my stomach and making a pillow out of my arms.

"Well, you made a pretty big scene. But then, so did he. You were also really drunk. He might come around." She shrugs and rolls her eyes.

"You think I'm weak, don't you?"

"I'm not one to judge weakness when it comes to assholes. I have a baaaad track record." She sighs and picks at her cuticle. My eyes turn wide at her admission. She's never admitted to me before that she falls for assholes. This is a big deal!

"And in all fairness," she continues, "Jake isn't an obvious asshole. He's just weird. I can't figure out why he doesn't just go for you. Or just *do* something."

I could cry at that statement. I can't figure it out either and it's killing me and the little bit of self-respect I have remaining.

"You think I should go apologize?" I ask, feeling sickly nervous for how he'll react to seeing me.

"I don't think you have anything to apologize for," she says, flatly. "But you could at least go talk to him." She looks over at me speculatively, and pounces suddenly, poking me in the ribs.

"Ow! Don't! My head hurts enough—I don't need ribcage bruises added to it." She laughs and rolls away from me, looking like she's going to go back to sleep. "What happened to Luke last night?"

"Ha!" A bark of laughter erupts from her mouth.

"What?" I say, sitting up and grabbing my head as pain slices through my brain.

She sits up and faces me. "I actually did it, Fin."

"Did what?" I ask, feeling nervous about what she's about to tell me.

"I dumped him!" she says, excitedly.

"Oh my God," I reply, and whoop with laughter. She looks at me confused, and I explain, "I thought you were going to say you did anal!" I burst out laughing at her horrified expression and it takes only five seconds for her to join in the laughter.

"You are such a perv! Anal?" she says, smashing her side into me and playing with a strand of my wayward hair. "Never. Ick! No, seriously, it was crazy. He was flirting so obviously with this dumb chick from one of my poli-sci classes, and I'd finally had enough. That shit about my clothes last night. Ugh, you have no idea how bad I let it get with him. There was so much you didn't even see. You were right, Finley. He's a total douche diablo, and he's been like that way too long. Last night was the straw that broke the camel's back."

"How'd you do it?" I ask, wiping tears out of my eyes from laughing so hard. I glance down and notice I'm in pajamas I have no memory of putting on last night.

She smirks saucily at me.

"What?" I ask, my eyes turning wide.

"I texted him!" She reaches over and grabs her phone off the tall dresser next to her side of the bed. "Read!" She thrusts the phone into my hands and looks at me enthusiastically.

I scroll through the texts and see Luke getting angrier and angrier—threatening to come over and talk to her. She silenced him with threatening to sic me on him. I frown at that text thinking I must have looked like a maniac last night if it scared him away. And sure enough, he doesn't reply.

"Holy shit, Angela! Was I that scary looking last night?"

"You weren't taking shit from anybody, Fin! It was awesome."

I sulk briefly, feeling sorry for myself and the display I put on last night. "Where did this newfound strength come from?"

She eyes me seriously. "It's not newfound, Fin. I've always been strong. I just don't always assert it in my relationships. And when I left with you and he didn't follow or even call to check on us, I don't know. I don't need someone like that in my life. And watching you go off on Jake last night just made me feel like I could do it!"

"That's great!" I say, and pull her into a hug.

"Yes, it is great. I don't know. I think, growing up, I always felt like I needed these certain guys in my life—poised, perfect, assholes. Ick! I don't know why the hell I think I need to find someone like my father. I'm so done with that life."

I smile at her. "I'm really proud of you, A." She begins to shake her head, attempting to deflect my serious and sincere compliment. I put my hand on her leg. "I'm serious. I'm proud of you."

She conceals a small smirk and I see her shoulders rise fractionally with confidence. "Next guy I date is going to be someone that peaks my interest. Not someone I think would act proper at a political event." She shakes her head in disbelief. "I will say though," she starts, turning her wide dark eyes on me, "It didn't take me being hammered to speak my truth!" She clears her throat pointedly.

That sinking feeling comes crashing back. "Yeah, alcohol does things to me, doesn't it?"

"You're telling me. What's your plan?" she asks, standing up and mussing her hair.

"I'm gonna go over there, I guess." I glance at myself in my closet door mirror. I look like death warmed up twice.

"Well, don't grovel. It's beneath you, Finley. You're stronger than that." She looks at me kindly and I grin in return. "Good luck," she finishes, exiting my room.

"Thanks, I'm going to need it."

CHAPTER ELEVEN

My nerves feel electrical as I walk across the parking lot toward Jake's door. The same door I've come in and out of so many times these past few weeks. I have to fix this. As annoying as Jake's mixed signals are, he didn't deserve to be publicly humiliated in front of a crowd. It's obvious now he doesn't want me for a relationship, so I need to settle for just being his friend. As sad as it makes me, I'm not ready to lose him completely.

I smooth down my thin gray hoodie and pull it over my daisy dukes. I take one quick breath and knock, feeling millions of anxious sparks firing in my abdomen. I hear the TV on, so I know he's here. Oh, God, what if he doesn't answer?

Just when I'm trying to come to grips with the idea that he may not want to see me, his door flies open, revealing a deliciously-rumpled looking Jake. He's wearing a pair of grey sweatpants and a white V-neck undershirt. Seriously, does he have to look hot in even sweatpants? As if having a mind of their own, my eyes drink in the tall, broad sight of him.

"Hey," I say, and jam my hands into the front pouch of my hoodie.

"Hey," he says, looking past me out into the parking lot at nothing in particular.

"What are you doing?"

"Nothing. I just woke up from a nap a little bit ago. I'm just watching some TV now." His voice is flat. Detached.

"That's cool. You have practice today?" I ask hoping to warm him up.

He shrugs his shoulders. "Weight training, yeah."

I look into his dark eyes, hoping to see a glimmer of friendliness, but I'm only greeted with indifference.

"Jake," I start, but he cuts me off before I can finish.

"I'm sorry, Finley," he says with a sigh and I look up at him confused. "I shouldn't have freaked on you like that."

"I'm sorry!" I reply, dubiously. "You didn't deserve half the shit I said to you. I was drunk and I didn't even know what I was saying…" I trail off, knowing what I'm saying is a total cop-out, yet somehow I can't help myself. At this point, I just want to minimize the honesty of my feelings last night. My ego demands it.

"Yeah, you were downing shots like someone who'd just broken out of rehab. I know your tolerance…you should stick to beer in the future." He offers me a lopsided smile, and I smile back.

"Still friends?" I ask, feeling myself cringe at the sadness that word brings me, but I know I need to get over it. It's quite obvious it's all we'll ever be.

"Of course," he replies, laughing, and pulls me into his apartment.

***

"You ready?" Jake asks, as I open the door to a blast of early morning sunlight.

"Yep, you have our book, right?" I ask, quickly throwing my lanyard over my head and pushing my arms through my backpack.

"Got it," he informs, backing away from the door with me following close behind.

We walk together to our Civic Duty class. It's a 10 a.m. Monday, Wednesday, and Friday class, comprised of mostly seniors. Jake and I hung out the rest of the afternoon yesterday, and almost the entire evening. Angela texted me several times to see when I was coming home. I felt ashamed at how easily I let Jake and I slip back into our old friendly ways. Here Angela is, finally being the strong, confident woman I always wanted her to be, and I'm being weak and pathetic. I feel like the biggest hypocrite.

For whatever reason, I just couldn't tear myself away from his apartment. When his roommate arrived, I tried to excuse myself, but Jake begged me to stay for pizza. Then pizza turned into a movie, and a movie turned into couch cuddling, and before I knew it, we'd fallen right back into our old habits. That wasn't the first time Jake and I cuddled, but it was the first time I'd fallen asleep in his arms. *Dammit all to hell, I loved it.*

Jake tosses his arm casually around my shoulders as we stroll through campus. I try to ignore the looks we get from the other girls, because despite how this may appear, I know it's nothing more than just a buddy being chummy with his friend. I know this. But damn, why does he have to smell so good? As we continue walking to class, I silently berate myself for the tiny glimmer of hope I'm letting seep into my brain. Hope is what hurts when shit hits the fan. Hope can be a bitch, and I need that bitch to give me a wakeup call before it's too late.

We find Martin's classroom and quickly nab two desks right next to each other. I glance around and see Jen, Olivia's roommate, sitting across the room with another girl. She gives me a subtle head nod and I wave back in response. I'm certain she saw the ridiculous spectacle I caused Saturday night and I feel a brief moment of shame. Jake leans over and whispers some crack about asking her for a smoke. I shove him away, feeling grateful we're at least back to normal again.

Professor Martin comes in, addresses the class, and assigns us a project. We need to pair off with someone and come up with a list of questions about what it means to be a critical thinker in today's society. The questions are due by Wednesday, so Jake and I pair off and plan to work on them tomorrow night, since he has a night class later.

After class, Jake offers to walk me to the computer lab because I have to work until my 2:00 class this afternoon. When we arrive, I glance in and see Parni at her designated computer. I nod and smile up at Jake.

"Your best friend is still here," he says, glancing past me into the lab.

"I know, I thought maybe her schedule would conflict with my work hours. No such luck I guess."

He rumbles a soft laugh and tucks a piece of my loose brown hair behind my ear. "What do you want for lunch, the usual?"

I shy away from his hand lingering in my hair, feeling my protective shield rise. "You don't have to bring me lunch," I answer. I need to stop letting him do everything for me. It's too much. I can't handle it.

"I want to. Same thing I always bring you?"

I look deeply into his eyes and see nothing but a thoughtful friend. I nod, and he pulls me in for a bear hug. I watch him turn and stroll out of the building. Why am I so damn weak? I have to stop letting him get so close to me. I would have thought after my scene Saturday night, he'd back off and give me some space since my feelings were blatantly on display. But if anything, he seems to be trying to get closer. If I was confused before, I'm baffled now.

CHAPTER TWELVE

The following night, Jake comes over to work on our list of questions. Typically, we'd be at his apartment, but now that his roommate, Tayton, is around, he figures he needs to give him some space to get settled. Tayton seems nice enough. He's the basketball team's manager. When I first saw him come in the other night, I instantly thought of *Andrew Garfield*. He's definitely got that attractive nerd look down pat, whether he was trying or not.

I let Jake into our apartment and we pass Angela, sprawled out on the living room couch watching a movie. She looks pretty mopey, and my heart aches for her. Despite being proud of her strength in breaking it off with Luke, she's still grieving the loss of a relationship. I tried talking to her last night about how she's doing, but she was pretty closed off about it. If there's one thing I know about Angela, you can't push her to talk about her feelings. I can't ask her for the cracks like I can with Lez. A talks when A wants to talk—and not a minute sooner. She did eventually tell me her new goal is to stay single for a while and start feeling okay without the presence of a man in her life. I smile at her customary way of tackling every area in her life with a concrete plan of action.

Jake tweaks my sides as I close the bedroom door and I squeal loudly, "Don't do that! I'm horribly ticklish." I laugh, and bat his hands away, following him to my bed where the contents of my backpack are sprawled all over the top of my gray paisley comforter.

Jake smirks cheekily at me, and pulls his bag off to grab a notepad and pen. I'm happy to see playful Jake again. We've definitely put our fight behind us. We even seem to be entering into a newer, deeper part of our friendship that I'm really enjoying. But I'm mad at myself for enjoying it because it's only causing sparks of hope to fly inside of me.

He sprawls out on my bed next to me, stretching his long legs down the entire length of my bed. Gosh, he's tall. He's wearing a pair of loose basketball shorts and a grey *Nike* t-shirt. I catch him eyeing me thoughtfully, and squirm slightly. Wondering if he noticed me checking him out, I brazenly squint at him. He beams back like he doesn't have a care in the world.

"When's your friend coming again?" he asks, rubbing his chin like he's contemplating something.

"Leslie?" I squeak, completely unable to contain my excitement. "Tomorrow!" I haven't been able to speak to Leslie as much since she moved to London, and I miss her like crazy. If anyone can help me through this Jake confusion, it's her.

"Cool. We should take her to The Tank to dance or something. I'm sure it'll be packed full of students by now," he says, fumbling the edge of my comforter as we both settle ourselves into comfortable positions.

"Yes, that would be awesome. Knowing her, she'll be ready to hit the ground running as soon as she gets here."

"Yeah, The Tank will be awesome."

"Good idea," I smile thoughtfully. I love that he's thinking of my friend's visit and suggesting places to take her.

"You should go visit her in London for Spring Break maybe." He states, deadpan.

"Oh Lord, that sounds cheap!" I laugh, half-heartedly.

"You're always reading those London books. You should just do it." He shrugs his shoulders nonchalantly.

I smile at him again. During one of our many late-night conversations, I rattled on and on to him, way too much, about my love for British chick-lit.

"Maybe someday," I say, placating his idea but not really considering it.

"Maybe I can come with you. I've never been outside the United States. It sounds like it could be fun," he says, as he casually begins flipping through our textbook.

I beg myself, my body, and my brain to not read too much into that statement. Despite myself, my mind flashes to us touring the streets of London, hand in hand, as a happy couple in love. *Freaking hell.* A female's mind is way too imaginative. *Friends, Finley! Jake just wants to be friends. Stop doing this to yourself!*

I clear my throat. "So, we gotta come up with some questions on what being a critical thinker in today's world means to us," I say, sitting crisscross on the bed.

"You look cute today," he drawls, clearly ignoring my urge to start working. I look up in confusion at the husky tone in his voice.

His eyes look meaningfully into mine and I fidget and look away, quickly. I glance down at my outfit, trying to see it through his eyes. I guess I do look a little cuter than usual, but since classes aren't yet stressing me out, I make more time to get dressed in the morning. Still, it's a simple pair of salmon plaid shorts and a white off-the-shoulder top. "You know, I haven't seen you all day. It was weird," Jake finishes, pulling the shoulder of my top up onto my shoulder more. It slithers down instantly and he bites his lip.

"I know. Did you go this morning?" I ask smiling in response to his comment. My classes start too early on Tuesdays for me to make it to Chaz's for my coffee. I told Jake that on Monday and he pouted for a good five minutes.

"Yep, I went. You weren't there. It was a sad day," he says, moping, as he playfully trails his finger on my kneecap. "Where'd you get this scar?" His brow furrows as he looks at the white bumpy area of skin.

The tickling sensation of his finger outlining my scar sends instant shivers straight to my groin. I clear my throat. "I, um," I choke out. *Get your shit together, Finley.* "I wish I had a cool story to tell you, but honestly, I was just a klutz. I was driving a moped on Leslie's farm and wiped out on the gravel. It was nasty. I was like a freshman in high school I think. Just another part of my awesome and talented coordination!"

His laughter rumbles in his chest. He then spreads all five fingers across my knee and strokes it affectionately. *Jesus.* I never knew a kneecap could be an erotic zone on my body, but I'll be damned. If it's Jake LaShae's large, warm hands doing the touching, it's erotic as hell.

"That tickles," I laugh, delicately shoving his shoulder. I hate how girlie I sound right now.

He captures my hand on his shoulder and holds it there, stroking his thumb over the back of my hand. I frown and look into his deep brown eyes. His expression morphs from friendly to lustful—needy. I exhale a shaky breath.

"Jake," I whisper, as he strokes his hand down my wrist, to my elbow and then slowly up to my shoulder. When his palm meets my bare shoulder and pauses, I lean into it and close my eyes, relishing in his touch. He rubs the pad of his thumb over my collarbone, and my lips part in response.

The need I feel in my core for Jake to kiss me is at an all time high. I feel like I'm free-falling off a cliff right now, waiting for this incredibly tumultuous feeling inside me to go away. I lean forward slightly, expecting to find his lips, but instead I feel the bed shift and his hand is suddenly gone. I flutter my eyes open and see him quickly tossing his stuff back into his backpack.

"What are you doing?" I ask, trying to register the expression on his face, but his head is dropped too low for me to get a good look.

"I...uhh, have to go," he clips out, awkwardly.

"What? We just started..." I reply, not sure what I'm referring to. Our homework or our—whatever the hell that just was.

"No, I mean, yeah," he stutters, and glances out the window, avoiding eye contact. "I just forgot I was supposed to be at open gym to shoot free-throws with Coach. I gotta run. I'm already super late."

"What about the assignment?" I ask, feeling my anxiety rise.

"I'll do some, you do some, and we can put them together in the morning before class. Just email yours to me, I'll do it," he finishes abruptly, and turns to exit. He comes back and drops a chaste kiss on the top of my head, completely avoiding eye contact.

"Jake!" I say, but he doesn't respond. He doesn't even look back.

I get up quickly and rush to the window and watch him walk swiftly to his apartment. I continue watching and see him enter his bedroom and immediately close his curtains. What the fuck was that all about?

***

This morning, I assumed Jake would pick me up at our usual time to head over to Chaz's, but when he didn't show up and the time on the clock was ticking away, I decided to just go without him. Last night, I emailed him the questions I came up with and he responded with one word—*Thanks*. I stared at that single, solitary word for ten minutes, willing it to explain this tangled mess.

My obsession over him is interrupted when my phone chirps and I open a text from Leslie.

Leslie: FIN FIN! On my way! Should be there after lunch!!!! I want to add more exclamation points to this message, but there's a guy at the gas station looking at me like he wants to wear my skin. See you soon!!!!!!!!!!!!!!!!!!

I smile sadly, and busy myself cleaning up my apartment to prepare for my best friend in the world's arrival.

After getting showered and ready for class, I wash out my morning coffee cup and hear a knock on the door. I swing it open and I'm surprised to see Jake standing on the other side. I smile awkwardly at him.

"Ready?" he quips, and avoids eye contact.

I frown, grab my stuff, and follow him out of Wildwood. Normally, Jake and I are chatting about anything and everything. He usually throws his arm around me—something. But today he's cold, detached, and completely avoiding eye contact. I can't make sense of it. He's the one who was touching me last night. Not the other way around. What's with the sudden mood swing?

"You didn't come get me for Chaz's this morning," I say, trying to break the awkward silence between us.

He shrugs nonchalantly. "I overslept."

Okay then.

We sit in the same spot, but Jake spends a lot of time talking to the guy on the other side of him, which feels an awful lot like being blown off.

When we leave, I decide I've had enough of his illusiveness. "Look, are you still planning on coming with us to The Tank tonight?" I turn to face him as we walk, hoping to get him to look at me.

He glances at me briefly, and looks ahead again before saying, "'Course. Why wouldn't I?" His dismissive attitude is pissing me off.

I glare at him, but he won't look at me to even notice. "Ooookay," I assent. "Do you want to come over and pre-game it with us? Meet Lez?"

"Um, I'll let you know. I might just meet you there. I don't know yet."

Well, fine then. I guess we'll see tonight. But I'm getting a funny sense of de ja vu.

***

CHAPTER THIRTEEN

"Finley! If this isn't your fucking apartment then I give up and I'm going to party with whoever the bloody hell lives here! Or I'll go back to the neighbors two doors ago—they had Captain Crunch."

"Leslieeeee?" I squeal, from the bathroom, quickly setting down the Windex and paper towels, and run out to greet her. She halts me mid-step with her hands up in the air.

"I, no joke, went into not one, not two, but *three incorrect* apartments before this one. What the hell kind of a set up is this place? All the apartment numbers are the same!"

"The building number Lez! Remember? I told you to make sure you had the right building number!"

"That's WILD!" She smiles, proudly. "Get it? Wild. Wildwood! Haysoos Chreeeest, I'm a funny buggar!" she chortles, unabashedly.

"I can't believe you kept just walking into places after you got the first one wrong."

"Fuck it! I made some new friends. YOLO!" She pauses, and looks me up and down quickly. "Uh, hellooooo, what the hell are you still doing over there and not over here hugging the shit out of me? I've been in England for crying out loud. It's not like I just got home from the grocery store!"

I smile at her and run across the small living room to hug her the way I've hugged her a million times before. She still smells the same and my brain seems really happy at the nostalgic memory. Her auburn hair is long and thick with extra long bangs swooped off to one side. Her clothes are more outrageous than I've ever seen. She's wearing red, crocheted shorts, with a turquoise button-down sleeveless blouse. How this girl can pair red with turquoise and look as fierce as she does is beyond me. But I don't even care because my Leslie is here!

"Let's go girl, give me the cracks!" she bellows, and pulls me toward the couch and we both collapse with big dopey grins on our faces.

"I need the cracks out of you too! You're the one living overseas as a designer!" I retort, and heave myself off the couch to run to the fridge and grab us both pops. "I don't even know where you're living!"

"Well, I just moved in with this fiery ginger. We had an interesting first meeting…I'll have to tell you all about it someday. It's a funny story!"

"Can't wait!" I hand her a Fresca—her favorite. I was sure to buy them just for this visit.

She smiles appreciatively at me. "So, what about you? That's what I want to hear about!"

I sigh deeply—thankful she's here, now more than ever.

"Uh oh…I don't like the sound of that sigh. Let's hear it," she says, looking at me seriously.

I unload the entire Jake debacle to her. Every little crack. I even unload the feelings I have deep down that I hadn't even admitted out loud—like the horrible insecurity in myself this situation is causing. The fact that he's clearly put me in the friend zone, but I still want him and can't force myself to stay away. I feel fifty shades of pathetic.

When I describe in great detail what happened with us last night in my room, I see Leslie's fiery anger peaking.

"Shit. Your drama makes my London adventures seem like child's play," she heckles kindly.

"What the hell am I going to do, Lez?"

She laughs, heartily. "Well, this guy sounds like a tease to me." I look at her sadly. "Alright, I'll try not to judge until I've met him. But fair warning, Fin—so far, I am not impressed."

"Fine, fine. Just tell me what I can do to figure this shit out!"

Her face contorts into an *oh, please* expression. "That's easy, Finny."

"What?" I look at her impatiently, like she's going to give me the key to the kingdom.

"You look fucking hot and show him what he's missing out on!"

I tell her the plan for tonight and I can see her wheels cranking at the fact that Jake will be out with us tonight. It's like I can picture the outfit she's designing in her head for me. Clothes were always the answer to everything for Leslie. She heads over to the door and grabs her gigantic wheelie suitcase.

"Point me to your room, lover!"

I point.

"So, *The Tank* you said?" Leslie asks, dropping her bag into my room and coming back out and heading for the front door.

"Yeah, but—wait. Where are you going?"

"Oh, I just gotta go tell my new friends where we're partying tonight real quick." I stare back, dumbfounded. "I promised!" she says, seriously, closing the door behind her. God, it's good to have her back.

***

Jake texts, saying he'll meet us at The Tank after practice. No surprise there. I wasn't expecting him to come over, but damn was I hoping he would. I envisioned him walking in the front door and getting a long, hard look at the incredible ensemble Leslie put together for me. But that won't be happening.

I'm wearing a pair of way too snug, way too short, white denim shorts. They are Leslie's, which is why they are scandalously short on me. Leslie is a good six inches shorter than me, but these shorts make my ass look great, and my lingering summer tan is on full display.

She pulls out what looks like a strappy scarf, and says it's a shirt. I respond with "Hell to the NO!" But she makes me try it on and I am eating my words because as soon as I put it on, I feel amazing. It was a black tank top with a slouchy scoop neckline, and makes my breasts look amazing. But the real showstopper is the back. Thin straps crisscross and meet at the small of my back, revealing the sides of my ribcage—and pretty much every other part of my back. I feel like I'm wearing nothing, but I can't deny it looks good.

"You fucking bitch! You're keeping that," Leslie bites out, eyeing me thoughtfully.

"What? No! I'm sure it was expensive, Lez!" I reply.

"You wear it better than me! It wasn't expensive, because I made it," she says, in a flat monotone, hoping to minimize the amazingness of what she just revealed.

My aqua eyes turn wide in response to Leslie's comment. I knew Leslie was talented. I have seen many of her designs, but this is a whole other level. Obviously, the move to London is proving to be beneficial for her skills.

"You do wear it well, Finley," Angela adds, looking me up and down. Angela got home from her night class shortly after Leslie and I cracked our first pre-game cocktails. The three of us have been primping and drinking wine for nearly two hours now, but we really need to get walking soon or we'll be stuck waiting in line at The Tank.

Leslie fishes a pair of black peep-toe ankle boots out of my closet. "Think you can shake your tail feathers in these?"

"Ahh, my 'Fuck Me' heels! Good call," I reply, confidently stepping into the high stilettos.

"You girls ready?" Angela asks, wearing a sweet dark blue sundress. Leslie is wearing a checkered vintage dress with a fitted bodice. The three of us couldn't look more different.

"Let's go show that pecker what he's missing," Leslie says, and we laugh as we follow her out the door.

CHAPTER FOURTEEN

The Tank is packed when we show up and the three of us groan at the sight of the one in, one out line. Before we even reach the back of the line, I hear a familiar voice calling my name.

"Finley!" Olivia bellows from the exit next to the entrance. "Over here!" She waves us over, and I see all the line-waiters turn to look at me.

Olivia gives a slight nod to the guy letting people in at the door. Angela, Leslie, and I walk in without another word.

"Thanks!" I shout, and follow Olivia through the swarms of people. She's tarted up to the nines in a little black dress, and she's slinking through the joint like she owns the place. The Tank is a hotspot dance club right near campus on the study strip, where everyone goes who is of age, or has a good fake ID. It's nice being a senior, not having to worry about getting into the bars anymore.

I glance around and see several familiar faces. There are always a lot of Wildwood residents at the strip since it's only four blocks away. We reach a large round high-top table that overlooks the dance floor. I look up and catch a glimpse of a really familiar face and blush at his blatant perusal of my body.

Jake. Damn. Why does he have to look so good? His nearly black eyes dilate as he takes in the shortness of my shorts and the longness of my legs in my tall 'Fuck Me' heels. I feel an ache in my groin when his eyes linger on my breasts before making their way up to my face. He offers me a sexy-as-sin smile, and I return it, eagerly. This is a different Jake than I saw in class today, and I have to say— I'm a fan.

I lick my lips and drink in his charcoal cargo shorts and fitted black tee. He looks tall, dark, and handsome. Olivia settles onto the barstool next to him and gestures for us to join. I sit directly across from him. Leslie and Angela grab the other two open spots.

"Everybody know Leslie?" I shout, over the loud music.

"Yeah, yeah," Olivia grumbles, and takes a swig of her beer. She grabs one of the pitchers in the middle of the table to refill. Olivia's roommate, Jen, fills three cups and hands one to each of us.

"I don't," Jake says, never taking his eyes off me.

"Leslie, Jake. Jake, Leslie," I say, with a smirk, and take a large swig of the cold draft beer to cool myself off.

"You're Jake?" Leslie shouts. He nods. "You would be," she adds, sarcastically.

"What?" he asks, breaking eye contact with me and looking at her curiously.

"Nothing. Fuck me!" she shouts randomly at no one in particular. She quickly clinks her beer with mine and takes a hearty swig. I laugh at her obvious approval of Jake's appearance. I'm not surprised. Jake just has that look about him. But I know that doesn't mean he's off the hook with Leslie.

After several beers and a ton of ferocious laughs, courtesy of Leslie's hilarious stories of her roommate, everyone seems to be getting along well.

"…Frank's naked bum is something I'll have forever drilled into my brain," Leslie laughs, finishing her hilarious tale of a guy she knows in London, getting his man parts waxed.

Emmet and a few of Jake's teammates show up and encourage him to join them at the bar. I feel butterflies in my belly when Jake refuses their offer. After they leave, he catches my eye and motions his head toward the dance floor. I nod in agreement. If Jake wants to dance, I'm dancing. This isn't the first time we've danced together. We've gone out a few other times this summer with his teammates. I quickly learned that Jake has some serious moves. Or maybe his moves aren't that great, but I don't notice or care because his body is rubbing up against mine, eliminating any chance at forming a coherent, unbiased opinion.

I give a nervous look to Leslie and she raises her eyebrows, encouragingly. Jake grabs my hand and pulls me through the crowd, right to the center of the mob of students. My pulse quickens as he puts his hands on my hips and grinds into me with an erotic rhythm. I crane my neck and look up into his dark hooded eyes and he smirks at me. His hands slowly move up, and I shiver at his touch on my bare back. Goosebumps pimple all over my skin.

"This is fun," I say, with a smile. He returns my pleased look, and then briefly glances around at the other dancers. "I was excited for Leslie to meet you," I add into his ear, attempting to get a feel for his mood. My inner monologue is warring with myself on whether or not I should ask him why he was so cold earlier. Damn it, maybe I should just man up and finally express my feelings to him— preferably sober this time so I can't blame the alcohol.

"She seems cool," he shrugs, with nonchalance, and continues grinding his hips into mine. God he feels good. My arms have to stretch for my hands to clasp behind his neck. Leslie, Angela, Olivia, and the rest of the gang join us, so we break apart to dance with the group instead of just each other.

Olivia seems to be paying more attention to Jake, now that she's on the dance floor. I have to forcefully hold down my green jealousy guns so I don't make a fool of myself. Leslie does her best to distract me from their obvious flirting, but I feel myself growing more and more anxious. Deciding I can't take anymore, I motion to Olivia that we should go back to our table for a shot, and she nods and smiles.

Back at the table, we all order a round of shots and the mood lightens considerably. Everyone chats about the start of school and class schedules. Jake continues stealing glances of me across the table. They seem to hold some meaning, but Olivia keeps yammering in his ear, distracting him.

Jen's boyfriend cuts into my thoughts, "We have to run the damn mile!" Phil barks, incredulously.

I look over at him and reply, "Run the mile for what?"

"That fitness class we all have to take before we graduate. I thought we were done with PE once we graduated high school," he adds, pulling his baseball cap down lower on his forehead.

"Oh, God. That. I haven't taken that class yet. I have it scheduled for my final semester," I say, groaning slightly.

"Ick! I can't believe they make you run the mile!" Leslie adds. "Finny and I wouldn't last a single lap!" She laughs and nudges me and I laugh back. Leslie's and my disdain for physical activity is no secret. We much prefer reading, watching movies, or in her case, sewing. The only form of true physical activity I actually enjoy, is dancing.

"What are you guys talking about?" Jake asks, over the chatter.

"The senior fitness class we all have to take. I'm not taking that class 'til the very last second. We were just laughing because Leslie and I both hate exercise with a passion," I stop mid-laugh when I notice Jake's confused expression.

"And sports!" Angela adds. I glare at her. "I still can't believe you ever played sports in high school, Finley," she says, disbelievingly, looking like she's well on her way to being wasted.

"Why? What do you mean?" Olivia asks, clearly not understanding Angela's accusation.

"Finley hates sports and exercise, yet she played basketball in high school! It makes no sense!" she teases me, and I laugh awkwardly in response. I know Angela, she's just drunk and giving me shit. It's what we do with each other.

"I did it for the social status," I say, and glance at Jake, who looks disturbed.

"What do you mean?" Jake inquires, seriously.

I continue laughing, but squirm at his serious expression. "Nothing. Just that...I don't know. I'm from a small town. It's just what people did to be social. You played sports or you were a band geek. I couldn't play an instrument so I went out for basketball," I confess, shrugging my shoulders and look over to Leslie for support.

"It's true! In Marshall, that's just what you did for something to do! It's funny to think about what we did back then. We'd never do that stuff now."

"Yeah, yuck!" I laugh, albeit a bit drunkenly. Those three bottles of wine we polished off before arriving, and the beer we're having now, have definitely kicked in.

"You guys are awful. You'll probably be super fat housewives someday," Olivia says, snottily. Everyone just laughs at her in response. "I run at least three times a week. I feel gross if I don't," she adds, snarkily.

"Good for you, Oli!" Leslie jeers. I can see Leslie's patience for Olivia's superior attitude wearing thin. "I'll be wearing moo-moos in my forties and you'll be in peak physical condition. The perfect *Stepford Wife*. I, personally, don't give a toss. I'll be designing and wearing the fiercest moo-moos you've ever seen!"

"I'll wear them too!" I say, excitedly. I laugh and look over and feel stunned by Jake's somber expression. He looks disappointed. Obviously, I'm a bit drunk right now, but I'm not making a total fool out of myself. I'm not smoking. What the hell is his problem now? His chest puffs upward, and he grabs his full beer and drinks the entire thing.

"Why so glum, Jake?" I prompt, feeling uneasy at his obvious change in mood.

"It's nothing," he answers, and refills his beer and begins drinking that quickly too.

I pull my eyebrows together but then shake my head. I can't figure this guy out. If he wants to be a moody bastard again, screw him. Leslie's here. I'm not letting him ruin my one night with her. He was just eye-fucking me a minute ago and now he will barely look at me.

"Let's go dance this drunk off, Lez!" I suggest cheerily. "Angela, you in? Anyone else?" I ask, but no one looks too interested.

Angela, Leslie, and I all finish our beers and head onto the dance floor to lose ourselves to the beat of the music. Honestly, I wish I would have taken dance when I was a child. Then maybe I could actually say I don't hate exercise. I love dancing and have pretty decent moves. It's just something that allows me to release all my pains and frustrations, and even my happiness. I can leave it all on the dance floor. And dancing with Leslie is always a riot because the girl has no pride, whatsoever. She couldn't care less if she looks like a total fool. If it makes anyone around her laugh, she's doing it.

All three of us have worked up a good sweat, so I suggest we go back to the bar and get a drink. Jake and Olivia appear to be deep in conversation as we pass our table. The green-eyed monster is screaming inside of me to claw her eyes out and get her away from my man, but I ignore it and decide another drink is a better idea.

We down a shot and head back out to the dance floor. Jen and Phil join us. They get a kick out of Leslie's moves too. Leslie has jumped on the empty stage area that most people are too embarrassed to dance on. Not only is she dancing on it, she's doing the Carlton dance move from *Fresh Price*—and she's doing it well. I join my friends and laugh harder than I have in a long time. Leslie grabs her crotch and the crowd erupts into cheers. I look around for Jake, but don't see any sight of him.

Honestly. Fuck him. I don't know if it's the alcohol talking, or what, but I am so tired of letting this mood-swinging jerk screw with me like this. I'm so much better than this. I know I am. I need to be honest and fess up, or quit hanging with him altogether. I have to be strong. I have to be confident. I have to be able to jump up on a stage and grab my crotch!

Before I can chicken out, I join Leslie and mimic her obnoxious moves. She hoots and hollers at me to continue, and we laugh and dance together like lunatics. This is me—this is the Finley I want to be. The self-assured, don't give a damn, do what you want kind of woman. I need to remember this.

***

CHAPTER FIFTEEN

Jen informs us that there's talk of after parties going on at Wildwood. We all gather and totter down the dark sidewalk past Chaz's to continue the party. Olivia left early to go to bed because she has to work in the morning. I look around briefly for Jake, but he is nowhere to be found. My hope is that he's back at Wildwood, because it's time we have a serious talk about our shit. I'm ready to just lay it all out there so I can move on—with or without him.

When we get to Wildwood, various clusters of students are staggered throughout the parking lot, drinking beer and socializing. Leslie and Angela stop at one of the previous buildings where several of Angela's poli-sci friends are hanging out. I hang for a moment, but then decide I want to go find Jake. I tell Lez my plan and she gives me a big thumbs-up as I take off the rest of the way toward his place.

Jake's lights are all out in his apartment. If he's gone to bed, he's nothing but a big party pooper, so I walk right into his apartment, assuming knocking would be a waste of time if he's passed out. The door is unlocked, so I wobble quickly toward his bedroom door and swing it open with a big smile on my face.

I flip on the lights so I can wake him, and my voice catches in my throat at the sight before me. I exhale a deep breath and look away, trying to get ahold of myself. My trembling hands grip the tiny bits of fabric on my shirt as my eyes focus in on Jake and Olivia, in bed together. My Jake. In bed. With my *friend*, Olivia. How is this even possible? How did this transpire?

I clench my stomach in pain. I feel like someone took a two-by-four and swung it at me just as I opened the door. I bite the inside of my cheek, hard, willing myself to look away from the intimate scene, but it's like watching a bad car accident—as upsetting as it is, I can't look away. Olivia shifts and brings her hand to her face to shield the light from her eyes. Her naked breast pops out from beneath the gray sheet. My already pained stomach rolls.

"What the fuck?" she croaks out, groggily, with her brown hair strewn all over Jake's pillow. Jake stirs in response to her voice, his arm draped protectively over her naked waist.

His dark chocolate eyes flutter and open straight to me, as if he could feel my presence in his sleep. His eyes squint for a second, and then turn wide.

"Finl..." he starts, but I cut him off.

"I...uhh..." I bark out an awkward laugh. I shake my head, trying to form a coherent response. "Sorry," I mumble, and turn to exit. My hand covers my mouth as mortification envelops me.

"What the fuck?" I hear Olivia grumble again, and I stop dead in my tracks, feeling her voice grate on my last semblance of control. I turn back to look at the two of them together. Once more. Just once more I need to get a good look at this scene. Jake moves his arm off of Olivia's waist and rubs the top of his short black hair.

"This is really something!" I hear myself say, from outside my body. My voice sounds manic and high-pitched, barely recognizable. "I never would have thought!"

"Finley, it's just…" Jake starts to get up, his chiseled chest on full display, and all I want to do is scrape my fingernails across it until they leave marks. I squeeze my nails into my palms to stop myself from rushing over and acting out what I see so perfectly in my head.

"No, Jake, really—this is all *my* fault! I'm *incredibly* sorry," I draw out the word with dramatic fashion and chagrin. Before either of them can respond, I add, "I had no idea you two were so into each other. That's really great. Special even. I'm really quite happy for you guys."

Olivia squirms to sit up, clutching Jake's sheet to her bare chest. Her expression looks pensive and uneasy. "It just happened, Fin. It's not like you were…" her voice trails off.

"It's not like I what, Olivia? It's not like I had any claim on him? You are *so* right!" I point at nothing and look up at the ceiling, deep in thought, preparing for a tangent. "I have zero claim here. Zip. Zilch. Nada." I stop myself and look seriously at Jake, all lightness evaporating from my expression. "We're just good buds, right Jake." It's a statement, not a question. He looks down, avoiding my piercing gaze.

I smile, meanly. "Please, excuse me," I say, storming out of his bedroom and through the living room. Holy shit, what did I just say to them? Humiliation boils over me as I rush out the apartment door and straight into the parking lot. I stop dead in my tracks outside his front door, glancing at his bedroom light through his window. His curtains are drawn—*thank God.* I can't let them see me like this. I need to get myself to the safety of my own apartment, but my feet feel frozen in place. Why? Why can't I make myself move away from his apartment door? Move, Finley! This is embarrassing enough without you having a nervous breakdown right in the middle of Wildwood!

I will myself to move and head straight across the lot toward my apartment door. I don't bother going to find Angela and Leslie. I can't. I can't face them right now. How am I supposed to tell the two friends closest to me that the guy I've been spending immeasurable amounts of time with, and daydreaming about a future with, just fucked one of my closest friends? How can I say those words out loud? How can I face such humiliation?

"Fuuuuuuck!" I scream, stopping suddenly in the middle of the lot and stomping my foot like a petulant child. I hastily wipe two wet tears off my cheeks. I could just kick myself for being such a fool and crying right now. I've been a fool for way too long. I've let Jake LaShae occupy my thoughts and time for way too damn long. Aside from the one intimate moment in my room, he hasn't given me any clear indication he wanted anything more.

I close my eyes, remembering the intimate touch of his hand on my collarbone and his hips grinding against mine on the dance floor. My mind is then assaulted with the image of Olivia's amble bosom popping out from beneath the sheets. *Fucking damn it all to hell!*

I grip my arms tightly across my chest, feeling suddenly ridiculous at the scantily clad outfit I'm wearing. All for what? For who? For a *friend?* Jake may not have been mine to claim, but he was certainly a good friend. Isn't there some sort of bro-code people follow that's kinder than the car wreck I just walked in on? And Olivia, Jesus. What the hell was she thinking? She knows about my feelings for Jake. We talk enough for her to know how close Jake and I have become the past few weeks. This girl has been my friend for nearly four years now. Does the girl-code in this situation not call for better behavior?

Jesus, Finley. Get a grip on yourself. Quit caring. It probably never would have worked, and it should have never gone on this long anyway. Guys and girls cannot be just friends. It never works. Someone's feelings always get involved. I deserve better than this.

I let myself into my apartment and head straight for the bathroom, stripping out of my clothes and jumping into the shower. I roughly scrub the makeup off my face, growing angrier and angrier at the fact that I did all this for him.

My anger morphs to sadness and shame. I've never experienced this level of rejection. The fact that it was a slow-churning rejection that began the minute Jake spoke to me that day at Chaz's, makes it all sting so much more.

I sit down on the floor of the shower and let the hot steaming water fall haphazardly all over me. Despite myself, my eyes burn with tears, flowing freely down my face with the rushing water. I brush back my thick wet strands and bite my knuckle, begging myself to stop crying.

I think back to the epiphany I had when I was dancing on stage with Leslie. That's the Finley I want to be. Not this crying, sniveling, mess of a woman, scorned by someone who's never even kissed her. Angela dumped Luke because she knew she deserved better. I can't be a hypocrite. Fuck them. Fuck them both. Jake and Olivia can have each other.

"Fin Fin?" I hear Leslie's voice shout into the apartment. The door to the bathroom opens almost immediately after.

"Yeah," I reply, my voice thick with emotion, revealing my true state.

"Shit. Thank God. She's in here!" Leslie calls out the door. "Holy fucking fuck, Finny. We just saw Oldie 'Oli!" Leslie says, once Angela joins her in our tiny bathroom.

"That's great," I mumble and haul myself up off the shower floor. "I don't know if I can talk right now, guys."

"Finny, do I really have to say *the cracks* right now?" Lez says, pressing her hand against the foggy glass.

I swallow hard, attempting to muster some strength. "I assume you guys heard?"

"Heard that Olivia is a dirty slut? Schyeah, no big shock there," Angela says, as I rinse back my hair one more time.

I cut the water off and let myself drip-dry behind the safety of the glass door for a minute. I shouldn't feel ashamed to face my friends, but damn it all to hell, I am. This is embarrassing as fuck.

I open the door and grab the towel off the hook, wrapping myself up tightly. I step out and look into four concerned and sympathetic eyes. "I'm fine," I say, as much for myself as for them. My chin wobbles.

"If you weren't, I would understand," Leslie says, reaching her hand out to touch my arm.

I shake her off and head over to the sink. I grab my comb and begin ripping through my hair, harder than necessary, but needing something to do.

"What did you guys hear?" I ask, looking at them both through the reflection in the mirror. It feels easier to look at their concerned faces through the safety of a mirror.

"Oldie 'Oli came out of Jake's apartment just as we came looking for you. Talk about the walk of shame," Leslie says, cutting a disgusted look to Angela, who nods in agreement.

"She was acting all innocent, like she didn't do a thing. I knew instantly what she'd done. A dog can't change its spots," Angela adds, with a sneer.

"She's a crinkly old grannie, Fin," Leslie interjects. "Honestly. If Jake thinks she's better than you, he's a damn idiot." The idea of being second best in the eyes of someone you've grown to care about stings something fierce.

Angela scoffs, "She acted like she had no idea you and Jake have been hanging out non-stop for the last month. What a royal bitch." I shake my head slightly in response and turn to face them.

"Guys, honestly. I have no claim on him," I say, flatly.

"Yeah, but jeez. There's code for this stuff! It's obvious to everyone you…" Angela trails off.

"It's obvious to everyone I like him. God, I'm mortified," I groan, feeling sick.

"Not everyone, everyone. I mean…" Angela trails off again, still unsure how to finish that sentence without further pounding a nail in my coffin.

"Listen. It's embarrassing enough this is going to go public and humiliate the shit out of me. Wildwood shit spreads like fire. I just want to minimize it all as much as possible. Jake and I didn't happen. He didn't want me. He just…" I shrug my shoulders and feel tears creep into my eyes again.

"I don't think he doesn't want you," Angela bargains, indignantly.

"Don't fill me full of bullshit, A. If he wanted me, he'd have me by now. I was so freaking obvious," I groan, and turn away from them. Damn this mortification. Damn it all to hell.

"He is a bloody lunatic, Finley!" Leslie reproaches. "You deserve ten million times better. Honestly, I'm just going to say it. He seemed like a shallow jerk to me. I didn't like him. I don't know what you saw in him." I look sadly at her.

"Let's order pizza!" Angela interrupts, with wide excited eyes.

"Honestly, I just want to go to bed." I smile sadly, feeling grateful, now more than ever, for these two amazing friends. Having Leslie here with me will hopefully help me get the hell over myself. I need to move on from Jake. I never had him in the first place, and this is the punch in the gut I needed.

***

"Come snuggle me, you sexy beast," Leslie says, after getting into her PJs and jumping into my bed.

I smile, flip off the light, and crawl into bed with her. A faint light creeps in from the parking lot and her green eyes look at me warily.

"I need more," she says, rolling on her side to face me.

"More what?" I ask.

"Finley, I know you like him, so I'm trying to be kind here. But he seemed shallow to me. I picture you with someone…" she pauses, looking toward the window, deep in thought. "Someone more like us, I guess." I purse my lips to the side. "And I sure as hell picture you with someone better than a guy who will fuck your friend. You guys may not have been in a relationship but he is a royal prick to be so selfish."

"I know. I know I need to just move on from him. It's hard to let go when I wasn't the instigator."

"You were always the one to break off relationships growing up. But this isn't you…fawning over a guy who's half of a man, at best. He was attractive, yes. But if you really look at what you two had together, was it everything you hoped to find in your future *lover*?"

She says lover with a French accent and I giggle softly. "Probably not. Maybe I just got swept up in the chase. I don't know. And I did like him, truly. He wasn't always bad. But I know what you're saying."

"You're better than this. Our mamas didn't raise no fools. But come on, Finny. You are beautiful, inside and out. You have a heart that opens so naturally to people. The guy that is meant for you is still out there."

I reach over and squeeze her tightly. "I'm so glad you're here Leslie. I needed you."

"That's what best friends are for," she says, and smiles. "To be here when your crush fucks your friend."

"Oh! Bad form!" I cry out, laughing heartily.

When Leslie stops laughing, she sighs. "Now I, on the other hand, am going to end up married to a gay man. My vajayjay will shrivel up and die because it won't be properly serviced. I'll die alone with my fifty cats, my sewing machine, and one fiercely designed moo-moo."

I laugh emphatically at the sight. "The guy that manages to capture you, Lez, is going to have to be tough as nails to break through your hard shell. But that's how we'll know he's worth it."

She rolls on her back and squints thoughtfully at the ceiling. "Night, Finny."

"Night, Lezzy."

CHAPTER SIXTEEN

I skip my morning class the next day so I can see Leslie off and sleep off a nasty hangover. I head to work after she leaves and manage not to see Jake. Either he's doing a stellar job avoiding me or he's actually busy. My mind wants him to just be busy—but then, my mind also wants to punch myself in the face for caring.

Parni is front and center at her computer when I come in, along with a sprinkling of several other students I don't bother acknowledging.

"Parni," I say, passing her and heading over to my desk. She just looks up at me in response. Radio silence from Parni even, man I'm feeling like a winner today!

Knowing I won't be able to concentrate on homework, I grab one of my favorite *Elizabeth Young* novels and start re-reading my favorite parts. The way she writes usually fills my soul with such giddy hope for falling in love, but damn, today it just feels depressing because shit in real life never happens the way it does in books. Ain't that a bitch.

Suddenly, *Taio Cruz's Dynamite* song echoes through the computer lab. My face flames red when Parni and several other students look up from their work. In our drunken pizza stupor last night, Leslie was messing with the ringtones on my phone, and the bitch made *Dynamite* my text notification. I stifle a smile and chance another look at Parni, who shoots me a furious gaze.

I slide the screen to unlock it and view the new text.

Olivia: Hey, what's up?

Me: Working.

Olivia: Fun!

Three minutes later.

Olivia: Wanna hang this weekend?

Me: I don't know what I'm doing yet.

Olivia: That's why I'm asking if you want to hang! Making plans…duh!

Me: I'm probably going to pass.

Olivia: Seriously? Is this going to be a thing?

Me: It's not a thing…I'm just trying to stay out of drama.

I begin to wonder if Jake and Olivia are going to start dating. The idea of watching her walk into his apartment, hanging out in the same places we'd hung out so frequently, makes my stomach roll.

Olivia: There's no drama. Let's not make a big deal out of this. I don't even like him like that.

She doesn't even like him like that. What a great reason to do that to a friend! I bark out a laugh and Parni shakes her head dubiously at me.

Me: You guys should date. You're perfect for each other.

Olivia: Oh for God's sake. We're not going to date.

I roll my eyes and try to come up with a response to stop this line of conversation because I just don't give a shit about them. Either of them. They can get married for all I care. After chatting with Leslie and Angela last night, I learned quickly that I've been putting Jake on a pedestal for months, and the hype did not live up to the reality. I'm done with Jake. I'm done with Olivia.

Me: I just think I need some space for a bit. Nothing major. Just want to focus on school and stuff.

Olivia: Sounds like bullshit.

Olivia can stew with no response from me for a while. I shut my phone off and jump back into my novel. After my little revelation, the pages don't seem quite so unbelievable now. That miraculous, epic love can happen, it just has to be with the right person, and Jake LaShae is most definitely not the one. Leslie's right—I need someone who gets me.

***

When I settle in for bed, I know deep down that Jake won't be calling for our nightly chat. I can't help but miss it. I had grown used to it. I don't miss the angst of trying to progress a friendship into a relationship though. That was hell on earth. And Jake's lack of contact all day just further reinforces the notion that he doesn't care about me and I need to get over him. Maybe I should feel grateful that he's allowing our friendship to end, otherwise I would probably just continue pining for him and suffering in silence. I need to be done with him and have a clean break so I can properly move on. Never mind the enormous humiliation of other people knowing I have these major unrequited feelings for Jake. Who needs pride anyway?

I wake up early the next morning, tossing and turning in my bed for a good hour, nervous Jake might show up to get coffee. When it's well past eight, I find the courage to get up. I patter out into the kitchen where Angela is spreading peanut butter on her toast.

"Morning," she says, head nodding at me.

"Hey," I reply, feeling uneasy and a bit mopey. "I think I'm going to skip class today." I pout my lip out dramatically.

"This is the day you have class with him?"

"Yeah." I sit up on the counter and take a bite of her toast.

"Stop being a pussy and go to class. I thought you had a quiz!" She looks at me sternly, waiting for me to dispute it. "You're better than that, Finley," she admonishes.

"Jeez, thanks for being so understanding," I mumble around a bite of toast.

"I'm not going to placate you on this one. He's an idiot, that's established. Your education shouldn't suffer for it."

"I hardly think my education is going to suffer for missing one little quiz."

She rolls her eyes. In defiance, I decide to go get my cup of coffee, Jake be damned.

CHAPTER SEVENTEEN

I walk out of my apartment, frustrated at Angela and in desperate need of air. Even though I don't care if he and Olivia start dating, it irks me that he's icing me out when I did nothing wrong. I mean, if he genuinely didn't have any feelings for me, why the silence? I kick a rock, angry that I keep tormenting myself over what Jake is thinking and why we're no longer speaking.

A sick feeling rolls over me as I think about the fact that the whole basketball team probably knows. And now that we're not ending up together, like they all assumed we would—I look like a total chump. Why did I have to have a class with him? This is hell. I'm in college hell. And I'm a senior for Christ's sake—I should be beyond this sophomoric drama.

I look up when I hear a door slam from across the parking lot and see a guy rushing down the steps of an upper-level apartment that sits kiddy-corner from my building. My eyebrows knit together as he pads across the concrete, straight toward me.

He looks slightly familiar. I've seen him in the computer lab before but I've never spoken to him. I look him up and down and feel annoyed at his cuteness. Honestly, that's how I feel right now. I'm annoyed. I don't need another cute guy clouding my psyche.

"Hey," he says, looking up at me and holding a half-empty black trash bag.

"Um, hi," I reply, figuring he's going to ask me where the dumpster is.

"You're Finley, right?"

"Yeah, that's me," I reply with a surprised expression.

I try my damndest to ignore the sudden stirring in my abdomen. This guy has somehow managed to pull off comfortably sexy. I didn't even know those two words could go together, but I'll be damned. I mentally restrain myself from rolling my eyes at the cruelty of the universe.

He looks down, nervously. He's wearing a loose pair of black athletic shorts and a white t-shirt that shows a nicely sculpted body underneath. I can see the outlines of his pecks through his shirt and I instantly want to see more. *Jesus, Finley, get a grip on yourself.* I'm impressed I'm even noticing him, with all the drama swirling in my head.

My eyes continue traveling downward and I see that he's barefoot. My perusal is momentarily distracted as I think about the nasty things that go down in this parking lot. Wearing no shoes is simply not safe.

"You work in the computer lab, right? In the business building?" he asks, scratching the back of his head.

"Yeah, in the business building," I answer, and silently curse myself because he just said business building. I eye his dark brown hair that has a natural curl to it. It's cut short on the sides with the top left slightly longer—long enough to comb my fingers through and yank on. *Whoa, where did that thought come from?*

I attempt to continue walking, but my feet are completely ignoring me as I take in his expression. The corners of his mouth are turned down like he's trying to contain a laugh. It's sexy as hell. Despite myself, I smirk back at him. I can't help it. That look on his face is unlike anything I've ever seen. It makes him look truly adorable. I'm suddenly feeling the urge to figure out more about this guy.

"You live here?" he asks, changing hands with his garbage bag.

"Yep, that building." I turn around and gesture back behind me, half-heartedly.

"I just moved here this semester. My friend Mark's roommate bailed on him, so he needed someone to fill the space."

"That explains why I haven't seen you here," I reply, fidgeting with the hem of my sweatshirt. I wish this guy would just get on with whatever he's after. His eyes follow my hands down to the invisible spec I'm picking at on my shirt, and then shoot back up to my face.

"I've seen you in the lab. I'm a business major—construction management. I'm graduating this spring. You?"

"Yeah, I'm a senior too. Marketing major. I actually don't have any classes in the business building this semester. I just work there."

"I figured out your name 'cause that one chick—the foreign one—is always yelling at you and stuff." He turns away and bites his tongue, appearing displeased with what he just said.

I laugh at his candid comment. It feels good to laugh. His expression brightens. "Her name is Parni. Yeah, we pretty much have a hate-hate relationship. I'm pretty sure she thinks I'm the bane of her existence."

He does it again. That concealed laughter face. It's really freaking sexy. I get a good look at his eyes and have to take a big gulp of air to calm myself. They are a gorgeous shade of navy blue with different hue intensities sprinkled throughout. They remind me of a really great pair of dark denim wash jeans. His eyes turn serious for a second as he catches me staring intently. I look away biting my lip, feeling foolish for ogling him.

"Where are you headed?" he asks, and I see a twinge of nervousness fleet over his face.

What is this guy after? I wish he'd just come out with it. "Do you need help with your computer or something, 'cause I know nothing about them—I just have to sit there."

His chest rumbles with laughter. "Why would you think that?" he asks, looking confused.

I shrug my shoulders, unsure how to answer that without sounding like a sullen idiot.

"Um, I'm going to Chaz's to grab a coffee or something. Honestly, my roommate was just driving me nuts," I offer with a shoulder shrug.

"I know how that feels. Mind if I go with you?" he asks.

I glance down at his feet, and as I look back up, my eyes collide into his sheepish smile. Another adorable look I wouldn't mind seeing over and over. Honestly, those eyes, his dark curly hair, and his creamy complexion are making one delicious package. How have I never noticed this guy?

"Yeah, I, uh, should probably go grab some shoes." He gestures for me to follow him and I can't help myself. I follow.

"You should probably never come out here barefoot again. Wildwood lives up to its name. Who knows what's out here in this nasty parking lot," I say, as we begin climbing the steps up toward his apartment.

He laughs softly and glances at me over his shoulder. His lips are pursed off to one side like he's thinking about something really hard.

"What?" I ask curiously.

"Telling you this probably totally ruins my cool factor," he says, cutting into my internal monologue of me warring with myself over getting away from this guy before I'm disappointed again. "But I've never been one to care about that stuff—or been cool, for that matter."

"What?" I ask, giggling. Gosh, this guy is such a breath of fresh air after the week I've had. Maybe he's not a total dick.

As we reach the top step, he stops and twirls on his heel, preventing me from ascending any higher. "I saw you out the window and didn't want to miss a chance to talk to you, so I grabbed the trash and rushed out here, like a barefooted moron, to catch you before you were gone again."

I laugh, doubtfully. "Why wouldn't you just talk to me in the computer lab?"

"You can hear a pin drop in that place! I hear every snotty thing that Pariah girl says to you, I don't need an audience when I'm trying to put the moves on a beautiful girl."

Beautiful girl screams over and over in my head, in that wonderfully warm tone of voice he has. I look down because I can't handle the intensely honest words he's just dropped on me. Not to mention, he has this adorable freckle below his left eye that somehow magnifies his sexiness. I fumble with the strings on my hoodie. That's a good activity for me right now.

"What?" he asks, laughing nervously.

"I just can't believe you're so up front about this." I look up into his curious gaze and hear skeptical disbelief laced in my tone.

"About you being beautiful?"

"Just, that…I don't. Jeez, don't make me say it!" I laugh, feeling agitated. I twist to the right and grab the railing for balance, to avoid eye contact.

"Um, I'm pretty sure I'm the idiot who just may have given myself hepatitis running out into a vile parking lot barefoot, so if you could even the score in any way, I would maybe feel like I got part of my man card back."

I roll my eyes. "Just being honest about…being interested in me, I guess. Unless I got this all wrong. If you just wanted to hang out, be friends or something, that's cool too!" I say, looking down and shoving my hands into my front pouch trying to fake indifference. I can't believe what's coming out of my mouth right now. How weak and pathetic am I, sitting here, blabbing about being friends? Once upon a time, I was just fine with being friends with a guy. This Jake stuff has thrown me all out of whack. But there is something about this guy that feels like I need more.

"Finley." He says my name so beautifully I can't help but look up. Even his voice is desirable. He moves in closer to me and pulls on one of the strings of my hoodie, pinching it between his thumb and index finger. His close proximity has my shield crumbling in nanoseconds. "I am interested in you," he finishes, staring deeply into my eyes with his gorgeous dark blue ones. "So let's just get that straight in your beautiful head right now."

My heart plummets. My lungs finally gasp for breath again, and I compose myself. "Okay then," I reply, the corners of my mouth turning down smugly.

He shakes his head and chuckles. "I risked hepatitis, or tetanus at the very least, so I wouldn't miss my chance to talk to you. That's definitely not something I would do just to make a new friend. I have enough friends."

He pulls away and turns to jog across the landing. He disappears inside his apartment door and reemerges a moment later, wearing a pair of sandals.

"What happened to your trash bag?" I ask, my eyebrows pulling downward.

"It was empty! I told you I just needed an excuse," he says, laughing. "Now I'm just giving you the real Brody."

Brody. I just realized I never cared to ask his name in our whole conversation. As far as I'm concerned, I could just call him Sexy Blue Eyes.

"Real Brody…" I nod. "Works for me."

He gently nudges my shoulder with his and we continue walking to Chaz's. Can this guy be real? He's so up front and honest about his feelings. It's definitely a huge change of pace from what I've been dealing with.

"So, what's the deal with this Chaz? Everyone talks about him. Have you ever met him?"

"Nope. Never. I know most of the counter clerks, but I've actually never seen Chaz."

"Interesting. Maybe we can invent a cool backstory for him. Something to get the rumors at Wildwood going." He lifts his eyebrows flirtatiously.

"Wildwood doesn't need any help starting rumors. This place is a glorified high school."

I groan internally at the thought of Brody hearing about the drama of Wednesday night with Jake and Olivia.

He chuckles softly.

"So, what's your story, Finley? Where are you from? What are your future plans?" he asks gently, squeezing my arm and dropping his hand down as we walk.

"I'm from Marshall, Missouri. Small town. I have a pretty cool family. Mom's a little high-strung at times, but cool. Dad's great. I'm really close to my sister, Cadence…and my two nieces."

"Plans after graduation?"

"Um, I kind of already have a job lined up in Kansas City. I had a really sweet internship opportunity last semester and hit it off really well with the creative director for an ad agency. I've been doing some freelance work for her this summer—and she's happy with it, I guess. She says I'm hired as soon as I graduate."

"Damn! Nailed it!" Brody says, with his eyebrows raised in admiration.

"I don't know…Val and I just seemed to click. She said she's been hiring interns for years and never met one like me. I just networked, is all."

"That's awesome. I have an internship lined up for next semester in KC too. I'm praying like crazy it turns into a job, because the timing would rock."

"Where are you from?" I ask, as we reach Chaz's front door.

Brody holds the door open for me, and says, "Topeka, actually."

I nod and smile, glancing inside. I'm suddenly frozen in place— stuck in a metaphorical mud, right in front of Alex at the counter. Jake is at the fountain pop machine. *Crap, crap, crap! I do not need this!* It's way later than our usual time. What the hell is he doing here?

Brody walks past me and looks back at my frozen state, his brow furrowed. "What's up?" he asks, taking in my alarmed expression.

"Nothing!" I reply, a bit too brightly. "Just trying to decide what I want to drink."

"I gotta grab milk," Brody says.

I try desperately to focus on his face, but I see Jake's eyes land on me. A look of discomfort instantly shadows his face.

"Milk's a weird choice," I reply, shoving Brody toward the aisle farthest away from Jake, which is conveniently where the milk is.

"Yeah, Mark told me to grab some 'cause we're out. Dude has to have his milk," he replies, glancing down at my hand still placed on his arm. I nod nervously, and release my grasp on his firmly-sculpted tricep. I look over my shoulder and about shit my pants when I see Jake standing right behind me.

"Jake!" I screech.

"Hey, Finley," he says in his familiar southern drawl. His voice sounds all wrong. Pained...pinched...different.

Brody turns around and they both exchange quick head nods. Jake is just a bit taller than Brody, but not by much. I'm certain Brody's a good four inches taller than me.

"Didn't know if I'd see you today," Jake says, looking into my eyes with an edge of uneasiness.

"I've been where I always am," I reply, coolly pursing my lips together and trying desperately to come off emotionless. I glance nervously at Brody and he seems intrigued by the current exchange.

"I was wondering if things were…" he pauses briefly, squints his eyes at Brody, and then looks down at me broodingly.

Confused at his expression, I reply, "Things are good. Thanks Jake. Anyways, I'm gonna grab a bottle of pop." *No more damn coffee! All it makes me think of is Jake now anyways.*

I shoulder through the two guys, feeling claustrophobic, and suddenly overwhelmed with anger. I reach the pop cooler and open the door allowing the cold air to blast my senses for a moment. Damn, I'm so pissed at Jake, but I know there's nothing I can say. Jake never made me any promises. But he also didn't have to just stop talking to me after the Olivia fiasco two nights ago. Now he's here trying to say something. *Frustrating.*

I grab a 20-ounce pop out of the cooler and hear the bell toll. I look up to see Jake's backside as he exits Chaz's. I sigh with relief, and jump when I glance to my right and see Brody standing next to me with a gallon of milk in hand. How do these hot men keep sneaking up on me?

"You good?" he asks, his eyes trained seriously on me.

I sigh again, "Yes, I'm good. I'm fine. Sorry." I grip the lid on my pop bottle and smile. He doesn't appear to believe it, but he lets it go for now.

We pay for our beverages and exit Chaz's. The walk back to our apartment is awkwardly quiet.

Brody exhales a frustrated sigh, stops and turns to me, "Look, I don't know what changed from now to the way here, but I don't care. I'd like to take you on a date, Finley. Would you like that?" He looks up at me with a scowl.

"Yes! I'd love that. Stop frowning!" I say without thinking. His face instantly relaxes and my stomach does a flip as he fights away a smile.

"Bossy much?" he half-smiles cockily.

"Not bossy, just don't like you asking me out with a frown, I guess," I reply, incredulously.

"Fair enough. So, yes then? A date?" he asks again, a little softer this time.

I nod and smile. "Yes. A date."

"Tomorrow night?" he reaches up and brushes a loose strand of my brown hair off my shoulder. His fingers barely graze my neck and I shiver in response, impressed with the reaction my body is having to his touch.

"I can do that," I rasp out, and clear my throat quickly. I conceal a smirk and he mirrors my expression.

He walks me back to my apartment. The silence isn't awkward this time. It's charged with something much more exciting and exhilarating. Can this really be this easy? In one single meeting with Brody, things feel so different. With Jake, I was constantly making moves to his counter moves. I was the driver, doing everything I could to push the relationship in the direction I wanted it to go. With Brody, I feel more like a passenger—and I like it.

We reach the door and I grab the handle. He nods and walks away from me backwards, before swiveling on his feet and jogging back toward his place. I lean back and enjoy the view until suddenly, the door swings open, and I'm lying on my back and groaning in sheer agony.

"Ow! Dammit, Angela!" I cry, and rub my elbow as she jogs past me to grab my pop bottle that's rolling into the parking lot.

"Enjoying the view?" she asks, swerving back to look at me as I amble up off the ground and look up, praying to God Brody didn't see. The door to his apartment is just closing. I sigh with relief.

"I was! Until you ruined it by opening the door!" I bark at her, and brush myself off sullenly.

"I didn't know you were leaning on the door!"

"Dang dude, my elbow hurts!" I rub it again and head inside.

"Who was that guy?" she asks, following me.

I sigh, suddenly feeling no pain again. "Brody," I smile saucily.

"Well that didn't take long!" she teases.

"Don't you even!" I snip at her playfully.

"Okay, okay, I won't." She laughs and walks into her bedroom. "Come in here and tell me all about him!"

I giggle and run into her room, feeling giddy as a high-schooler again.

CHAPTER EIGHTEEN

Studying for this quiz before class is impossible because a denim-eyed hottie keeps creeping into my thoughts. I stare ahead dreamily, waiting for Professor Martin to pass out the quizzes.

"Finley," Jake whispers over to me. I look over at him curiously. "Can I bring you lunch after this?"

I shake my head and accept the paper from the classmate in front of me. Jake doesn't say anything in response. Hell no, he can't bring me lunch. I couldn't be less interested in his lunch.

I'm the first one to finish the quiz, so I leave class quickly, not glancing back at Jake's piercing gaze. I stroll into the computer lab and quickly take my seat behind the monitoring desk. After rereading the same sentence in my textbook five times, I opt to stare out the huge bank of windows on the opposite wall of the lab.

The windows overlook a big patch of grass with curving sidewalks broken in throughout. It's a busy area with lots of student traffic and I probably people watch way more than I should. I hear Parni clear her throat, and I steal a glance at her.

"How do you not have anything to do? You're in *college*," she bites at me.

"Parni, have you never heard the phrase *stop to smell the roses?*"

She stares blankly, "You smell the roses too much."

"People watching is a great pastime Parni, you should try it." I look back out the window and am floored when I see Brody standing there with a big goofy grin on his face. I stand up in shock and walk through a row of computers closer to the window to figure out what's going on.

He smiles even bigger as I approach, then holds up a finger, indicating to wait one minute.

He fumbles in his backpack lying on the ground next to him, and presses a white sheet of paper up against the window. I squint to read it.

I FORGOT TO GET YOUR NUMBER.

I laugh out loud at his message, to which Parni and a few other students look up at me and train their eyes on the Brody Spectacle as well. I run back to my desk, grab a notebook, and quickly write my number down. I return to Brody's eager eyes and hold my paper up. We're now separated by two feet and one pane of glass.

He smiles, then quickly grabs his phone out of his pocket and enters my digits. He holds up one finger again, and reaches into his bag and presses another sign against the window.

DOES THIS MEAN I CAN CALL YOU?

I laugh out loud again.

"Oh for the love of God!" Parni reprimands, but I ignore her and nod enthusiastically to Brody's dark blue eyes. He reaches into his bag and pulls out another piece of paper.

JUST MAKING SURE.

I continue shamelessly beaming back at him, and he swaps his paper with another.

YOU LIKE SAILING?

I furrow my brow and shrug my shoulders, unsure how to answer that.

ME NEITHER.

He shakes his head and gives me a look that he's disgusted. I laugh out loud at his adorably comedic expression.

SERIOUSLY, WHO SAILS?

Before I can even get a chance to laugh again he presses another sign up against the window.

I MADE GOOD USE OF MY TIME IN CLASS TODAY.

I give him my best impressed look.

I'LL CALL YOU.

I bite my lip and nod, returning his wave goodbye. I turn on my heel and my Brody-buzz is pummeled at the sight of Jake standing in the doorway with a brown bag of food in hand, looking visibly shaken. We lock eyes and my smile fades instantly at his somber expression.

I walk over to him in the doorway and his expression transitions into indignation.

"Who the hell is that?" he says, none too quietly.

I shove him out of the lab and into the hallway. "His name's Brody. What's your deal, Jake?" I ask, crossing my arms over my chest and pointing at him with a hard stare. I'm over being embarrassed about anything related to Jake.

He shakes his head, quickly. "I've just never seen that guy before and now I see him twice in one day. How long have you known him?"

"Jake, you went from speaking to me several times a day, to nothing for two whole days. Now you want to be chummy again?" My voice rises at the end. "Maybe if you weren't so hung up on yourself, you would have noticed Brody before—not that it's any of your business anyways...I don't want your damn lunch."

He glares down at the bag in his hand like it has completely betrayed him. "Finley, I just thought...you know what, you're right. This is for the best." His eyes travel down my body, looking positively mean and nasty.

I raise my eyebrows and nod, dismissively, not giving two shits how *Jake LaShae* looks at me anymore. I'm done with his mood swings. I don't know what the hell he's trying to do right now with his lunch, but he can give it to Olivia for all I care.

Without another word, he turns and exits. I force myself to think back to Brody in the window, and how freaking cute that was. That's the kind of man I need in my life—someone who will put it all on the line for me. Or, in Brody's case, all on the window. I smile as my pulse quickens at the anticipation of our upcoming date. *This is just what I need.*

CHAPTER NINETEEN

Brody calls to arrange a date for Saturday night. All he says is that he'll be by around 6:30 and that I should be hungry. Angela leaves for KC for the weekend, so I don't have her around to help me obsess over what to wear. Without knowing what we're doing, I select a pair of floral print denim shorts. The weather in Manhattan is still warm, and these shorts can go casual or dressy. I throw on a loose white tank and a long pendant necklace. I run a straightener through my hair, and I'm considering having a drink as the clock ticks closer to 6:30. My nerves are getting the better of me.

There's a knock on the door at 6:31, and I wish I would have said no to this date. I'm a ball of nerves right now. I've been on lots of first dates before, but this Jake situation has me feeling insecure and twitchy.

I open the door and I'm greeted with a lopsided smile on Brody's adorable face. His curly hair is perfectly mussed on top of his head. He eyes me appreciatively.

"You look awesome," he says, with more sincerity than I've ever heard from any other date.

"You look awesome too," I say and laugh, slightly. He's wearing a pair of loose khaki cargo shorts and a soft charcoal-gray t-shirt with a faded graphic design over the top. The sun is just beginning to set, and the golden hue gives him a dreamy backlight that gives me instant butterflies.

"I tried on like four t-shirts." He laughs, and shakes his head. "I don't know why I said that."

I smile and tuck my hair behind my ear nervously. "Should we go?" I ask. He nods and leads me down the parking lot toward his car.

"Bye, Brody!" a male voice shouts from afar. I look up at Brody's apartment door where a shaggy-haired guy stands in nothing but a pair of boxers. Brody nods his head sternly, refusing to acknowledge the guy. "Just be yourself!" the man adds, pressing one hand to his mouth in an extreme motherly fashion. Brody's face morphs into a glare and he turns to look up at his apartment door.

"Mark! Honestly!" Brody bellows. Mark smiles like the cat who ate the canary, and retreats into his apartment. Brody turns a mortified expression to me.

I laugh and shrug my shoulders. "It's good advice!" I say, and he scoffs and opens the passenger door of his black Acura.

I hop in and glance around his car. I'm pleased to see it's clean. Dirty cars drive me nuts. Brody slides into the driver's seat, and I peek over at him nervously. "So, what are we going to do?" I ask, trying to calm my nerves.

He looks at me out of the corner of his eye as he backs out of the stall. "It's a surprise."

I smile at his sneaky look. "It's not sailing is it?" I ask, sounding more serious than I felt.

He barks out a quick laugh. "No. Sorry to disappoint. It's not sailing."

"What if I would have said I loved sailing?" He glances at me, quickly. "What?" I snicker curiously at his expression, completely unable to contain the big smile on my face. *I am digging how I feel with this guy.*

He glances to the backseat, and then motions with his head. I look back to see several more pieces of white paper. I twist and grab the scattered sheets and bring them up front.

OH, WOW! ME TOO! #soulmates

COOL, DO YOU HAVE A BOAT?

YOU WOULD.

I laugh hard at the last one, sort of wishing I'd said yes to the question of whether I liked sailing or not.

"Like I said…I made really good use of my time at class that day." He grins wickedly at me, and I bite my lip to contain my excitement.

"What are you listening to?" I ask as I reach for the volume knob on his stereo.

"Local radio…oh, yeaaaaa," he drawls out in a deep voice, and purses his lips into a cocky pucker. I raise my eyebrows.

"Any particular station?"

"Nope. I surf. I love lots of stations."

"Why's that, you think?" I ask, turning my body to face him. "Indecisive?"

"I like to think of it as being extremely open-minded. That, and it's too much pressure for me to buy an album and listen to one band constantly. I like so many different kinds of music. "

"So, local radio satisfies your every need?" He cuts me a look that has me blushing at my unintentional sexual innuendo. He looks forward and exhales slowly, appearing to collect himself before responding.

"I like giving the power of music to the DJ behind the mixing board. I like witnessing the unexpected. I like being surprised by things. You surprise me."

My jaw drops slightly at his last statement, but before I can ask what he means, he pulls the car into a residential driveway.

"Where are we?" I ask, looking around. The house appears to be a new construction building. The lawn is a mess of lumpy dirt. There are several large pieces of construction machinery and various tools and dumpsters strewn all about.

Brody hops out of the car and opens my door before I have a chance to open it myself.

"This is a house I've been working on. I did construction for a local contractor this summer. He said I could use it for the night."

"It doesn't look like it's done," I say, noticing the lack of a front door and windows. "Is there even furniture?"

"It's not finished. Not even close. But we're not going inside."

He pops the trunk and grabs a cooler out and reaches his free hand toward mine. I give him my hand and he instantly laces his fingers between mine. I'm surprised by the quick and intimate hold. *But I'm not complaining!*

He leads me around the side of the house into the backyard

where there's a huge in-ground pool with no water. We walk across the bare concrete patio area and stop at the edge of the pool.

"Feel like going for a dip?" I tear my eyes away from the bottom of the pool and am greeted with a sexy smirk.

"That's where our date is?" I ask, pointing to the huge stack of blankets in a heap down below.

"Yeah…come on, Fin," he tips his head boldly at me. "Bet no one has ever asked you to a picnic in the bottom of a pool before."

I love how he calls me Fin already. I nod my head incredulously, and walk over to the pool ladder. "This is a definite first." I grin up at his tall frame as he turns around, cooler in hand, and makes his way swiftly down the ladder, jumping the rest of the way once he hits the last rung. He sets the cooler down and looks up at me expectantly with that same audacious smile. I bite my lip and turn around to make my way down. *I hope he's enjoying the view of my ass right now because I know for certain that's what that cocky smile meant.* When I reach the bottom rung, he grabs me on either side of my waist and effortlessly eases me down to the ground. *Oh, he's smooth. Real smooth.*

"I brought a ton of blankets 'cause this concrete is hard as hell. But the view is worth it," he says, slowly removing his hands from my waist.

"What view?" I say, twirling in a circle as I gesture to the four sides of light-blue concrete.

"I stand corrected. Two views." He raises his eyebrows at me flirtatiously as his eyes drink me in.

I cock my hip provocatively. "Okay, Mr. Fresh. Seriously. What view?"

"Seriously…that view!" he says, moving closer to me, blatantly staring at my legs.

I shove him back playfully and his chest rumbles with laughter. He reaches out and strokes my arms in response. It feels nice.

"Come here. Let's eat…you'll see what I'm talking about soon."

I kick off my flip flops and he does the same. His massive stack of blankets is actually really comfortable. He opens his cooler and pries a lid off a *Corona*.

"What I like to drink wasn't on your signs," I say, taking a swig of the bottle he hands me.

He smiles, "I took a guess."

"Good guess."

He pulls out two massive subs wrapped in white paper and two bags of kettle chips.

"It's not fancy, but this place has the best subs off campus."

"Looks good."

We waste no time digging in. He's right. It's the best sub I've ever tasted. I laugh when he holds a finger up and produces napkins with little words written on them. He lines them up so I can read his full message. They say:

I

THOUGHT

OF

EVERYTHING

I grab the *everything* napkin. He watches as I carefully fold it and tuck it into my pocket. His smile turns from curious to smug. I blush in response.

Suddenly, he breaks our silent flirting session. "It's getting late. Here, lay back, we're kind of missing it."

I wipe my hands off on the *of* napkin and lay back next to him. Our shoulders are touching and his arm hairs graze the back of my hand. When he points toward the sky, I finally understand the view he's talking about.

The sky is lined with thin ripples of barely visible clouds, but wisps of white are just enough to give the mixture of reds, oranges, pinks, and purples something to latch onto. The sky is a beautiful burst of color.

"Most people sit up on a hill and watch the landscape at sunset. It takes a special kind of person to watch a sunset from the bottom of a pool." He turns and raises his eyebrows expectantly at me.

I look at his face and smile. His blue eyes are glittering with golden flecks from the sky, dancing back and forth between my eyes.

"You have great eyes," he says, looking suddenly serious.

"I was just thinking the same thing about you."

"Naw, mine are just blue. Yours are awesome. They look like a turquoise ocean you'd see in Mexico or something." He reaches his hand across his chest and brushes a strand of hair off my forehead. "And they are so big and round. I like that." I slow blink my eyes, relishing his touch. "Expressive," he adds, looking deeply into my eyes.

"Mmmm, yeah, expressive. They get me in trouble sometimes."

His warm breath blows across my face as he laughs softly. "I bet you can't hide your emotions very well, can you?"

I purse my lips and shake my head. "Your eyes look like denim," I say, ready to take the attention off of me and back onto him. His hand drops as his chest rumbles with laughter.

"I've never heard that one before."

I laugh, feeling slightly foolish. "It's weird, but true, they are like this perfect swirl of a great pair of jeans. Nothing better than a great pair of jeans, right?"

"Depends who's wearing them," he says, grinning his wicked grin again.

I look back up at the sky, nodding my head shamefully. "So, how did you discover watching a sunset from the bottom of a pool was this beautiful?"

"I don't know. I was working late nights out here all summer. I was spreading the liner on this pool, and yeah, I guess I just kinda checked the sky out 'cause I was losing daylight. It seems like from down here, there's less distractions. You only see the sky."

I nod, thoughtfully, and say, "Like tunnel vision."

"Exactly." He appears deep in thought for a moment and then turns on his side to face me. "At the risk of sounding creepy...I've had tunnel vision on you for over a year now."

"What?" I ask, my jaw dropping. I turn on my side to mirror his position.

He avoids my piercing gaze, looking past me toward the house. "I had some shit go down with my ex sophomore year. She was...something." He shakes his head. "I'm not going to go there. I just...I wanted to ask you out for forever, but I needed to get my shit sorted." He swings his eyes back onto my face and looks serious and sincere.

"Why me?" The words come out of my mouth before I can stop them.

He flinches slightly, like he doesn't understand how I would ever ask such a question. "Are you kidding?" he pauses, waiting for a response from me, but I just shrug. He sits up and rakes his hand through the side of his hair and rests his forearm on his bent leg. "Besides the fact that you...look like that..." He shakes his head, appearing almost frustrated. "You have this..." he pauses, seemingly collecting his thoughts. "You know that Parni we were talking about at your lab? The real bitchy one?"

I bite my lip to contain a snicker.

"See, look. You won't even call her that. She is always such a bitch to you but you always seem to somehow find the humor in whatever she says to you. Like she can be going off on you for the pettiest shit and you just let it roll off your shoulders."

I stare in amazement at his detailed description of my interactions with Parni. The raw honesty of his confession stings like something I've never felt before.

"And I can tell you think it's funny when she's throwing one of her tantrums," he continues. "Most people would let that shit get to them. They'd get riled up about it or snap at her. You don't. You see the funny side of it all. I love that. Fuck...it's just...it's cool as..."

Before he can finish that thought, I sit up and kiss him. I didn't even know I was going to kiss him. My body just took over! This man, this beautiful man is like no one I've ever dated before. He's open and honest and sexy as hell. Maybe if I wasn't so obsessed with Jake, I could have noticed him sooner—*really* noticed him.

His hand instantly grips the back of my head and his lips respond with enthusiasm. His fingers squeeze around the hair at the nape of my neck. He pulls my head back slightly, further opening my mouth to his.

I may have started this kiss, but Brody is in the driver's seat now. His tongue enters my mouth and I swoon at the erotic feel of it. He furthers the pressure of his tongue and I feel completely commanded by him. And I like it. I more than like it. *This is a kiss.*

As he works passionately on my mouth, I can sense all of my previous week's feelings of insecurity evaporating. The thoughts of my worthlessness engrained in my brain by Jake are now entering into the mixture of swirling, curling colors in the sky.

My insides flutter as Brody pulls me down on top of him. His hands rove over the sides of my breasts and down my ribcage. He cups my ass in both of his hands and my groin screams for more.

I break the kiss, panting hard against his mouth. "I just...I...huumm..." I swallow hard, trying to tame my obvious arousal, albeit, not as obvious as his.

"Yeah, sorry. I probably kicked that up a notch too far."

I nod, unable to form a coherent thought. I roll off of him and sit crisscross, facing him. Worried my sudden interruption will give him the wrong idea, I scoot closer to him so our legs are touching.

"That kiss was..." I purse my lips. "It was good. I definitely want more of that."

He huffs with a quick laugh and brings his hand to my cheek and kisses me sweetly. I press my hand against his chest.

"Yes...definitely more. Just not right now," I say, and his hand instantly drops. My heart breaks at the loss of his touch on my cheek. I quickly grab his hand and put it back on my face. "No, I just mean I want to do this right."

"What about what we just did was wrong?" he asks, looking wounded.

"Nothing!" I squeal, and kiss his lips quickly. His eyes open, taking in my expression. "Seriously, nothing. I just…I want to do this right with you."

Understanding blankets his facial features, and he half-smiles at me in that adorable way he has. I bring my hand up to his cheek and rub my thumb over the freckle that's been taunting me since yesterday morning.

"I just…I haven't had the best luck with guys in the past. I feel like…this could maybe…really be something." I look down, feeling nervous about being so honest about my feelings. What if I'm coming on too strong, too serious? What if this scares him away?

Or what if I'm totally getting played? My mind clamors back to the one-night stand I had with a football player my sophomore year and I internally cringe at the disgusting memory. I was drunk as a skunk and flirting shamelessly with him all night. One thing led to another and I slept with him. He swore he'd call and he never did. I still see him on campus occasionally and he gives me the most disgusting looks.

"That's cool with me. I want this to be something too. Something real…I don't know, maybe even major." He looks away shyly. "What I mean is, slow is fine, Finley." He reaches in and kisses me again. When his fingers comb through my hair again, I push him slightly away.

"You're going to have to stop doing that hair tugging thing if we're going to take this slow. Seriously." I shudder. "*It's shit hot.*"

He laughs loudly and pulls his fingers out of my hair and tweaks my nose. "Sorry. I've been thinking about touching this hair for a while now."

"You can touch it all you want, just not when we're kissing...for now at least." I smile saucily at him and he returns it with his own.

"Come here." He tucks me in under his arm and lays us back down to continue watching the sky change colors.

"I'm glad you brought me here," I say, relishing in how perfectly I fit in the crook of his arm.

"I'm glad you said yes. I want to take you on more dates, Fin. A lot more."

I shake my head in amazement. We lay there talking and laughing until the sun is completely gone and the sky is replaced with several stars. Before we get up, he leans over me and kisses me deeply again, paying careful attention to where his hands are. My locks almost cry at the denial of his touch, but I appreciate him taking my request seriously. His kisses are like none I've ever experienced before. They are sexy, all consuming, and reverent at the same time.

I could kiss this guy forever.

CHAPTER TWENTY

"So, what are you doing tomorrow?" Brody asks, playing with my hair. My back is pressed against my apartment door as he delivers me back home from our date.

"I got nothing. I mean…schoolwork, I guess," I say, and roll my eyes.

He huffs with laughter. "You should come over. Would you want to? We can do school stuff together," he says, biting his lip, knowing what he just said was complete and utter bullshit. And I couldn't care less.

"Sounds good," I nod, grinning, and he leans in and kisses me again. His hands cup both my cheeks softly. He breaks the kiss and murmurs against my lips.

"See you tomorrow, Fin." I shamelessly stand there, watching him walk across the parking lot. He looks back, grinning. I smile back, turn around and go into my apartment, and sic my grin on an unassuming Angela.

"Oh, God. Don't bring that shit in here," she says, looking annoyed and unimpressed when I enter her bedroom and flop onto her bed dramatically. "I'm nursing a tragic break up and you're going to come in here and rub *that* in?" she says, gesturing toward my face.

"A!" I squeal. "Please, pleeeeeease let me tell you about him!"

She looks at me and smiles, then jumps up and down on her knees and says, "Okay, spill! I want every detail!"

So I tell her every last bit, even the sub toppings. I literally have to stop myself from squealing at the end of every sentence so Angela doesn't think I've gone completely mad. She giggles and laughs with me and we map out the perfect too-good-to-be-true future for Brody and me. But damn it all if I don't want every last bit of it!

***

"I'm coming over with you," Angela says, strolling into my room, eating a bowl of cereal.

"No, you're not!" I reply, pulling my hair up into a high, messy top-knot.

"I want to meet him! I don't want to wait. I must ensure we're not dealing with more Jake LaShae ridiculousness."

"We're not. Not even close. Oh my God, not even in the same league!" I roll my eyes and continue doing my hair in my closet door mirror.

"Just let me come over for a little bit. We're practically neighbors, what's the big deal?"

"Alright—whatever. It's going to be awkward as hell," I groan.

"No, it won't! Let's bring over beers and food and we can watch some football! Make it more like a fun gathering. Guys love football and food."

I turn my lips down and nod, liking that idea, even though I hate sports. I still love the food and beer. I am American after all.

I text Brody, informing him of mine and Angela's plan. I giggle when he texts me that if I'm a good cook, I'm stuck with him for life. He says his roommate, Mark, will be around, so it sounds like fun. I'm looking forward to meeting this Mark character after his shouted words of encouragement to Brody last night.

Angela and I head over around noon with a crockpot of cheese dip and chips and some dill pickle wraps—classic Midwestern high-end cuisine. Angela looks ridiculous, insisting on wearing her Chiefs jersey. Really, I just feel annoyed because I don't have a jersey to wear, so I look pretty plain in comparison in my skinny jeans and white tee.

Brody answers the door in all his comfortably-sexy glory of jeans and a t-shirt. I don't know if it's because all I can think about is that kiss, or if his outfit really is that sexy, but I'm instantly feeling butterflies from being in close proximity to him again.

"Oh, good, you brought food," he exclaims. "Mark, see? They really brought food!"

"I said I was going to bring food, why would you think I wouldn't?" I inquire feeling confused.

"Because all women are liars and cheats!" bellows Mark's voice from the bedroom to the right.

Brody grabs the crockpot out of my hands and rolls his eyes. "Don't listen to him. He's an idiot."

"You won't be calling me an idiot when we taste that food and discover it to be poisoned!" he yells again. Angela comes in behind me and looks at me like *are you serious*, and I shrug. I'm just as confused as she is.

Brody pulls me into a hug and Angela breaks our little moment by shouting back at Mark. "Yeah, you're right, it's poisoned! You know us college girls *so* well. We have *dark passengers* inside of us just screaming at us to poison people!"

I hear a commotion inside Mark's room and he comes rushing out the door and into the kitchen, mere inches away from Angela's face.

"Was that a Dexter reference?" he asks, with a deadly serious expression. "Or do you simply know what a dark passenger is because you are truly possessed?"

"Which answer would you be more impressed with?" Angela asks, placing her tiny hand on her hip.

"Sweet Snow White. Are you wearing a Chiefs jersey? Answer: Yes, yes you are."

She shoots Mark an incredulous look and his eyes rake over her entire body. "I'm glad you figured that one out on your own. If you hadn't, I would have even more fears for your clearly questionable IQ." Angela begins to squirm under his discernible scrutiny and I'm fighting back an uncomfortable giggle bubbling inside of me.

"Could you be more obvious?" she says, sneering and looking over to Brody and me for help.

"Probably. Could you be more beautiful? Answer: No. No, you couldn't." Mark states, deadpan.

"Alright, I'm going to leave if he doesn't stop acting so creepy."

"Did you just ask a question and answer it?" I ask, looking at Mark and taking in his haphazard appearance. His medium brown shaggy hair is straight and swept off to one side, curling slightly at the ends. He's wearing a pair of camouflage shorts and a black sleeveless t-shirt, revealing well-sculpted arms and a distinctive tattoo on the inside of his wrist.

"Mark, cool off. Why don't you offer the ladies a beer?"

"What is your name beautiful? Is it Raven? Answer: No, but close, I imagine."

Angela's face twists in confusion. "I'm Angela. Are you fucking with me? Because seriously, I'm about to leave."

"Don't leave. I have beverages. Please, come peruse." Mark gestures dramatically toward the fridge and Angela shoots me another *WTF* look but heads over anyway.

She brings me a *Corona* and I officially introduce her to Brody. Brody smiles and is polite and perfect, just how I imagined he would be. While he makes small talk with Angela, he continues eyeing me, pulling his lower lip into his mouth and scraping his teeth against it. When conversation lulls, he laces his fingers into mine and pulls me toward his room. I look at Angela for assurance she's comfortable being left with her admirer. She smirks and gives a nod toward Brody to signal I should follow his lead.

"We'll be right back," he says, to Angela and Mark. "Mark, be good. I'm not kidding."

"I'll be a prince to this raven-haired enchantress."

"Honest to God, I will punch you," Angela states, straight-faced.

Mark's face ignites in excitement and his hands shoot up in surrender. "I'll turn the game on. Please, make yourself comfortable, beauty."

Brody pulls me into his room, shuts the door, and presses me up against the back of it. His lips connect with mine and he strokes his thumb tenderly along my jaw. I groan into his mouth at the forceful entry of his tongue. Brody doesn't kiss like a college boy, *he kisses like a man.*

"I thought about you all night," he moans against my lips, and comes back in, pulling my lower lip into his mouth and gently scraping his teeth along it as he releases it.

I instantly pull it into my mouth, sucking off the remnants of the searing kiss he just laid on me. "Damn," I whisper.

"Damn what?" he whispers back.

"Damn, this is going to be so hard." I scrape my hands through the sides of his hair and kiss him passionately, taking control and showing him that while I love the power of his kiss—I can match it. He presses his hips against me in response and I let my hands fall down to my sides, feeling at a loss with the epic arousal approaching.

He strokes his hands softly down my arms, then grabs my wrists and pushes them up above my shoulders, pinning them to the door. *Holy Jesus, this is too much.*

I pull my mouth away, panting heavily. "Okay, okay, okay…"

"Okay," he concedes. He drops one more kiss on my mouth and releases my hands. He turns away from me and adjusts himself and smiles back at me over his shoulder sheepishly. "Do we have to go back out there with them?"

I grin and reply knowingly, "Not right away. But is Angela okay out there with him?"

"Mark's harmless. Come here," he says, as he pulls me onto his bed to sit beside him. I glance around his room and it seems normal enough. He has a double bed with a khaki down comforter, a desk and lamp in the corner, and a bookshelf stacked with DVDs.

"Who's in the frame?" I ask, nodding over to the picture on his desk.

He rolls his eyes. "My two sisters. They are crazy. Honest to goodness, crazy. But they're pretty cool too."

I laugh at his affectionate words for his sisters. "So, what's Mark's deal? He seems funny," I offer, trying to dig more info out of this new guy of mine.

He nods, appreciatively. "He's funny alright. He's my best friend actually. Has been since we were kids."

"I kind of dig him digging on Angela. Is he a good guy?"

Brody looks down, contemplating something. "Yes. For sure. He's really good. He's super smart, but a bit of a slacker, so that's caused him some trouble with relationships in the past. But haven't we all struggled with relationships?" he says, with a faraway look in his eyes. For the first time, I feel him pull away from me, and I don't like it.

"What's up?" I ask, folding my legs up onto his lap. He chews his lip thoughtfully while thumbing the tattered holes on my jeans.

"I don't want to scare you away," he replies, softly.

"Scare me?" I ask, knitting my brows together and wishing he'd look at me to give me an inkling of where he's going with this. The anxiety of rejection is rearing its ugly head.

"I've just...I've had my heart broken." He lifts his dark blue eyes to mine. "I don't trust easily."

"What happened?" I ask, despite myself. This feels a little early to have discussions about exes, but so far my feelings for Brody are at warp speed, so maybe this is the next natural step.

"Oh, the usual shit. I've been cheated on…by two of my more serious girlfriends. It starts to fuck with your psyche after a while. Makes you think it's something you did."

My heart aches at hearing him admit he thinks he's the cause behind why someone would cheat. "That's crazy."

"Yeah, no. I get it. I know. But it makes me kind of irrational at times…and insecure. And I have two younger sisters, so I already have this, like, over-protectiveness kinda programmed into me. With my last girlfriend, from a couple years ago, I was just a mess. She was a huge flirt and it got to me. She kept telling me I was crazy but I kept beating myself up about it."

"What happened?" I ask, pulling his finger out of the hole of my jeans and holding it tightly, for reassurance.

"What always happens…she cheated. Mark saw her and one of our buddies leave a party together. They weren't leaving just to chat, if you know what I mean." His upper lip curls like he's still disgusted by the ordeal.

"You're lucky Mark told you. It's hard being the messenger sometimes," I offer, not knowing what else to say.

"Yeah, I trust him with everything. I already had an inkling she was fucking around on me. Turns out, I was right."

I rub his back encouragingly, and he looks up and half-smiles at me. "So, what's your baggage, Fin? I'm sure you have something, right? I shared, now you have to share."

I exhale a big breath, and release an awkward cackle of a laugh. I see a nervous expression fleet across his face.

"Well," I begin, not knowing where to start. "I've had a one-night stand before."

"Yeah? You skank!" he snickers, and I shove him. He captures my hand in his and threads our fingers together. He presses a soft kiss to my fingers in silent encouragement.

"It was dumb and it was a football player…I'm a total cliché." I screw my face up in disgust.

"A *K-State* player?"

I nod. He looks like he wants to know the name but doesn't ask.

"Well, that's not so bad," he says.

I nod again, feeling instantly guilty for not telling him about Jake. But what's there to tell, really? Unrequited love hardly makes for a juicy history. And then I'd have to tell him what happened just a few nights ago and the last thing I want to do is sully this beautiful start we have going.

"Should we go save Angela from Mark?" I ask, slapping Brody's leg and smiling brightly.

"I guess," he grumbles, and we head out to survey the damage.

"Hello love birds!" Angela says, as we return to the living room. She's seated on the big sectional couch eating a plate of nachos.

I smile shyly, and then my emotions are shocked by the odd demeanor of Mark. Angela is on one end of the couch and Mark is on the opposite. But he's not sitting on the seat. He's sitting on the arm rest with his eyes firmly locked on Angela.

"What's going on, Mark?" Brody asks, warily, walking into the kitchen and shooting a quizzical look at him.

"He's been staring at me since you guys left. Seriously. He is weird as hell."

Mark takes a chip off his plate that's resting on his knees and chews it thoughtfully, all while continually staring at Angela.

"See something you like, Mark?" I ask casually, sitting between the two of them to break the awkward tension.

"Who is a beautiful eater? Answer: Sweet Snow White, with Raven Hair. They call her, Angela." He says her name so reverently, I burst out laughing.

Angela's hand freezes midair, and she instantly drops a chip. Her wide eyes turn scornful as she shoots daggers at Mark. She leans over and whispers in my ear, "Okay, he hasn't said a word to me since you guys went into the other room. Now the first thing he says is that I'm a beautiful eater. Honestly, Fin, if Brody is this weird, I have serious fears for your taste in men."

I giggle and sputter slightly, looking at Mark, who seems completely at ease staring at her. I think it's kind of sweet, actually. Mark is the complete and total opposite of any guy Angela would normally go for. Maybe he's the perfect match for her.

Brody pulls Mark into the kitchen. It appears he has some strong words with him, because Mark returns acting like the perfect gentleman. We all make idle chit-chat for the afternoon. Angela and Mark both seem interested in the game. I barely even notice who's playing because I'm too busy laughing and cuddling with Brody. I try to just sit next to him, but he yanks me over onto his lap, so I laze with my legs draped over him.

It feels great. It feels defined. Brody likes me. A lot. There's not even a question. I'm reciprocating that feeling to him as well. It blows my mind that this guy has been around me for three years and I'm just now getting to know him.

Angela and I finally decide we need to head back to our place to get some school work done. Brody all but begs me to stay and do homework with him, but I know I won't get anything productive done, so I refuse. I'm going to have a hard enough time focusing on homework with him across the parking lot, let alone in the same room.

He walks me out his apartment door. When I begin to walk away without a kiss, he grabs my hand and pulls me into him roughly, scorching me with another hot and sexy kiss. Angela barks something obnoxious about getting a room, and takes off without me. He pulls away and my cheeks feel like they are on fire with need.

"So, can I see you tomorrow or something?" He pulls his fingers out of my hair and brings them down to my waist. He tugs my hips into him but continues looking downward.

"Yeah, sounds good." I bite my lip in excitement and he finally looks up into my eyes. His expression looks serious and I see a moment of hesitation, like he wants to say something, but he doesn't. I retreat into the safety of the parking lot and eventually my bedroom. I grin the whole time I try to study, feeling pretty excited that for once I'm actually excited for Monday morning to roll around.

CHAPTER TWENTY-ONE

I wake up Monday morning and instead of having instant thoughts of Jake, Brody's denim eyes pop into my mind. I smile and stretch, feeling giddy at the prospect of seeing him. I brush my teeth and shove my feet into a pair of tennis shoes and head out to get my morning coffee. I briefly glance at Jake's apartment out of habit. All seems quiet. I don't give a shit anyway. I'm not letting Jake ruin my morning trip to Chaz's. Chaz's was my turf long before it was his.

"What up, Finley?" Alex says, as I stroll past him with a bright smile.

"Alex!" I cheer back at him. He looks up from his phone and furrows his brow at me, obviously unimpressed with my chipper morning attitude. I grab my coffee and pay. I breathe a sigh of relief when I don't run into Jake. Maybe he'll be a gentleman and quit coming to Chaz's, so it's not horribly awkward all the time.

I head out to campus a bit earlier than usual. When I walk into class, Jake is already seated in his usual desk. I hesitate for a second, and then push my chin up high and walk in.

"Finley!" Jen says, coming in behind me. I stop and turn around and see her wide brown eyes looking at me, assessing. "How are you?" she asks, and steals a glance around my shoulder.

"Fine," I reply, trying to figure out what her deal is.

"I wanted to talk to you Friday, but you finished that quiz so damn fast, I missed my chance." She looks at me sympathetically. "I'm really sorry about what happened Wednesday night."

I shake my head, wishing we were talking about anything else. Jen is nice. I like her well enough. But she's still Olivia's roommate and friend. I highly doubt I register highly on her loyalty chart.

"It's fine, Jen...it's," I look back over my shoulder to see if Jake is listening, and he looks away quickly. "Seriously, it's nothing...less than nothing," I finish softly.

"Well, not really. I mean," she laughs briefly, and leans in close to me. "It was pretty fricken' obvious you had it bad for Jake."

My cheeks flame red hot at her blatant lack of propriety in this moment. "Um, yeah, that's really no longer an issue. In fact it was almost a blessing in disguise." Her lips sneer together in disbelief. I cross my arms defensively. "I'm not lying, Jen. I'm kind of...seeing someone now."

"A new guy?" she asks, louder than I'd like. I grit my jaw in response.

"Can we just not talk about this? I feel like everyone is listening and it's weird." I gesture my head slightly behind me and she gets a sneaky look in her eye and nods curtly.

"Check ya later, Finley," she says, and strolls over to her desk.

I roll my eyes in annoyance at the whole exchange, and turn to make my way to my desk by Jake. I'd really rather not sit by Jake anymore, but since we're sharing a textbook and have assigned seats by now, I don't really see a way around it.

I feel his eyes on me as I slide into the desk and pull out my notepad and pen.

"How are you, Finley?" he asks, with his deep timbre voice. I've listened to that voice for hours upon hours, and now it sounds like a stranger's.

"Great, Jake!" I say, a bit too brightly. "You have a nice weekend?"

He shifts uncomfortably in his seat. "Uh, yeah. It was fine. I was home at my parents' all weekend."

I nod in response. Normally, I'd ask him all about his visit and whether or not his siblings were home too. But I'm done being that girl to him. He did fuck my friend, after all.

"So, I uh, that guy at the lab…" he says, sounding nervous and unsure of himself. This is a whole new side to Jake.

I smile saccharinely and continue staring straight ahead. "What guy?"

"You know what guy," he grumbles, and I still refuse to look at him. This is awkward as hell. I can't believe he's asking me about this right now. I don't know what to say, so I chose to say nothing at all.

"Are you going to tell me who he is?" he asks, leaning over to me.

I smile, internally debating whether or not I should tell him.

"Would you at least look at me, Finley?" Jake growls. I turn, just to get a glimpse of the sudden outburst. He looks angry and disheveled. His normally bright chocolate eyes look tired and a bit mopey. He looks strung out.

"It doesn't concern you, Jake." I sneer at him and turn away again.

He mumbles incoherently beneath his breath and sits there in stony silence through the rest of class. I decide that after I get off work today, I'm going to go buy my own textbook. The fewer reasons I have to speak to Jake, the better.

***

"Hi Parni!" I offer brightly, as I walk into the computer lab.

"Finley," she responds, without glancing up from her computer to look at me.

I drop my bag by my desk and see a white sheet of folded paper on my chair. I smile instantly, hoping it's something from Brody. I unfold it and it's completely blank. I turn it over, looking at the front and back, and there's nothing.

I sit at my desk, feeling disappointed. I turn to shake my mouse and wake up my computer monitor and a sheet of paper is taped to the screen.

GOTCHA

I smile at his silly smiley face scribbled next to it and quickly grab the paper from the monitor and glance around the lab hoping to see Brody. No sight of him. That makes me feel a bit deflated, but at least I know he's thinking of me. I sort of love this note thing he's doing. So much more original than the texting every other guy I've dated in college does.

I busy myself with schoolwork for the next two hours and my stomach begins grumbling with hunger. I didn't even think about packing a lunch this morning. Mondays were the day that Jake brought me something to eat. I only have to make it 'til after my 2:00 class, so I just need to suck it up.

"Hey," a familiar sexy voice breaks my concentration.

I look up, smiling, as Brody strolls into the lab. "Hey," I repeat.

"Parni!" he booms loudly. Several heads turn away from their monitors to see what all the commotion's about. The computer lab isn't a library, talking is allowed, but typically it's really quiet.

Parni gives Brody a *what the fuck* look. I bite my lip to stop myself from laughing. Brody grabs the chair nearest her and wheels it right up next to her. "What are you working on?"

Her lips curl up in disgust at his close proximity. "Why are you speaking to me?" she inquires, in her thick Indian accent.

"What do you mean? Aren't you a friend of Fin's?" he asks, not taking his eyes off of her and looking honestly confused. She looks past him, at me, obviously having no clue what he's talking about. "I'm not messing with you, Parn. Fin talks about you. A lot! She's always saying how smart you are!"

Her words inch out between her crumpled lips, "I did not know that."

"I think it's pretty cool you come here of all the labs to choose from. Finley says you're going for you masters...that's sweet!" Brody gives her a boyish, All-American smile and I look on amazed as the normally icy demeanor of Parni begins to melt beneath his charisma. Parni looks at me like I'm going to reveal the big joke, but I just smile kindly at her.

"I do talk about you, Parni. You're a really hard worker." I nod sincerely, meaning what I'm saying. As rough around the edges as she is, I've never seen a student dedicate as much time to their studies as she has. Her commitment is quite remarkable.

"That's very nice of you to say, Finley," she says softly, looking down. Holy crapoly, Parni just said something nice to me!

Brody gives Parni one more pearly-white smile and gets up from his seat to make his way toward my desk. I glance at Parni and swear I see a semblance of a smile on her lips. I've never seen Parni smile in the entire time I've known her. Leave it to Brody to charm the pants off the toughest broad on campus.

I grin devilishly at Brody and he comes around my desk and leans against it facing me.

"How are you?" he asks, with a sexy, sneaky smirk.

"My day's looking up."

"Oh yeah?" he asks, raising his eyebrows cockily. "What are you doing tonight?"

"I'm cramming for a test I should have studied for this weekend, but I was otherwise occupied," I say, with a smile.

His chest rumbles with a soft laugh and he tries to conceal a smile. Damn, I love that. "I'll help you study," he propositions, innocently.

"Hmmm," I glower. "Yeah, okay. We can try." He laughs outright and I beam back in response.

"You want to come over to my place? Or should I come to you?"

"I think...we should go to the library," I conclude.

His expression turns to disgust in a nanosecond. I laugh at his disgruntled look. "Please tell me you're joking." His nose furrows even further.

I shake my head. "I'm not. Library or bust."

He puckers his lips in deep thought. "Library...I guess," he grumbles. He shoves himself up off the edge of my desk and stretches lazily, revealing a strip of skin between his jeans and his t-shirt. I have to physically contain myself from reaching my hands out and running my fingers along his pant line. I fear this *taking it slow* thing is not going to last long.

He leans over and kisses me sweetly on my cheek. My eyes close briefly, savoring the adorable gesture. Before walking away, he drops a white folded piece of paper on my desk and strides out of the lab.

I quickly grab up the paper and unfold it.

YOU'RE WORTH THE WAIT.

My heart soars at his sweet words as I bite my lip in anticipation. I look briefly around the room, and see Parni watching me with a small smile on her lips. *My God. Did Brody thaw out the frosty Parni into actually being nice to me?*

"Glad you guys are done pawing at each other," she says flatly.

I frown at her, "Pawing?"

"Isn't that like...flirting?" she asks, looking uncomfortable.

"Um, I guess. Sort of. But pawing is more physical."

She shrugs her shoulders and turns her focus back to her computer monitor.

***

CHAPTER TWENTY-TWO

Brody finds the perfect spot for us to study inside the library. It's on the third floor on the far wall that has large windows and old wooden desks that face each other. At first, I assume he's going to sit in a desk straight across from me, but he just pulls a chair over and tucks it closely up next to mine. *I'm not complaining.*

As we work quietly on our own stuff, I find myself grinning at his serious concentration face. Then I feel silly for being the one who can't focus, after demanding we come to the library to focus. I keep looking at that freckle beneath his eye, feeling desperate to kiss it.

"Hey," I whisper, and he looks at me sideways, the corners of his mouth turned down, holding back a smile. "Can we make out?" I giggle, softly, at his admonished reaction.

He shakes his head and continues staring at his textbook. I

continue staring and smiling at him until he stops what he's doing and looks at me.

"You were the one that wanted to come *here*…to focus on school work. I would have much rather studied in my bedroom, where making out is much more comfortable." He glances around nervously, looking for other studiers.

I take a quick look too, and see no one in sight, so I raise my eyebrows at him playfully. He lets out a breathy laugh. He nods his head in a *come hither* way, and dammit all to hell, I come hither! He pulls me in for a deliciously soft kiss. I melt into the touch of his hand on the back of my neck. I'm still shocked at how easy and carefree it is to be honest about my feelings with Brody. I hung out with Jake for weeks, and never once would have considered just being honest about my feelings, let alone asking him to make out. With Brody, there's such an ease because he put it all out in the open from the very beginning. It's freeing.

I break the kiss and bring my hand up to touch his freckle. "I like this," I whisper against his lips, as he pulls me in for more. I pull back before he can catch me and place a small peck on his freckle.

"You're fucking weird," he murmurs against my lips and captures my mouth with his again. Our tongues dance together for a moment before he breaks the kiss suddenly, just as we start ramping up. We remain close, drinking each other in as quietly as possible.

I look up from his mouth and am surprised to see his expression turn serious.

"Fin," he begins, and a nervous feeling spreads over me. "I want to say something, but I don't want to freak you out." I pull back and Brody's face looks pained and uncomfortable.

I turn away from him and look forward, casting my eyes downward to look at the pages on my book. Mentally, I begin to prepare myself for him to tell me some reason we can't be together. Or that he just wants to be friends with benefits or something.

I pull away from his lingering embrace. He scrapes his chair against the wood floor, moving closer to me with his legs spread around my chair.

"What? What's the deal?" he asks, seeming confused at my sudden change in body language.

"Just say it, Brody," I whisper, looking down at my open textbook.

"Well, I'm feeling like it's a bad idea now, with how you're reacting, but…"

I turn to look at him, suddenly feeling courageous. He swallows hard and I see a muscle in his jaw tick rapidly twice. That's something I've not seen on him yet.

"I heard some shit on campus today about you and that Jake guy, the basketball player." My lips part in shock. This was not where I was expecting him to go. "I don't know what's true and what's not, but screw it. I'm just going to lay it out there because I told you I'd be real."

"I can't freaking…" I start.

"I want you to not date anyone else." He cuts off my sentence before I have a chance to finish.

"What?" I ask, feeling like I didn't hear him right.

His voice is quiet and low, "I want you…to not date anyone else. Especially that Jake guy."

"You're asking to be exclusive?" I feel the heavy, uneasiness lifting off of me in slow swoops.

"Yeah, I mean. I don't know where you're at, or how available you even are. Are you like, seeing him or something?" There's that tick in his jaw again.

I shake my head, my eyes wide in amazement.

"Well, were you? 'Cause I heard he slept with your friend behind your back or something." His face is surly.

"Oh, my God, would you please stop?" I ask, placing my hand over his lips.

"Well, I just need to know," he mumbles against my hand, barely coherent.

"Don't ruin this," I say, widening my eyes seriously at him. When he relaxes, I remove my hand.

"I don't want to see anyone else. And I need you to want that too," he adds, sullenly.

"I'm in," I say, nodding my head with a grin and threading my fingers with his.

"Are you sure you're ready or whatever?" He looks down at our hands with a sad expression on his face. "'Cause I don't want to be strung along again. I can't take it. And I can't take the idea of you still having a thing for that guy. If that's the case, you need to tell me now because I'm serious about this, Finley. I'm serious about us."

"You asked me out for the first time with a frown. And now you're asking me to be my boyfriend with a frown. Is this really how our relationship is going to be? If so, I need to have a word with my boyfriend," I say, my eyes wide in challenge.

He attempts to conceal a smirk. His face looks so damn sexy, I can't help myself. I grab his cheeks and lay a hard, smacking kiss on him.

"If it means you'll keep saying yes, I'll be a pouty bitch as often as it takes," he murmurs against my mouth.

"You're lucky you're hot." We both laugh and he pulls me into his chest.

"I like you calling me your boyfriend," he says smugly. Relief washes through me at the clear label he just put on us. The uncertainty of our relationship is gone. We are defined. And it feels damn good.

***

CHAPTER TWENTY-THREE

Time flies for the next month and a half. Brody and I slip into a comfortable routine with each other—typically involving him in my bedroom, doing homework, or at least attempting to. We go out to eat a lot, and sometimes order in. We've become hermits, but I can't help it—I'm smitten!

And my time with Brody feels so important. I feel myself becoming more confident and at ease with myself. I laugh more with him than I ever have with past boyfriends. It's like he brings out the best parts of me. The parts that make me confident, and happy—even when we act like total idiots. Yes, I'm doing the typical, *falling off the face of the planet because I have a boyfriend* thing. And Angela is giving me the stink eye quite frequently. But this feels right. It feels major.

Brody pulls me out of that awkward and uncertain place Jake dropped me in only six weeks ago. Six weeks ago feels like *years* ago in my head now. That's how changed I feel. That is what I love most about my time with him.

Thankfully, Jake doesn't attempt to call or text. Class is still slightly awkward, but getting easier. I think I wounded him when I cracked open my own textbook in class one day. He pretty much iced me out completely after that.

Jake is a sore subject for Brody, especially after he found out through someone else that we have a class together. That was the first time I'd seen a glimpse of Brody's jealous side—the part of him that had been so damaged by his cheating exes. How two girls could cheat on him is beyond me. Brody is *everything*. He is sexy and funny as hell, what more could you need?

Angela constantly gives me shit about all the giggling behind my closed door. Truthfully, I feel embarrassed thinking of her hearing all the dumb stuff Brody and I do together. One night, I dared him to speak in a British accent for the rest of the night. At first, he didn't even consider humoring me, but I upped the ante by offering a sexual incentive. He jokingly told me to buggar off because we were supposed to be taking it slow, but when I whispered in his ear what I had in mind, he suddenly became very fluent in Brit.

Not having sex with Brody is killing me. It feels like a slow, painful death. I have to put the brakes on several of our heavy petting sessions because I know if I don't, we'll be kicking ourselves later. Even Brody is on board with this waiting game. We both know, the longer we wait, the more special it will be. The buildup is exhilarating.

***

Brody and I are supposed to be in my bedroom studying, but so far, all we've done is discuss the last episode of *Dexter*. We're sprawled out on my bed, like most nights. I'm wearing a simple camisole and linen pajama pants, and Brody is in his standard jeans and white undershirt. Damn, I love him in those undershirts. They are thin and soft and leave little to the imagination. I've seen him without his shirt on a few times by now, but since I can't very well ask him to walk around shirtless, these thin undershirts are an excellent alternative.

"Why do you wear stuff like this?" he asks, stroking his thumb along the hem of my teal camisole. "It shows your bra."

I frown hard at him. "And what—seeing my bra is so offensive to you?" I grip my leg around his hip in challenge.

His eyebrows raise at my reaction. "Never, babe. Never. I just don't see the point of wearing something that shows off your bra."

"So, what are my alternatives?" I inquire skeptically. *This should be good.*

"I'm glad you asked," he chortles shamelessly and hops up onto his knees, preparing himself for a speech. I grin at his adorable enthusiasm. "You see...I think you're better off just going completely without. I mean, your breasts are very likely to stay inside the tank top, correct?" The corners of his mouth turn down, unsuccessfully attempting to conceal a smirk.

"Are you asking me if my bosoms will spring out of this tank top if I remove this bra—like they have a mind of their own?" I ask incredulously.

He sits back on his haunches and closes his eyes hard, like he's in pain. "Babe, easy on the descriptions, please."

I giggle at his pained expression. "Well, you can forget it. I'm not taking my bra off," I mock indignation, and Brody cocks an eyebrow.

"Seriously...I feel like this would be a really good experiment, for future snuggle sessions. Or even just fashion tips. That tank top looks like it can hold your tits in just fine on its own. But since you seem to be unsure, I think it's best to just test the theory."

He crawls over top of me and I ball my arms and hands in front of my chest. "No way! What are you doing? Get awaaaay!" I squeal and squirm as he attempts to squeeze his hand between my back and the mattress to my bra clasp.

I wiggle free from his grasp and jump off the bed, standing in a defensive stance. "Down, Fido!" He turns on his side, his lips puckered in determination.

Because I don't know when to quit, I say, "We both know you're not nearly smooth enough to unclasp a bra with one hand, so what did you think you were going to get done there?"

His playful face turns suddenly serious. "Oh, Fin." He tsks and snickers, moving painfully slow to get up off the bed. Now I'm feeling scared. "Those be fightin' words, babe," he says.

He lunges at me and wraps his large arms around my waist. He hauls me down onto the ground, pinning me beneath him. With one hand, he pins my two wrists above my head, while the other is snaking under my cami and up my back to my bra.

"Brody! You jerk!" I laugh at the tickling sensation his calloused, construction-worker hands cause on my bare skin. Happy tears form in my eyes. I feel the clasp on my bra break free, and my jaw drops in shock as he looks down at me with the biggest shit-eating grin I've ever seen.

"Oh, Lord, you're totally proud of yourself right now, aren't you?" I ask, deadpan, rolling my eyes.

"You should know better by now, babe." He bites his lower lip playfully.

I giggle, feeling those happy tears slip down my temples as he nuzzles his nose softly into my now freed breasts. "Oh I love it here, Finley. So much."

I groan and bring my hands to his cheeks. Feeling overwhelmed with an intense feeling of contentment and pure happiness, I pull him close to me. His dopey smile only furthers the emotions bubbling inside me. Before I kiss him, I say, in a happy sigh, "*I love us.*"

Brody's smile falls and his face turns stony serious. My eyes widen as I realize the words that just dribbled out of my mouth without thinking. I've been feeling this *love* word inside of me for nearly a month now, but we've only been together just under two. It's early to be saying things like love! *Dammit.* Brody's serious expression makes me sick to my stomach. Why? Why did I have to say that? *Jesus.*

Brody's eyes remain fixed off to the side, not even glancing at me. I squirm to get out from under him. I can't believe I said that so fast. He obviously doesn't feel the way I do. Oh my God.

Slipping back into my old habits, I try to figure out a way to minimize what I just said. I can't lose Brody over this. I can't. I have to figure a way out of this. He rolls off of me easily and I awkwardly attempt to get up, my loose bra and breasts feel suddenly embarrassing. I first need to figure out a way to get him to leave without making things awkward.

Before I can straighten myself, he grabs my wrist and yanks me back down on top of him. I frown, and avoid eye contact, feeling horribly uncomfortable. He tucks my loose brown hair behind my ear.

"Hey," he says, breathing against my face. I continue avoiding his gaze in no way prepared for whatever he's about to tell me. "Hey," he repeats, and I fix my eyes on him, ready for whatever he's about to say that's going to ruin this perfect bubble we've been living in for almost two months.

"*I love us, too.*" He moves more hair off my face, and secures it behind my ear. "Actually, I think I love *us*, more than I love you—does that make any sense at all?" He's nervously gauging my reaction.

I offer a small smile because it's all I can do at this point. I swallow hard, trying to contain the intense emotion growing in my heart. I nod silently and blink. Two wet tears slip out of my eyes and slide down my cheeks. He rolls us over and holds himself over top of me.

"Do you understand what I'm saying, Finley? It means more to me to say it this way. I hope you know what I mean. I need you to understand how this feels. I want to be clear." He exhales a shaky breath, and says, "I love *us*. I love what you make me feel. I love what we have become together. I love how you don't let me get away with shit." He laughs slightly. "I love what we are together. Now. Right this minute. I love...*I love us.*" His dark blue eyes dance nervously between my own aqua ones.

I cradle his face in my hands. My eyes glitter with tears. The intensity of his words feel like they hold the key to everything I've been feeling. Hearing him say those words is all the validation I need in our relationship. Brody and I are for real, and being *us* is something I never ever want to lose.

"I love us too, Brody." My voice is thick with emotion. He kisses me in a needy, desperate kiss. As the kiss deepens, I feel something in it that I've never felt before. His lips move against mine with a purity and honesty, unlike anything I've ever experienced in my entire life. I open my mouth further, and with that, I open my heart as well. I'm allowing all of his emotions and promises to envelope me from the inside out. I don't know how anyone is ever worthy of this type of love, but I'm taking it.

Feeling desperate for more, I bring my hands up into his hair and yank slightly, inadvertently breaking our kiss. His eyes flutter open in question. I give him one quick nod, silently telling him I'm ready. I am *so* ready to make love to Brody and experience sex with someone who consumes my heart.

He eyes me with adoration for a second, sits up on his knees, and pulls his shirt over his head. I follow him up and drag my hand down his sculpted chest and abs. He combs his fingers through my hair, tugging gently at the nape, just how I've told him I love. The first time he did, it was lustful—and sexy as hell. The sensation of him taking control of my body makes me feel safe and desired. I trust him entirely.

"This is us, Finley," he says, in a breathy whisper. "Just us."

I cry out in an aroused gasp as he locks his lips on mine again. I reach down and pull my tank top and unclasped bra over my head, my hair sprinkling back down onto my naked shoulders.

Brody looks down at my chest and brings his two hands to my breasts, cupping and massaging reverently. I arch my back into his grasp, letting my head drop back. God, I love my breasts played with. Nothing feels more erotic than arching into his rough hands cupping me. An exaggerated moan exhales out of my mouth.

"Brody," I say, looking sensually into his eyes. "I want you. I—I want *this*."

He shakes his head slowly. "You have no idea, Finley. I've wanted this like I've never wanted anything in my whole damn life."

I bite my lip, trying to maintain some semblance of control as our bodies flush together again. Brody's hand trails slowly down the side of my breast, down my ribcage, and to the hem of my pants. He tickles and teases my hipbone until I'm bucking against him in frustration.

He laughs against my desperate kiss and slips his fingers deep into my needy center. I break the kiss and cry out, unable to focus on his face or anything but what his hand is doing to my body. We've been intimate like this before, but feeling it now, with our love out in the open, brings the intenseness of the act to a higher level. My hands find my breasts and squeeze desperately to get a grip on the building climax inside of me.

"Babe…are you seriously doing that right now?"

"What?" I ask, panting, and my eyes flutter open in confusion.

"I'm not going to last two seconds if you keep touching yourself."

I half-smile and bring my hands to his back, grazing my fingernails over his sculpted muscles. He groans slowly and kisses me softly. "Do I need to get a condom? I'm clean, I was checked over a year ago and I haven't been with anyone since."

"Um," I croak, trying to clear my foggy aroused brain enough to respond coherently. His hand is still inside me for God's sake. I hate this needed buzz kill in the throws of passion! But I'm glad he cares about this. "No. No, I'm on the pill, and I'm clean too. It's been even longer for me."

He smiles. "I'm glad. I love the idea of our bodies waiting this long for each other."

I nod, urgently, "I'm yours, Brody. I'm yours." I press my hips forward and he pulls back to unfasten his jeans. I would help him but I'm too busy enjoying the seductive image of shirtless Brody and his unzipped pants sliding down his perfectly formed V-region.

This isn't the first glimpse I've had of his ample erection, but knowing that it's going inside me this time makes it all the more exciting. He tosses his jeans and my pants. It dawns on me that we easily could have moved to the bed, but the floor seems like a special place now.

Brody holds himself over top of me, his erection nudging my center.

"Are you sure, Fin?" he asks, gently nipping at my neck. "Are you sure you're ready?"

"Yes, I'm sure." I pull his face away from my neck to look at me. "I love us. I'm sure."

He smirks and his lashes fan his cheeks. He presses himself slowly inside of me. It's tight, almost painfully so. It's been so long since I've been with someone, my body needs a minute to adjust. As soon as Brody begins rocking back and forth, the pain shifts into pleasure and I cry out.

"Oh God, Finley," he croaks. "I'm sorry, baby, I'm not going to last."

"Just another minute, just another…" my voice catches when he reaches his hand between our bodies and places pressure on my sensitive nub, rubbing back and forth. I silently scream, biting down onto his shoulder as my orgasm rockets through me. Seconds later, Brody's climax follows and we both lay still. Our labored breathing is the only noise in the room.

A soft chuckle vibrates Brody's chest, "You freakin' bit me!"

I laugh and look down at his shoulder and the perfectly oval teeth marks I left on him.

"Sorry! You kind of surprised me there with your Jedi hand trick."

"That's called close-up magic, babe." I bark out an unattractive cackle and he pulls back to look into my eyes. The crinkles around his eyes display his sincere happiness in this moment. "I love us, Fin. I want to say that instead of I love you. I kind of want it to be our thing. Don't get me wrong, I love *you*. Like crazy, I love you. I just love *us* a bit more. Is that weird?"

I rub his cheeks affectionately and feel the sting of tears forming in my eyes at his beautiful words. "No, it's not weird. It's us."

He smiles proudly and kisses me. "Get ready, round two is going to be even better."

I don't know how it could get any better than that. This all is more than I ever anticipated. This beautiful man loves us more than he loves me. I get it. I feel it in my core, and in my heart…it's exactly what's right for us. Finding Brody has made me feel like a better version of myself. Saying I love us means more in our own remote and perfect little world. It means so much more.

CHAPTER TWENTY-FOUR

Brody took off early this morning to go home and cram before a big test he has today. It was hard letting him out of my bed after we shared such an incredible night, but I knew he'd been neglecting his schoolwork since we met.

"Welcome to the land of the living!" Angela greets me as I stumble out of my bedroom early Friday morning. She's sitting on one of our vinyl red barstools, eating a bowl of cereal.

I frown at her. "What's that supposed to mean?"

"You've been in Brody Loversville and I've been in the real world, wondering when you two pervs were going to come up for air."

"Well excuse me for being over the moon, basking in the glory, happy!" I squeal and run over to her, poking her ribs. This giddiness inside of me needs to come out, and Angela is the perfect target.

"Quit! I don't want your happiness to rub off on me," she scowls at me, rubbing the areas I poked.

I frown, "Why the hell not?"

"Well, while you've been in your own little love bubble, I've been getting stalked and harassed."

"For real?" She nods. "Who?"

"Mark."

"Brody's roommate, Mark?" I ask, attempting to conceal my smirk.

"Yes! He's ridiculous!" She tries to look truly disturbed. I laugh and shake my head. Mark is definitely one of a kind, but he's not scary. I head over to the cupboard to pour myself a bowl of cereal.

"I'm serious, Finley. He's somehow figured out my class schedule and he's everywhere! He's taken to escorting me from class to class, or back to our apartment. It's weird! He's always asking me questions and answering them himself before I even get a chance to reply."

"Well, maybe he likes you?"

"Oh, I *know* he likes me. He makes that very clear."

"What's he done recently?" I ask, propping my elbows on the counter and readying myself for a juicy story.

"Oh my God, what did he say the other day? Oh yeah, okay. So I was coming out of my comparative politics class, and he was standing waiting for me...like he has been for the past couple of weeks. Before I even got down the steps, he strolled over to me and said, *Your feet shouldn't ever have to touch the same ground as mere mortals.* That's how he talks! And he kind of throws in this weird accent.

Then he said that my face was too luminous, or something, to be human. He's freaking weird, Fin!"

I laugh, not feeling the least bit sorry for her. "I think he sounds sweet!"

"Sweet, yeah, right. Can you imagine him at a family dinner at my house? Coming home to meet the parents. Good grief."

"Hey, you said you were going to start dating guys you were interested in, not just guys that your family would approve of. And Brody says Mark is really smart. Like crazy smart."

"Yeah, I can kind of tell that. It's not that I think he's dumb or unattractive. He's just…ugh! He's so weird! He says the weirdest things!" She scrubs her hands over her face in frustration.

"Has he asked you out?" I ask, bringing my bowl of cereal over to sit next to her at the breakfast counter.

"Only like nineteen times."

"Aw, sad! What do you say to him?" I feel myself getting sad and defensive for the poor guy.

"Well, I haven't said flat out *no*. I probably should have. I told him I'd think about it."

I beam at her. "A! You like him!"

"I do NOT like him! Ugh. He's too…he's too…"

"Too cute?" I smirk and shove a spoonful in my mouth.

She ticks her jaw off to one side. "You think he's cute?"

I nod and smile.

"I don't know." She looks away like she's thinking about him, so

I decide to pounce.

"Maybe we could go out this weekend? As a group. Is there anything fun going on around campus?"

She eyes me speculatively. "Do you really think you can tear yourself away from the Brodster long enough to socialize with the rest of us?"

"Yes, dick," I glower at her.

"Cool, well, I know Jessica and Veronica are having a theme party at their apartment. I guess we could all go to that maybe."

"Cool, what's the theme?" I ask, slurping the last of my cereal.

She giggles. "You'll never guess."

"What?" I demand frowning.

"Beastiality."

My face twists in disgust. "Are you messing with me?"

She shakes her head and giggles. "Those girls have a warped sense of humor."

"So, what, we dress as animals?" I ask, fearing what else this theme could involve.

"I guess." She laughs heartily at my face. I wonder what Brody will think of this theme.

***

Brody: You're fucking with me. That is not the theme of this party.

Me: I wish I was.

Brody: So, what am I supposed to wear?

Me: Just bring that beast you have in your pants.

Brody: You are such a perv. Besides, I highly doubt you want me sharing this beast with anyone but you.

Me: Good point. That beast is mine. Surprise me.

Brody: Surprise you with my beast tonight?

Me: Not tonight, I'm laying low with Angela. I owe her a girl's night.

Brody: A pillow fight will turn my sad face into a happy one.

Me: In your dreams.

Brody: My dreams typically involve just one girl. She's hot. Spoiler alert, her name sounds like Rinley.

Me: Parni?

Brody: liaksdfjkdalldkjafldvbaidoalknvcpoewri

Me: hahahahaaaaa

Brody: You just fucked up my dreams for the night.

Me: I'll make it up to you tomorrow.

Brody: Can't wait. So seriously, what should I wear?

Me: Surprise me!

Brody: Oh God, this is going to be bad.

Angela and I make a trip to the store to find something for our animal costumes. There's a really quirky shop right next to The Tank that I've actually never been to, but Veronica told Angela they have Halloween costumes in stock already.

After a lot of giggling and flat out hell noes, we settle on a fox and a duck. They are slutty, as most Halloween costumes are these days, but I don't care. I'm just excited to see Brody's eyes bug out of his head.

CHAPTER TWENTY-FIVE

"We're really going to wear these? No turning back, right?" Angela asks, poking her head into my room and holding up her yellow fuzzy duck costume.

"It's a little late to change your mind now, A! The guys will be here in like, ten minutes!" I say, sitting in front of my closet door mirror, and applying one final layer of mascara. I drop the tube of makeup and stand up.

"I wish I would have grabbed the fox costume. You look great," she pouts.

"Oh, my gosh, would you stop? You were the hottest duck I've ever seen! Go put your shit on and stop complaining."

She grumbles and stomps out of my room. I turn to check myself in the mirror. I feel about as ready as I'm going to get.

The costume I selected is a one piece bright orange mini-dress with a hood that has two furry triangular points for Fox ears. A furry tail hangs from just above my behind. The dress is definitely not designed for nearly six-foot tall girls, so it hits much higher up on my thighs than I'm comfortable with.

I slip my feet into my tall brown boots and swipe some clear lip gloss over my lips.

"Let's see it!" I shout, grabbing my beer off the floor and heading across the living room into Angela's bedroom. I conceal a smirk at the sight of Angela's yellow fuzzy-covered behind sticking out as she's digging in the bottom of her closet.

"I'm going to wear wedge sandals with this. That should work, right?" she yells, turning around. I look her up and down and nod, approvingly. Her costume is a yellow fuzzy bodysuit that cuts high up on her thighs. Her arms are covered in the same fabric, with wings. Her costume also has a hood with a duck beak on top. Her jet black hair spills out the sides of the hood and her face shimmers in a golden dust make up she's applied all over.

"You look great!" I offer, trying to calm her nerves. "Your skin looks great. Fresh...and dewy!"

"Dewy?" she crumples her nose at my choice of phrase. She really does look great. She's petite enough to pull off something so skimpy. I would look way too hoochie in the same outfit, but Angela looks adorably sexy.

"We're here!" Brody announces through a partially opened door. "Are you decent?"

"Yes!" I answer back, and make my way out to the living room.

Brody's eyes move around the room and then find me. His brow furrows deeply and he tugs the hood of his gray wolf sweatshirt off. "That's what you're wearing?" His voice sounds pained.

"No, these are just my Saturday lounge clothes," I say, placing a hand on my cocked hip in blatant challenge.

"Jeez, Fin. That's like…crazy short." He walks over to me and pulls at the hem. "You look shit hot, don't get me wrong—but fuck, Finley. I can't take you out like this."

"The hell you can't!" I bark back, incredulously.

He groans and runs fingers through both sides of his hair. "Damn, babe. This is going to be a terrible night. Why couldn't you have purchased a big ol' cow costume or something?"

"I thought you'd like it! I wanted to look good for you!" I glare at him, feeling annoyed and pissed at how excited I was to show off my outfit to him. Now I'm feeling like ten times the fool. He grabs my hand and pulls me into him with a pleading look on his face.

"You didn't even dress up," I say. "A wolf sweatshirt? That's hardly a costume," I pout, shamelessly sticking my lower lip out.

"It has ears," he says, and pulls his hood up, revealing similar furry ears like mine. "I'm sorry. You just look so damn good. I'm just feeling a little nervous about everyone looking at you tonight."

"Who cares? We're going to a party Brody. Everyone is going to be dressed up." I cross my arms in front of my chest and he snakes his hands around my hips, resting them on my bottom.

"I know. I'm sorry. It's my own shit. I'll get over it," he says, attempting to tear my pouty gaze off the floor. "Come here, my lil fox. Give me a kiss."

I scowl at his joke, but then offer a halfway smirk. He brings his hands up, stroking my cheeks—effectively stroking away my anger and kisses me sweetly.

"Damn, foxy lady," he murmurs against my lips. I laugh and

shove him away. He captures my hand and keeps me close by his side. "I'm sorry, okay?"

I nod, silently.

Angela clomps out in her four-inch wedges and itty-bitty fuzzy onesie. "Where's Mark?"

"Where is Mark?" announces Mark's voice as he enters. He's wearing a bright purple adult-sized *Barney* costume. Like the children's show, *Barney*. "Answer: Here I am." He smiles at us all, proudly.

"What the hell are you wearing?" Angela barks at him.

"What? I thought it was a beastiality theme party!" Mark shoves the head of his *Barney* costume back and gives her a wounded puppy dog look.

"Beastiality is supposed to be about people fucking animals or something. Who wants to fuck *Barney*, Mark?"

"Uhh, who doesn't? He's purple. Purple's cool. He's prehistoric. Last I checked, prehistoric was fucking bad ass. And he can sing. I'd kill to fuck a dinosaur right now," Mark says, ticking off all of his points with his purple-covered fingers. His expression is so serious, I can't stop laughing.

"Please tell me you didn't think that little speech through. And that you'd now like to take it all back and have a do-over." Angela says with her jaw dropped.

Mark eyes her seriously. "Nope. I'm owning it. I want to fuck a dinosaur." He smiles proudly, and then frowns, briefly eyeing Angela's bare legs. "Correction, I'd first like to fuck a duck."

Brody and I burst out laughing, and Angela's stony glare softens to a smirk as she glances down at her yellow-feathered ensemble. I swear I'm going to fall off my barstool watching her instantly soften toward Mark. *Holy shit.* Mark might just be finding his way into Angela's good graces!

"Should we have one drink and then head over?" Angela suggests, and we all nod and make our way toward the refrigerator.

***

Three beers later, we clamor out of our apartment and across the Wildwood parking lot toward Jessica and Veronica's place. I can hear the music from two buildings down and a crowd has already formed outside the door.

Several college students dressed as animals are standing around, drinking, and talking. Costumes range from sexy kittens, to cows, and even a flock of penguins. Angela leads us all inside, where there's a keg and really loud music playing.

We belly up to the keg and continue the party that we had a good head start on back at the apartment. Jessica and Veronica are part of the penguin pack that's scattered throughout. They are fun and smart, like Angela. I've hung out with them a few times around Wildwood gatherings.

The music is loud and my buzz feels good. Brody keeps seductively stroking my lower back, nearing dangerously close to my behind. It's sending all kind of woozies to my whatsits, so I decide to distract myself. If I don't distract myself, I'll grab Brody and drag him to my bedroom, where we've been spending all of our time the last two months. In fact, this is really Brody's and my first social gathering together. I promised my roomie a group night, and I'm going to give it to her!

I grab Angela's hand and pull her into the living room where a few girls are dancing up on the coffee table. They instantly reach their hands out for us to join them. I don't even hesitate.

I turn around to grab Angela's hand and she shakes her head, silently indicating she has to go to the bathroom. I shrug my shoulders and begin shaking and shimmying along with the girl next to me. We sing the words to a popular *Ke$ha* song as we bob our heads to the rhythm of the music. Damn, I love dancing. It's been too long. A's right, I've been way too cooped up in my love nest with Brody.

I smile over at Brody and notice he looks uncomfortable. Where the hell did that look come from? I raise my eyebrows suggestively at him, hoping he'll lighten up some. He appears to be trying to communicate something to me with his eyes, but I'm suddenly jostled, nearly falling off the coffee table. A big guy, who looks like he plays football, has joined me and the girls up on the table. He grabs my waist to steady me. Once I nod I'm okay, he begins grinding between me and the girl next to me. I laugh at his sudden intrusion and he makes a filthy gesture with his tongue back my direction.

I'm suddenly yanked from the coffee table. My face shows disgust when I look up and see a brooding Brody, shooting daggers at the football guy on the coffee table.

"Brody!" I shout. I press my hands to his chest, shoving him away from the coffee table. "Stop! What the hell is wrong with you?" I try to hold his hands but they are fisted into tight, angry balls. His expression looks angry as hell. I can't even get him to look at me.

"HEY!" I yell, louder this time. He breaks his glare with the guy above and looks down at me. "Would you stop?" I say, pleadingly.

He exhales harshly. "I'll stop when you stop, Finley," he says my name like a swear word. "Stop freaking shaking your shit on coffee tables."

My jaw drops and my eyes turn into saucers. "Tell me you're

fucking kidding me right now, because I don't even know this guy in front of me," I grate through clenched teeth.

He looks down at me and I see his seething anger break for a brief second and then return. He scrubs his hand through his hair roughly. "Why do you have to dance on the damn coffee table, Finley? It's hard enough watching guys look at you in this dress. Then you have to jump up on a stage and put on a show?" His jaw muscles tick rapidly as he glares at me.

Is this a fucking joke? Maybe Angela's right. Maybe we have been way too antisocial. I had no idea this side of Brody even existed. He warned me he had insecurity issues because he'd been cheated on, but I didn't know it was this bad. This is ten times worse than he was when he found out about my class with Jake!

"Listen, Brody. I wore this dress…for you! I danced on the coffee table…because I'm in college. And I'm fighting with you right now…because you're being a psychotic ass!"

He looks at me with indignation, his jaw ticking furiously. "A psychotic ass? Are you fucking serious? Awesome, Finley. Go on. Go back up on the coffee table and shake it all you want. Let that guy grind on you. I wouldn't want to sully your college experience." His voice is harsh—guttural.

His words cut me deeply. In our two months together, he's never spoken to me like this. We've discussed fun things, like our future. Both of us have job prospects in Kansas City, so it's hard not to look to the future and get excited about our lives together as adults. But regardless, I'm still in college right now. And I was under the impression we were both very secure in our relationship, but this harsh statement about my actions cuts me to the quick and rage flares inside of me.

"You're full of *shit*, Brody." I sneer at him and turn on my heel to head back toward the coffee table. If he's going to make bullshit comments about me being a bad girl, I'll show him just how bad I can be.

"Finley!" he growls, and grabs my arm, pulling me toward the door. "We're leaving." The room grows quiet around us as everyone watches in rapture at the ridiculous scene we're creating.

"Why don't you chill and let her dance, man. She's a fox. We're all enjoying the show," a random guy says from beside me.

I glance briefly at the guy. He's dressed in normal clothes, but has an ape mask pushed on top of his head. *Is this guy an idiot?*

I quickly avert my gaze back to Brody, who looks positively murderous. Using all my might, I shove Brody's chest toward the door. He doesn't even look down at me—he just continues glaring daggers at Mr. Apeshit over there.

When I finally get him out the door, he turns and storms down the parking lot, back toward his place. I follow him because I sure as hell refuse to let him off the hook that easy.

"Hey!" I call out, but he doesn't even turn to look at me. "Are we going to discuss this?" I ask as we reach his apartment door. Just when I think he's going to slam the door in my face, he steps back and gestures for me to go in first.

I storm in and twirl on my heel, folding my arms over my chest, ready to rip him a new one. Before I get a chance to open my mouth again, he's on me—kissing me and working feverishly on my shocked and unresponsive lips. For a brief second, I respond because kissing Brody is so natural to me. Abruptly, I get a hold of my senses and turn my face away.

"I can't handle this, Finley," he rasps. He tries to kiss me again but I push him back. His face looks pained, even in the darkness of his apartment with just a soft blue light streaming in the window from outside, I can see something is tearing him up inside.

"What can't you handle, Brody?" I ask, despite myself. I should be steaming mad at him and not forgive him, but shit. I love us too much not to care.

"These feelings. They are too much," he says as he backs away from me, raking his hand through his now shaggier dark brown curls. I asked him a few weeks ago to hold off on getting it cut because I love rubbing my hands through it so much. He was more than happy to oblige.

"I know I'm acting like a psycho. I can hear myself. But shit, Fin! I've never cared about anyone the way I care about you. And watching you on display like that, for all those dudes…it feels like…like…"

"Feels like what?" I ask, my voice rising in alarm.

"Like it's only a matter of time before you cheat on me," he groans, and stomps off into his bedroom. I stand there a moment, stunned by his admission.

"Cheat on you? What the hell, Brody. I've given you no reason to think I'd cheat on you!" I say, walking into his room. He's looking out the window, shaking his head like he's trying to stop himself from saying more.

"Don't hold back now! We're here. We're fighting. Let's lay it all out on the table," I tell him.

"You're telling me that if Jake," he pauses, and swallows painfully. "If Jake came running to you and telling you he wants you…you wouldn't consider it?"

Just hearing Jake's name after everything Brody and I have said to each other feels like a slap in the face. I shake my head violently and turn to leave his bedroom.

"Finley, wait." He rushes up behind me, pressing my front up against the open doorframe, encasing me in his arms.

"I don't fucking deserve that, Brody," I croak out, my voice thick with emotion. *How could he say something so cruel about me?*

"I know, *I know*. But I think about it all the damn time." His statement shocks me. He sounds desperate, hurting.

"Why wouldn't you say something?" I ask, turning my head to look over my shoulder at him. I need to see his face. I need to see where this is all coming from.

"Because it's too fucked up to admit," he replies, sounding desperate. His mouth is dangerously close to mine. "I'm a freaking mess, Finley. I'm scared to tell you any of this because I don't want to lose you. I thought I was over all the shit with my past. But with you, I care even more. Everything feels even scarier. The stakes are higher."

I turn in his arms to face him and drink in his glassy eyes, swimming with torment, pain—fear. "That's because it's real, Brody." My hands instinctively go to his waist, even though I'm still pissed and hurt. "We're for real. I want a future with you. I love us. That means something to me!" I add.

"It means something to me too, Finley. It means everything." He sighs and presses his forehead against mine. "I love us so damn much…I can't keep my head on straight."

My anger softens at his vulnerability. Even in his desperate, wrong, messed up way, it's all still good. He's still letting me in. He's being open. "Brody," I croak, "You can't get all caveman every time I want to have a little fun. We are still in college ya know?"

"I know," he whispers against my face. He brings his hand up and strokes his fingers from my forehead to my neck. He started doing that after only a few weeks. He said he loves the feel of my soft face on his fingertips. I'm pretty sure I gave him crap about being weird, but the sensation is toe curling. I love it almost as much as when he tugs my hair.

As if reading my mind, he slips his fingers into my hair and squeezes softly. "I'm sorry, Finley. I'm so sorry." He kisses me. It feels real this time—not desperate like before. It feels honest. I open my mouth and accept it—what else am I going to do? *I love us.*

Brody deepens the kiss and presses his hips into mine. I'm surprised to see he's already aroused.

"Does fighting turn you on?" I ask, looking at him with wide eyes.

"*You* turn me on," he says, seriously, not allowing me to lighten the mood with teasing. "Seeing you in this tiny dress has been driving me mad, Finley. I need you."

I smile. "Then what are you waiting for?"

CHAPTER TWENTY-SIX

Brody grabs my thighs and hoists me onto his waist. I instinctively wrap my legs around him and hold on. Instead of going to the bed, like I thought he would, he walks us to the bathroom and sets me down on top of his sink.

My hands fist in his sweatshirt, feeling achy and desperate for him to be all over me all at once. He tosses me a naughty grin. "This is our first make-up sex, babe." He steps back, kicking out of his shoes and pants, and heads over to the shower. "I'm going to make it count."

I laugh as he turns on the water. "Don't make a habit of it, alright?"

He looks down sadly for a moment. His eyes darken as he takes in my spread legs. "That dress is hot, but it'll be even hotter on the floor." He pulls me off the counter and drags the dress up over my head, revealing my matching pale pink panty set. The bra is sheer and shows the sharp pucker of my nipples.

"Fuuuuck," he exhales, drinking in my body. Goosebumps pimple over every spot his eyes touch. "I'm a fan," he says, leaning down, and wraps his mouth around my nipple over top of the see-through fabric. He scrapes his teeth gently, tugging on my nipple and I cry out at the painfully, erotic sensation. His hands reach behind me and make quick work of my bra. "Let's ditch these too," he says, pulling my panties down. I'm now completely nude, except for my high stiletto-heeled boots.

I lean down to remove them, but he stops me, and walks me back to the counter. He drops down on his knees. I lean against the edge of the counter, feeling ten shades of excited for what's about to happen.

He strokes my boot-covered calf with his hand. "I'm sorry I doubted you," he says, dropping a soft kiss to my exposed kneecap. I instinctively close my legs. He eyes me seriously—like he's a dog and I just took away his bone. I open my legs back up to him.

When he places his mouth on my sex, I squeeze my thighs tightly around his face. He doesn't seem to notice or care. He works his tongue feverishly, pushing me toward climax. In a matter of moments, I'm coming apart all over his mouth, my head slamming back onto the mirror. If I hurt myself, I don't even notice because my body is consumed with the intense pulsating pleasure between my legs.

"Jesus, Brody," I exhale. I drag my eyes up to him as he takes his shirt and underwear off.

"Am I forgiven, babe?" he asks with a small smirk.

"What were we fighting about again?"

His chest vibrates with laughter. "Let's take a shower."

A shower? Oh, ummmm, let me think about it. Yeah, okay.

***

It's completely dark, except for the glow coming in through his curtains from the security light outside. After Brody's very thorough bathroom antics, I'm feeling completely sated and deliriously happy.

"Do you ever wonder how the heck it took us so long to find each other?" I ask Brody, as we cuddle completely naked in his big king-sized bed.

"Not really." He snakes his arm around my waist and pulls my back tightly against his chest. He nuzzles my hair, inhaling deeply. "Damn, I love the smell of my shampoo in your hair."

I giggle and turn around to face him. Our legs are tangled together intimately. He sweetly strokes my wet hair away from my face, and looks into my eyes adoringly.

"I'm serious. Don't you ever wonder?" I ask again.

"I'm glad we didn't." I scowl at him and he chuckles and kisses my brow line. "I would have hated to meet you a year ago. If you think I'm a pain in the ass now, you should have seen me then."

"You never talk about her. Or your other ex. Not really at least. You don't get that detailed about your past. I don't want to pry, but after tonight, I'm a lot more curious."

He sighs, looking sad. "I'm not keeping anything from you on purpose. It's just kind of embarrassing, I guess."

"Embarrassing? How?" I'm clueless as to how an incredible man like Brody can feel embarrassed and insecure.

"It's just a real ego blunder when you have not one, but two, serious girlfriends cheat on you. It makes a guy feel like he's not good enough. Like he's not doing things right. He's not...I dunno...satisfying, I guess."

"That's ridiculous, Brody." I drape myself over his chest. "You are completely satisfying."

"No, I know," he answers dismissively, like he barely registered what I said. "Thank you, babe. It still doesn't change anything though. Like, Cora, my high school girlfriend…we never fought…nothing. We never said anything bad to each other. We never even disagreed about what movie to go to. She was the nice girl that got along with everybody. And then she was so damn nice that she told me immediately after she cheated. She thought that was kinder or something, I don't know. She slept with her friend's boyfriend at a party the night before. She practically ran straight to me when she was done to tell me everything. I didn't even know she went to the party! She totally blindsided me."

I remain silent. I'm not sure what to even say in this situation.

"Then, Lyndsay. Lyndsay was like, the total opposite of Cora. She was loud and flirty and all over the damn place." He swallows hard. "I think that's why I flipped so bad tonight. A lot of what I saw just brought me right back to her shit."

"Yeah, but I'm not her. You can't persecute me for something someone else did."

"I know, Finley. You're not her. You're so much more. I'm so damn sorry. I hate that I did that. I guess I still have shit to work through." He shrugs and looks down. "I don't know why I even stayed with her as long as I did. She was constantly messing around on me. I was such an idiot."

"And she had sex with one of your friends," I finish, reciting what he'd told me previously.

He nods and I see that muscle in his jaw tick. I rub his cheek and sigh, trying to muster up the courage to open up.

"I kind of know how that feels," I offer. His frown relaxes and he looks into my eyes, curiously. "I don't know how much you heard about me and Jake. I mean, there's not much to hear. We never hooked up or dated...nothing."

"So, what was the deal then?" Brody asks, and his voice sounds thick. Forced.

I shrug. "He slept with Olivia. I walked in on them. It was freaking mortifying."

"But you guys weren't even dating?"

"That's correct. And I know I had no claim on him. It just seemed like people thought...I thought..."

"That you two would end up together," he finishes for me.

"Yeah, I guess. Jake and I were best friends. We spent so much time together in such a short time span. I fed into the fantasy of it all, I guess."

Brody shifts away from me and lays on his back staring at the ceiling. "Babe, I hate hearing you call him your best friend."

I groan. "Brody, I'm sorry. I'm just being honest here."

"I know...and I'm glad. But hearing you care that much about another guy is fucking painful as hell." He closes his eyes like he's trying to compose himself, and it tears me up.

"You have nothing to worry about, Brody. Jake's not even in my life anymore. I love us. That's not something I say lightly. I've never even said *I love you* to a guy before. And I was kind of a serial monogamist through the years, so that's saying something."

"I feel the same," he says, as he turns back to me so we're face to face. He pulls my hips into his so our bodies are completely flush against each other. "My two exes," he starts, "I said I loved them, Fin. I said those words, and now, thinking back to the moment I said them…It doesn't even compare to what I feel when I say them to you."

My heart swells. I close the small gap between our faces and meld my lips to his. How did I find this guy? I don't know how I could possibly deserve it, but I'm taking it anyway. I'm taking it all.

CHAPTER TWENTY-SEVEN

A couple weeks later, campus is buzzing in anticipation for Homecoming. Homecoming at *K-State* is huge. It always has been. Wildwood and the study strip are the two of the biggest party scenes. Everyone who doesn't go to the football game tailgates in the parking lot all day long. People are drunk and puking before the sun even goes down.

Brody and I manage to actually socialize with our friends without murdering each other. It's nice. It feels right. Being able to look at him from the dance floor at The Tank and have him bring me drinks and not glare at every guy within a five-foot radius, shows that we are growing and developing together. Maybe he is beginning to feel more re-assured in our love.

Angela and I decide to invite a few friends over to pre-game at our place before we head out to the study strip later in the night. Brody and Mark stroll into our apartment with several cases of beer. I smile and drink in Brody's tall frame. He's wearing skillfully distressed jeans and a purple *K-State* t-shirt that hugs his biceps. I find my way over to him and pull him in for a kiss.

"Well, hello to you, too," he mews, attempting to conceal a pleased-as-punch smirk. Damn, I love when he tries not to smile.

"I missed you," I say, reaching my hands up above his shoulders, and hugging him tightly. Brody and I have been spending a few nights apart every week, because both of our studies were starting to suffer as a result of our whirlwind romance. As much as I hate it, the nights we are together, we more than make up for our time apart.

"Do I smell food in this apartment? Answer: No. Did you girls seriously not make any snacks?" Mark drawls, standing next to the fridge.

"No, we didn't make food, Mark. We don't have to make food for you guys every time we see you," Angela answers, slamming the fridge door and crossing her arms across her small chest.

Mark cocks his head to the side and says, "Is purple your color? Answer: Every color is your color, you beautific modern-day maiden." He pinches her sides and she yelps and swats at his hand.

"Could you be any more weird? Answer: No!" Angela smiles clearly pleased with her impersonation.

Mark shoots her a challenging look and sprints after her. She giggles and runs into her room. He follows. Mark is definitely getting under her skin, in a good way. Maybe soon that will be more than a metaphor.

"We drinking?" Brody asks, pulling me into the kitchen with him.

"Does a bear shit in the woods?" I ask, and he scowls at me.

"Damn, my woman says the sexiest things."

***

"LET'S GO TO THE BAR!" Angela shouts over the swarms of people that have packed into our tiny apartment. A sudden downpour forced all the parking lot partiers inside. And since our place isn't nearly big enough for the amount of people that were congregating outside, we've all overcompensated with our cozy discomfort, by drinking—heavily.

The rain lets up for a bit, so we all file out of the apartment and head over to the study strip. The study strip, during homecoming, reminds me a bit of Mardi Gras in New Orleans. The partying happens on the streets outside the bars, just as much as it does on the inside. Since we're all pretty hammered, Angela, Mark, Brody, and I, opt to just walk around and socialize with everyone wilding out.

As we're loitering outside of The Tank, a familiar voice calls out from behind me. "Finley? Damn." I turn and see Rider Grayson, my huge, massive, one-night-stand nightmare, standing right in front of me in all his jock glory.

Rider was not one of my finer college moments. I was a sophomore and had been doing fine, hopping from short-term boyfriend to short-term boyfriend, sowing my wild oats. Rider caught me fresh off a recent breakup, and I got that dreamy-eyed look in my eye. He wasn't particularly gorgeous, but he had that air about him because he was a football player. It's hard to put my finger on it, but that player-confidence was enthralling to me as a sophomore.

The worst part of the whole situation was that after we slept together, he went right back to ignoring me on campus. He never even acknowledged me with a head nod. He'd pass me at the dining hall, walking to class, and his eyes would glaze over me like I wasn't even there.

I remember telling Angela that maybe he forgot we had sex

because he was drunk. How pathetic was I to be hoping a guy was too drunk to remember having sex with me. The alternative was that he had sex with me, and it was so bad, he couldn't stomach talking to me again. So for him to be addressing me like he knows me is just completely weird.

"Rider, hiiii," I rasp out, and do a quick glance around for Brody. I see him down the sidewalk a ways, his back turned to me, chatting animatedly with Mark and a few other guys.

"How you doing, girl?" he asks in a thick southern accent, brazenly looking me up and down. I'm suddenly regretting the K-State tank, mini skirt, and tights I matched together.

"I'm fine. I thought you graduated?" I look into his baby blue eyes and feel like he's aged more than time should have allowed. His kinky blonde hair is still shaggy and shoved into a ball cap. I get none of the same feels I got for him two years ago.

"I did. It's homecoming. Gotta come back for homecoming. Pshh…who you hanging with tonight?"

"My boyfriend, actually."

"Oh, snap, you got a boyfriend now? That's a shame…for him!" He laughs, looking back to his friends for support, but they are too busy talking to one another and typing into their phones.

I sneer at his nasty statement. Rider is still just as big of a prick as ever. But I'm no better. I let him sucker me into his bed. We had such a great time talking and flirting all night—sex was just a natural step to keep the momentum of the evening going. I'm the typical cliché though. I believed him when he said he'd call—he didn't.

"It's not a shame for him. We're really good actually. Amazing even."

He laughs, meanly. "I would have remembered *amazing*." His

buddies snicker from behind him, barely looking up from their phones. I love how his lackeys are laughing at his joke, without even caring who it's directed toward.

"Who's amazing?" Brody's voice cuts through the awkward tension between Rider and me. Brody's scent fills my senses, and I instantly relax now that he's standing next to me.

"You're amazing." I kiss him chastely on the lips, and he scowls at me.

Rider hoots obnoxiously and Brody cuts him a mean glare. Brody may not be a football player but he's still taller than Rider. However, what Rider lacks in height, he makes up for in muscle.

"Something funny?" Brody pulls the words out slowly, menacingly.

"Brody, don't," I defend. I'm not particularly happy with Rider's ridiculous comments, but I'm coherent enough to not let it get to me. The last thing Brody should be doing is picking a fight with a psycho like Rider Grayson. Rider is the type of guy that has absolutely nothing going for himself after college. He has nothing to lose.

Brody's eyes glance over to me, telling me to buzz off. I grab his arm and haul him away from Rider, and away from a potential police situation. "Let's go. You're going to end up in jail," I say, pulling him down the sidewalk with me toward the place Angela and I bought our costumes. He jerks his arm out of my hand and glares at me. The red, orange, and green glow of the multicolored bulbs around the window cast strange shadows across his face.

"Overcompensating much?" Brody reprimands, looking hard into my eyes.

"What do you mean?" I ask, my face screwed up in confusion.

"With that…calling me *amazing* shit. I felt like you were trying to convince yourself as much as him."

"Are you high?" I ask, and he continues staring at me, stonily. "Seriously! I'm asking. Did you walk down the strip, smoke a joint and then come back up here and that's why you're saying crazy shit?"

"It's not crazy, Finley. You fucked him! You told me!"

"Yeah! And I fucked other guys before him! Who gives a shit?"

He scoffs, turns, and walks across the street packed with people, to join Mark and Angela on the other side. This jealousy shit is getting really old. I was willing to throw him a bone when I was dancing on the coffee table, but right now, he's acting like a child.

I stomp over to join them and overhear Angela and Mark inform Brody of an afterhours party happening at a house right behind the Wildwood complex.

"Sounds fun!" I offer brightly, my smile saccharinely sweet. Brody doesn't even look at me, but nods his agreement. Normally, I would push the Rider incident, and demand Brody apologize, but I'm too damn annoyed. Rather than say something I'll regret—I figure staying out with our friends is the wiser alternative.

CHAPTER TWENTY-EIGHT

The house is a small duplex, and packed wall to wall with people when we arrive. The tension radiating from Brody is palpable. He's upset—and hopefully kicking himself right about now. I refuse to baby him about this again. We've been here before and he has to realize that I will talk to other men from time to time. Granted, past one-night stands aren't prime pickings, but I need him to know I'm not ever going anywhere.

Desperate for a moment of peace and quiet, I head down a narrow hallway in search of a bathroom. I see a bedroom door open and step inside. It's empty, so I go in and shut the door. My ears are instantly thankful for the break. The room is tiny with a twin mattress. The door doesn't even open all of the way because of the dresser situated right behind it. It looks more like a small office. I actually can't believe anyone even lives in here, but the mess of clothes and toiletry items beg to differ.

I sit down on the mattress and exhale a heavy sigh. A small reading lamp on the bedside table illuminates a soft yellow glow. It's soothing. I need soothing right now. I need to think. I love us so much, but I really need to get Brody to relax with me when we're at these parties. We're so good together when it's just us. But I hate all the macho caveman stuff he thinks is perfectly okay.

I look up when I hear someone struggling with the doorknob, and am about to get up to investigate, when the person swings the door wide open. I freeze momentarily, because I'd know that silhouette anywhere.

"Finley," he says. He stumbles over to the bed, and falls down in a heap.

"Jake, what do you want?" I ask, feeling tired and not in the mood. I haven't spoken to Jake in weeks. He barely looks at me in class, and we never run into each other at Chaz's anymore. It's been nice.

"You're just gone all the time now. I mean...yer here, but yer not really *here*. Do you know what I mean?" he slurs, heavily, and looks at me through half-glazed eyes.

"You're drunk," I say, and try to get up, but he grabs my wrist and pulls me back down.

"I am. I'm not gonna lie. But I just wanna talk to you for a bit," he slurs, his southern drawl more pronounced with the alcohol.

"It's not a good idea," I say, shaking my head sadly.

"Just for tonight, Finley, please. Just for tonight, let me actually talk to you. Like truly talk. 'Cause it feels like I never...get to. Not anymore anyway."

"You're too drunk, Jake. You can talk to me when you're sober."

"No! No," he says, and shakes his head as if clearing his thoughts. "You won't talk to me later, cuz you got that new guy, who's all like...*oooo, look at me.* I hate that guy, Finley."

"Jake, stop." I feel suddenly uncomfortable sitting here with him. Especially if he's going to speak poorly about Brody.

"I gotta say this 'cause it's important, an' you never lemme talk to you in class." I look at him expectantly, assuming that letting him say his piece will get me out of this room faster.

"See, Finley...I'm supposed to end up with a certain someone. My family makes it feel that way. My Dad..." His eyes bug out slightly. "My Dad is like..." he makes an explosive noise and gestures his hands out wide.

"Jake, I'm leaving."

"My family is all alike, and it's all they talk about." He looks at me, seriously. "I have plans for my life, Finley. I have to be with...with...an athleeee."

"A what?" I ask, having difficultly following his slurred speech.

"An athlete," he repeats, perfectly clear this time. "I wanna end up with an athlete. I wanna have athletic children. I want...I want professional sports to stay in the family. I wannnt. I neeeed more than..."

"More than me," I state. I'm reading him loud and clear and my mind is blown as the final puzzle piece is put into place. I feel sick to my stomach at the disgusting shallowness of it all.

"No, Finley, you just don't understand. The pressure. The pressure of my family. They are all athletes."

"God, Jake. I couldn't care less about what you're telling me right now. I mean, honest to God. The fact that you're saying any of this to me right now is just so incredibly pointless." I feel a moment of pride swell in my chest at the truth behind my words. What a freeing feeling.

"It's not pointless, Finley!" he says, turning his dark eyes on me seriously. They are rimmed red around the edges and drooping.

"It *is* pointless!" I move to get up.

"It's not!" he says, and grabs both my arms with his large broad hands to stop me from moving. I instantly feel uncomfortable at the intimate hold. These hands used to be so comforting and exciting to me. Now they just feel like stranger's hands. "You're fricken'…you're all…you're someone, Finley." He pauses, and his eyes glance down to my lips.

"Jake…"

Before I can finish my thought, he slams his lips onto mine. I'm stunned by the pain of his sudden kiss, our teeth actually clinked together. The smell of alcohol permeates strongly from his mouth and nose. This. This right here is the kiss I'd been longing for, for weeks. All that time I wasted pining for a guy that meant nothing. Less than nothing. All that energy I used wishing Jake would see me as more than a friend. It doesn't even compare to what I have with Brody.

Suddenly light blasts into the room.

"You've got to be fucking kidding."

I pull away from Jake and swerve around to see Brody. My eyes bug out of my head at the sheer horror of this situation. I shudder at the homicidal look in his eyes. It's scary.

"Brody, just…" I stand up and hold my hands out, defensively attempting to defuse the situation.

"Just what, Finley? Just let you fucking kiss this dick-fuck in a bedroom, while I'm out there trying to get my shit together and be a better guy for you?" He barks out a laugh, incredulously. Manically, like he's one second away from going completely berserk.

"Hey, man," Jake starts.

"I wouldn't…even…consider…" Brody swallows hard and his face contorts like he's in physical pain. "…it," he says, slowly, paying special attention to every syllable.

Jake stands up and I feel Brody next to me actually grow taller. The anger radiating off of him is palpable.

"Sit the fuck down, Jake!" I shout, and shove him backwards onto the bed. I have to get control of this situation. This is nothing. This is less than nothing. I need him to see that. "Brody, don't even worry about him. He is nothing. He's drunk and I'm an idiot for giving him the sixty seconds I gave him."

"You kissed him for sixty seconds?" he roars, and I flinch at the loud volume.

"No! He said he had something to say. I shot down everything he said, Brody! He kissed me for less than five seconds, at most. He's just…just…a dick!"

My words don't placate him at all. He turns around suddenly, and punches the wall next to the door in one fail swoop. I wince in response to the frightening cracking sound of the sheet rock breaking.

He swerves back around and turns a steely gaze on me. "He's a dick, I'm a dick. And you keep letting us all kiss you—and fuck you. Why do you keep attracting dicks, Finley?" His words are mean and menacing. Without waiting for my answer, he storms out of the little room. I begin violently shaking my head back and forth, stunned by the words he just threw at me.

"You okay, Finley?" Angela's concerned face enters my blurred vision, where I remain frozen while Jake attempts to get himself up off the bed behind me. "What the hell did you do, dick face?" she hollers in Jake's direction.

"Huh?" Jake mumbles.

"I have no clue what the hell he just meant, but I'm sure as shit going to find out," I grind out, finally finding my voice and reeling.

I storm past Angela, out of the small room and squeeze through the masses of people. I don't see Brody anywhere, so I head outside. I catch a glimpse of his tall frame storming through the narrow alley back to Wildwood, so I follow.

"Brody!" I shout down the alley, tottering after him in my ankle-heeled boots, barely noticing or caring about the cold, misty rain. "Brody!" I repeat. "What the hell did that all just mean? What do you mean about me attracting dicks? So now I'm the problem?"

He stops, looks at me approaching, and shakes his head without speaking. The dark parking lot has one single security light casting angry shadows over his face.

"I'm not messing around right now, Brody. What the hell did you mean by that?" I cross my arms over my chest, attempting to warm myself from the cold, damp air.

He sneers at me. "Just seems like you sure know how to pick 'em, Fin." He glances briefly up at the sky, the light rain-beads dotting his facial features. "And I..." he laughs, "I thought I was different. I thought I was better. That I was the guy for you. That I could change and be worthy or some shit. Worthy to be the guy to make all the dicks you've met be forgotten. I'm not though. I'm just as big of a dick. And I'm just as big of a chump as I've always been." He swipes at the rain collecting across his face.

"Just stop, Brody. Just stop!" I cry, but he continues anyway, clearly on a roll.

"I tried so hard, Fin. I tried to make you want me more than any other guy. I tried to make myself feel like I was enough, like you'd never want to cheat. But seeing you..." he pauses, breathing heavily, and a faint ghost of smoke puffs out of his mouth with his hot breath in the cold, wet air. "Seeing you kiss that guy makes me feel like I'll never be enough. I'll never be enough for you."

"You're wrong, Brody!" I yell, stomping up to him and punching my finger as hard as I can into his chest. He flinches. "That shit with Jake was nothing. Less than nothing. If you can't see that…if you don't see more in me than that bullshit you walked in on…then maybe you're right!" I pull away from him and hug myself again, trying to stop the pain from slicing through me right now—and prevent freezing from the cold rain collecting on my clothes.

He huffs hard and turns to continue walking away. I let him this time. I'm hurting just as much as he is right now. My heart is ripping in two at him thinking so little of me and not trusting me.

Suddenly, he stops about ten feet away, twirls back toward me, throwing his arms out wide, and says, "I feel like loving *us* is just going to waste, Finley! It's wasted, because we're too fucked up to appreciate any of it. To cherish it, to keep it safe! I'm sitting here feeling like I've got this amazing thing that no one else can ever even understand. *Us…our love…*it's special but it's slipping right out of my damn hands!"

"It's not, Brody! Not even close!" I fight back, despite myself. No matter how angry I get, I know something will always bring me back to him. I'll still fight for us.

"I don't know how I can be the guy for you, Finley," he says, looking sad and pained.

"You already are, Brody! Don't you get that?" I ask, my voice cracking as the tears fill my eyes. "You are the guy for me."

"I want you forever, Fin. I want you *in my* forever. I want…God, fuck it. I want kids with you! I want a life with you! I want to know your family and for you to know mine. I want more than this college bullshit. This cheating. I can't stand this! I hate being this dick!" he growls, and turns away from me.

Feeling everything he said all at once, I rush over and shove him hard from behind. He turns around and scowls accusingly at me. "I didn't cheat!" I scream and use all my might and shove him again, right in his chest. He captures my hands and holds them against himself for a second as we both breathe heavily.

One second, we're both reeling with anger, and in the next we're grabbing each other's faces. Our lips slam together so quickly, there's a painful bite to my teeth hitting the inside of my lip. But I don't care—I welcome it. It's a despondent, aching kiss. The pain of our forceful encounter further emphasizes our desperation for each other. We explore each other's mouths and find new areas of pain and sorrow. The kiss hurts my heart, but I can't stop it. I can't break it. It's angry, and bruising, and punishing, and everything we both can't say with words.

It's *the* kiss. *The* kiss to change us. *The* kiss to fix us. *The* kiss to keep *us*. Becoming us wasn't wasted. Fuck that. I don't accept that.

Our clothes feel damp and heavy from rain. Arousal takes over and our bodies are pressed tightly against each other. I lift my leg up onto his hip and he digs his fingers into my thigh in response. His grip is hard and punishing. His other hand ventures up to my cheek and our kiss ignites even further. Our lips rub together, like two pieces of silk, with centripetal force powered by undeniable desire.

I break away suddenly, and stare down at his raw, swollen lips. "You are not a dick, Brody. You are mine." I moan and connect our wet lips again. He responds by grabbing my other leg and pulling it up his hip to pick me up off the ground. He moves us swiftly across the rest of the parking lot, my skirt bunched up around my waist.

He breaks our kiss briefly, pressing me up against the door to my apartment and fumbling awkwardly with the locked door. "Keys?" he asks, his eyes looking frantic and desperate.

I dig into the front pocket of my skirt, and in seconds the door flies open. He deposits me on our kitchen countertop. With his hands free now, he grasps my face between his two hands and kisses me so hard my legs squeeze him into my center in response.

"Finley," he says, against my lips.

"What?" I reply, my voice scratchy and uneasy.

"Say it again."

"What?" I ask, in a slight moan, as my ache reaches an unbearable level.

"Tell me I'm yours," he growls against the side of my neck while attempting to pull off my tank top. His whiskers on my neck are sharp, and make me cringe. But his voice sounds pained and angry. I need to fix this. I need to reassure him.

I look at him seriously, and he stops what he's doing, lifting his denim-blue eyes to mine. "Who else's would I be?" I ask, my eyes dance desperately around his face, and I long to see understanding, but I still only see fear, of what I'm still unsure.

He bites his lip and strokes his trembling fingers down the side of my face. He cups my jaw and kisses me softly, stopping only to pull my tank top over my head.

"I love us, Finley," he whispers, so faint, I hardly hear it. I reach down and cup his firmness with my hands.

"I love us more. Forever, Brody. Always."

"Dammit, why did you wear tights?" he asks, looking frustrated.

Feeling frantic, I snip out, "Rip 'em!"

"What?" he asks, his brow furrowed.

"Grab 'em and rip them. Now Brody, just do it!" I groan out the last bit, feeling overwhelmed with the anticipation of him inside of me. I shift my hips toward him in permission.

His face transforms, and his eyes hood with arousal. He reaches in between my legs, grabs a handful of tights by my inner thigh, twists the thin fabric, and pulls. Hard. The soft tear of the material sends a warm wetness straight to my center. I cry out a moan as he tears more, to clear the area for his entry. If ever there was a day I was glad I don't wear underwear with tights...today is that day.

I fumble the button on his jeans and in less than two seconds, he enters me hard and we both mew in ecstasy at the tight, wet welcome. He pumps in and out, slowly at first. His glossy eyes are locked on mine, allowing my body to adjust around him. When he captures my mouth with his lips again, he picks up speed and I break the kiss to release a loud, uninhibited moan.

I lean back and pull his shirt off over his head, desperate to feel the skin-on-skin contact. I stop to kiss his chest quickly, before hugging him close to me again.

"I need you to come," he says, sounding demanding and angry. I look up into his serious gaze. I hate the frown I see on his face.

Before I can think much more about it, he brings his hand between us and rubs roughly against my sensitive clit.

"Brody!" I scream his name, feeling an almost painful orgasm rocket through me. The pleasure pain is all consuming. His serious expression turns menacing as he follows me with his own orgasm. He attempts to pull out, but I grip his hips with my legs and hug him closely to my naked chest as our breaths equalize.

"I love us," I whisper in his ear.

He pulls his face back to look into my eyes, "I love us, too, Fin." His expression looks sad and despondent. I hate it. I hate that I helped put it there.

CHAPTER TWENTY-NINE

I wake the next morning feeling unusually cold. I come to and Brody is nowhere to be found. I frown, looking around for him. I check my phone to see if there's a text from him informing me of where he went. Nothing. That's strange.

After our kitchen encounter last night, Brody carried me to my bedroom and tucked us both in. I wanted to talk more about what happened, but he said he was exhausted and just wanted to hold me and fall asleep.

Taio Cruz's Dynamite ringtone blows up in my hand. I unlock it and see that it's my sister.

Cadence: What are you doing today?

Me: Ummm, I was sleeping off a crippling hangover.

And wondering where the hell my boyfriend is.

Cadence: Not anymore! You're meeting me in KC! George is staying home with the girls. Get yer ass up. Ditch the hot new boyfriend and get moving, I wanna do lunch.

I glance over and see a white sheet of paper folded up and sticking out from under the blanket. I smile, knowing instantly it's another special Brody note. I love Brody notes.

Me: Okay, maybe. I'll call you in a sec.

Cadence: Hurry up!

I lay back, getting comfortable and unfold Brody's note.

Finley,

I'm sorry I'm not there to wake up with you this morning. It kills me to leave you sleeping in bed without me, but I couldn't sleep all night.

I frown and sit up, feeling suddenly nervous.

I just don't know if I can do this. All I can think about are his lips on yours. Seeing his hands on you. That killed me last night. You know my past now. You know this has happened to me before. I never would have expected it from you. That's what hurts the most. Anyone, but you.

I meant everything I said last night. I did want a forever with you. Kids, all of it. I've never had what I had with you in a relationship before. I didn't even know I could feel this way. I've never met anyone that lights me up the way you do. You are amazing, beautiful, funny, strong, everything. Your heart opens so willingly. You are everything I always expected you to be.

I thought waiting a year for you was enough, but last night just brought me right back to that ugly place I've been before. I hate that. I hate that I want to kill that guy right now. I hate that I look at you differently. I hate all of this.

I need time to think right now. I can't shake that image of you kissing him and I hate myself for it. Please, don't come over. Don't call. I need time. ~Brody

I re-read the *look at you differently* line eight more times. My eyes sting with tears and I blink furiously, attempting to clear my vision. He's seeing me differently now? I glance around my room, frantically. I don't know what for. My hand quickly crumples the letter and I slam it against my chest, trying to relieve the instant ache that's forming there. I slide off the bed and my legs give out from beneath me and I crumple into a ball on the floor. A loud sob explodes out of me. I rub the letter roughly over my head, trying to stop myself from hearing the words over and over in my mind. No. No! This can't be happening. Brody can't need time away from me!

Anger suddenly boils up inside of me. I jump up and shove myself into some clothes. I storm out of my bedroom door and out into the Wildwood parking lot. My thoughts are wild and frantic. My feet carry me on a familiar path, to a place I've walked in and out of more times than I can count.

I pound loudly on the door. "Open up! Now!" I shout as I continue to pound, not once stopping the rhythm—I actually bring my other fist up to pound more. "Come on! I know you're in there! Open the hell up!" I shout even louder. I see a few other apartment doors open, trying to figure out what all the commotion is this early in the morning. The morning after homecoming is usually a ghost town at Wildwood as everyone sleeps off their hangovers. I'm definitely shaking things up.

Finally the door swings open and I shoot daggers into a sleepy looking Jake. He rubs the top of his short dark hair and squints against the early morning sunlight.

"What the hell, Finley?" he croaks out in a raspy morning voice.

"Who the fuck do you think you are, Jake?" I yell loudly, only securing the stares of the curious neighbors.

He looks at me, confused, his eyes drooping and haggard. He looks like shit. He looks hung over and sick. I could just punch him right now.

"Stop fucking with me, Jake!" I screech, my temper boiling over. "Stop fucking talking to me! Stop fucking looking at me! Stop fucking moping in the desk beside me in class. Sit somewhere else! Just stop! Stop acting like you give two shits about me! FUCK!"

"Finley, I…" he starts, but I cut him off.

"You're a shallow asshole. I'm not even friends with you anymore and you've figured out a way to ruin my life!" I scrape my hands into my messy brown hair, knowing I probably look like a mad woman right now, but not the least bit concerned.

"I meant what I said last night," he steps out of the doorway toward me.

"I. DON'T. GIVE. A. FUCK. JAKE!" I shout, and then pause momentarily, trying to catch my breath. "I tried to say that to you last night but you wouldn't listen. I'm in love with Brody. I'm in *love*. *Real*, tangible love. The kind of love that deserves my *everything*! Not this!" I gesture snottily between the two of us.

Tears fill my eyes as I picture my beautiful Brody walking in on Jake and me last night. That would have killed me if the roles had been reversed. Brody's right. Anyone but I could have done that to him and it wouldn't have mattered as much. We're supposed to have this special *us* love that's different and unbreakable. On a level above the norm. *Perfect*.

My chin trembles as a sob escapes out of me. I cover my mouth, shaking my head manically. I glance around and see several people standing outside their front doors, staring at the huge spectacle I'm creating. I back away from Jake even further. I'd be humiliated right now if I cared about anyone else. But I can only think of Brody right now. His opinion of me is all that matters and I've tarnished that. I've tarnished his love for me. His love for us.

Jake's face looks sad and uncomfortable. I scoff, "You don't get to get me back, Jake. You don't get to come back into my life and fuck things up. You mean nothing to me. Stay the *fuck* out of my way," I bite out, for good measure. I turn and jog across the parking lot toward my car, tears now streaming freely down my cheeks.

I catch a glimpse of my face in the reflection of my car window. I hardly recognize myself. Who is that horrible looking person with round, saggy eyes? I sob more and grip the handle of my car door until it hurts. I scream out in effort as I throw every last bit of my strength onto the door handle. Physical pain on my hand feels better than the mental anguish in my heart.

I retch open the door. My sobs are loud and shocking in the confines of my small car. I take several shaky breaths, trying to get control of myself. I click *Call* on my phone.

"Hello?" Cadence's voice fills my car.

"Cade," I cry, my body suddenly wrecked with sobs again at the sound of my sister's voice.

"Finley, what is it?" she asks, sounding alarmed.

"I need you," I cry. My sister's voice provides comfort and safety, but the comfort is more than I can bear right now.

"I'm coming. I'm coming right now, Finley."

Before I'm too far away from campus, I get a text and check it quickly at a stoplight.

Angela: OMG Finley, I saw the whole thing go down with Jake. Are you okay?!?!?!?!!!!

Me: I'm heading to KC to see Cadence. It's a long story…I'll talk to you when I get back.

Angela: Okay, I love you. Drive safe!

CHAPTER THIRTY

Cadence and I make plans to meet in Kansas City. Marshall is a three hour drive to Manhattan, so KC is a good central meeting point. Throughout my years in college, Cadence and I often met up in KC. We love window shopping at the Plaza, and of course, eating at our favorite restaurant, *Oklahoma Joe's BBQ*.

I need to get out of town anyway. Away from Wildwood and away from Brody. If he saw me now, I'd just further secure his decision to leave us. *He just needs time. He just needs time.* I continue this mantra over and over in my head on my drive to KC.

I grab my phone to let Cadence know I'm only a few minutes away. I blink rapidly to clear my eyes. The tears haven't stopped the entire drive. Even though I'm trying to convince myself he just needs time, I still can't shake the idea that I've dirtied this beautiful love we have. He's trying to end this now before he hurts me too much. Little does he know, I'm already ruined by him. Now even the radio makes me think of him!

Everything after that happens so fast. One second, I'm texting my sister, the next, I'm feeling myself being tossed around within the confines of my seatbelt. My knees hit the dash on either side of my steering wheel and I hear a loud smacking sound as my head hits the plastic area to the left of my windshield. My airbags deploy, eliminating any lines of sight I had. I have no idea what I just hit.

I come to a slamming stop on what appears to be a huge metal electrical pole. My vision blurs. I blink hard to see where I am. A moment of sheer panic slams into me as realization sets in that I just crashed my car. I scream out, "Noooooo!"

A loud, creaking noise from the pole catches my attention. I look up and see it falling toward me in painfully slow motion. I throw my hands up to shield myself and the large steel beam comes crunching down beside me into my car. A searing pain shoots into my arm as it makes contact with my right side. An odd sensation radiates from my face and I bring my fingertips up to touch it. A horrified feeling rolls over me as I feel a huge golf ball sized lump forming near my temple. I inspect my blood-covered hand.

The On-Star agent's voice inside my car is speaking, but I can't hear her over the roaring in my ears. I can't hear anything. I glance around for my phone, feeling the urgency to call my sister, but I can't find it anywhere. Suddenly my door is ripped open and a man is looking at me and talking to me but I can't make out anything he's saying. I blink slowly and feel my brain swirl inside my skull. If only the pounding could stop. If the pounding could stop, I could hear what these people are trying to say to me. I squint, trying to make sense of his words. My right eye doesn't offer much visibility. I reach up and touch it, feeling confused by the mass stuck over my eye.

I try to get out of my car and the man places his hands on my shoulders to stop me from moving. I frown at him, confused as to why he won't let me get out. Black spots pop up over his face and my eyes blink slowly, trying to focus. One final blink and they refuse to open again.

***

I wake up to a squeezing sensation on my arm. I blink, slowly, and a tightness stings on the right side of my face. Only my left eye opens. I see a blood pressure cuff attached to me. Soft voices murmuring catch my attention. I look around and see my sister, Cadence, in a rigid stance, talking to someone in green scrubs.

I glance around and see I'm in a small hospital room. I look down at my body and see my arm is secured in some type of large square brace. I cringe looking at it because it's so horribly messed up.

"We won't have to operate on her arm. The X-Rays show a hairline fracture, so bracing it will be all we can do for that. Provided there are no complications, she should come out of this just fine. The rest of her injuries are superficial. They look bad, but they'll heal with time."

"Okay, okay. Our parents are on their way. How long does she have to stay here?"

"She should be able to leave in a few hours. We'll come back and fit her for a brace. Someone will need to drive her home. She shouldn't drive with that wrist fracture for a few days."

Cadence nods quickly and covers her face with her hand.

"She'll be just fine. It could have been a lot worse, so she's very lucky." He pats her shoulder and exits the room.

"Cade?" I croak. She turns to look at me with wide eyes.

"Oh my God, Finley!" she says. She rushes over to my bed and grabs my unbraced hand.

"What's going on?" I ask, my voice quaking.

"You were in an accident, Fin. You crashed your car. Don't you remember anything?" Her blue eyes are wide and assessing. The age difference between us has never seemed so obvious, but she looks like a worried mom more than my big sister.

I blink, and wet tears slide out from beneath my lashes. I nod slightly, feeling horrible. "Yeah, I remember it, I think," I pause, unable to admit the cause. "I was just getting off the exit ramp and…"

"And what? What happened, Finley?" She pushes her dirty-blonde hair out of her face to focus more intently on me.

"Was anybody else involved in the accident?" I ask, feeling anxious and panicky.

"No, no one. Just your car and a light pole. They said you went off the ditch on the exit ramp and hit the pole. The pole landed on top of your car."

"Yeah, I remember that. Thank God no one else was involved." I look down, feeling ashamed. "Cadence, I was distracted. I wasn't paying attention. I…" My chest starts shaking with my sobs and she leans over, hugging me gently.

"Shhh, Finley. Shhh, you're okay. You're fine. You're going to be okay. No one else got hurt. The doctor said you just passed out from shock."

"Oh my God, Cadence, my car. Mom and Dad are going to be so mad."

"Mom and Dad are just happy you're okay. They are on their way here now. A car can be replaced. You can't." She nods her head, solemnly. "I'm so glad I was here, Finley."

"Me too," I cry, bringing my free hand up to mask my face. "I'm so embarrassed Cadence. I can't believe I was so stupid. I can't believe I did this!"

"What happened, Finley? Why were you so upset when you called me earlier?"

I swallow, feeling dryness in my throat. "I was a mess. I was bawling the whole drive. Brody..." my voice cracks, and I stop myself before making a total fool of myself.

"Damn it, I should have just come to Manhattan. You shouldn't have been driving."

"No, no. God. Don't take the blame. I was going to get out of Manhattan one way or another. This is all my stupid fault," I say, biting my lip and wincing at the open wound I taste on my tongue.

"What's going on with Brody?" she asks, pulling up a chair and getting comfortable beside me. My sister's wide blue eyes pierce me for more information. Cadence and I talk on a regular basis, so she knows a good deal about Brody and how in love I am with him. She gave me a load of crap when I told her about how we say *I love us*, instead of I love you. But I could tell she was really happy for me.

I gently swipe my tender cheeks dry. "I fucked up, like seriously fucked it up," I reply, my voice coming out raspy and pinched. "Things were awesome...we were awesome...and I, we, both of us I guess...just screwed it all up."

"So, what happened?"

I fill her in on the events of the party.

"You are such a fool, Fin. As soon as Jake came into that room, you should have gotten the hell out of there!"

"I tried," I reply, feeling defensive, but also feeling guilty for not trying harder. He was drunk—I easily could have gotten out of there if I really wanted to.

"Not hard enough. Brody seems to be actively trying to get

through his issues with relationships and his unfaithful exes. The least you could do is meet him halfway."

I groan and look away, unable to take her judgmental look any longer. My body aches all over, along with my heart. I'm feeling like the worst kind of shit right now. Why did I give Jake the time of day? Why didn't I just leave? Now I'm lying in a damn hospital bed because I keep making stupid choices in my life.

"I just want Brody back. He's the one." My chin trembles and with one blink, tears stream quickly down my cheeks. "But he said he looks at me differently now."

I swallow around the huge knot in my throat, trying my damndest to hold myself together. I've made an ass out of myself enough for one day.

"How can I ever get him to see me the way he used to? I feel like I've ruined this perfect little bubble we had."

"No relationship is perfect, Finley. Hell, George and I fight all the damn time. We were high school sweethearts. I've only ever known George. Even though we grew up together, it doesn't mean we don't have our own issues. It's not easy, but it's messy and extraordinary, ya know? Extraordinary is better than perfect any day."

I look sadly at her. My head is pounding. My heart is aching.

"This could actually be good for your relationship," she continues, glancing out at the noise in the hallway. "I think sometimes a relationship has to be broken before it can become what it should be. And you're broken as shit right now."

I laugh and cry at the same time. It's an odd emotion.

"Sorry, hon, but jeez, look at you." She glances down at my arm. "Sometimes you need a little drama to appreciate what you have." I nod, allowing her words to blanket me in a small shred of comfort.

"Remember when Mom and Dad bought the acreage? I was fourteen, so you were only four, I suppose. Anyway, they did a bunch of remodeling to it first and you cried like a baby because they were tearing everything out. The carpet, the cabinets." She laughs at the memory I have no recollection of. "Mom told you it was going to look a lot worse before it looked better." I frown, contemplating that. "You can get back what you lost, and make it even better."

I swallow, feeling the tiniest bit better. "So, what should I do, you think? He said he wants space."

She smiles. "Give him a little space. You need time for your face to heal anyway. You look terrible." She giggles and I laugh softly in response, and then wince in agony. "Then I think you need to do something big. Something to make him look twice. See the beauty after the storm, maybe?"

I half-smile at her advice, thinking back to our fight in the rain and how true her words are right now. Despite lying in this hospital bed all messed up, this is the first time in hours I haven't felt completely miserable. I can make him look twice. I can make him see this mess I made as something that will make us better. I can do this.

"Thanks, Cadence. You always manage to be around just when I need you."

"You mean any time you're an idiot and crash your car and nearly give me a heart attack?" she says with mock indignation and then smiles. "I'm around any time you need me, Finley. Always. Just please...don't let the next time you need me be an EMT calling me from your phone! That is scary as shit!"

I smile sadly at her.

"So, can we stop talking about you and your stupidity for two minutes?" I cut her a glare and she laughs. "I have news," she says excitedly, and her fair skin flushes a deep red.

"What? Oh God, you're…"

"I'm pregnant!" she finishes, with a huge smile.

"You are?" I screech back in reply, and then wince. "You're telling me your exciting news when I'm lying in a hospital? That's so weird," I groan, shifting slightly. My eyes instantly go to her belly for confirmation.

"Well, it seems as good of a place as any." She shrugs her shoulders. "It's early, but it's official." She lifts her eyebrows at me playfully.

"That's awesome, Cadence. Congratulations!" Damn, I feel like an even bigger ass for scaring her like this when she's in a fragile state.

"Thanks, McKinley is acting so grown up lately. She won't cuddle with me at all anymore, so I'm ready for another little baby."

I smile, thinking of sweet McKinley. She's four now and her older sister, Megan, is nine. My nieces are my whole world. I miss them like crazy. With Cadence being ten years older than I am, her oldest daughter is only eleven years younger than me, so she looks up to me a lot. The shame enveloping me for this careless behavior only furthers the disappointment I already feel in myself.

"I'm really happy for you, Cade," I say, sadly. "I promise to try to set a better example for them in the future." My chin wobbles again and Cadence looks at me severely.

"Stop feeling sorry for yourself. Everything will be okay." A text notification pings on her phone. "Mom and Dad are here. I'm going to go bring them back."

"Kay," I nod.

As she leaves, Brody's words about wanting kids with me flash into my memory. I feel slammed with guilt. Brody and I having our own little *us* baby would be the happiest moment of my life. Sure, we've only been together for a couple months, but I can feel it in my bones that I want forever with Brody. I just have to be deserving of our love. I hope it's not too late to fix us.

***

Cadence offers to drive me back to school later that night after I get discharged. I accept quickly because I'm not sure I can handle another hour with my parents. My mother was an emotional mess when she saw me with my swollen eye and cut up face. That pole crashing on my car really did a number on me. My dad hugged me and then gave me a stern talking to about the importance of paying attention when driving. Both of them decide I don't need a car at college for a while. Everywhere I need to go is walking distance, so this is their form of punishment, I guess. I'm not exactly rolling in the dough, so I have no choice but to accept their decision. Honestly, driving doesn't sound very appealing to me right now anyway.

CHAPTER THIRTY-ONE

I check my phone incessantly on the way back to campus, praying Brody will call or text. I considered calling to tell him about the accident, but I am taking Cadence's advice to give him space.

"Thank God you're home." Angela comes out of her bedroom and her face drops when she takes in the sight of me. "What the hell happened to you?" Her horrified expression is too much to take, so I look away from her and walk slowly toward the bathroom.

"I crashed my car," I answer, putting my pain meds up in the medicine cabinet.

"Finley, your face! Oh my God, what happened?"

I tell her all the details of the crash.

"I wanted to call you so bad today but I didn't want to interrupt your time with your sister. Jesus! Why did no one call me?" she shrieks, walking over to me by the sink to inspect my injuries.

"It looks worse than it is," I say dismissively. "It's painful as hell, but the doctor said it's nothing that won't heal on its own. Just a fracture," I say when she turns my braced wrist over for inspection.

"I should have gone with you. I'm such an ass."

"Stop. This is all me. One-hundred percent my fault. I'm an idiot and I deserve everything right now." My right eye is still extremely swollen but I can see out of it now.

Finley," Angela groans and hugs me softly. Her embrace breaks my cold reserve and tears slip down my cheeks onto her shoulder.

"Oh, A, I'm such an idiot. I feel like such an ass. First the shit with Jake, then my fight with Brody, and now I wreck my car. Damn it, why do I keep screwing things up so bad?" My watery eyes look anxiously into hers for any type of answer she can give me.

"They say bad things happen in threes! If that's the case, you're done. You're good now."

I shake my head dismissively.

"So, what the hell happened with Brody? All I know is that you ripped Jake a royal new asshole, which was epic, by the way." She giggles and I giggle back, wincing at the pain in my head. "Five-star performance...hands down. So, what's the deal?"

I motion for her to follow me to my room and she saddles up next to me on my bed.

I sigh, heavily. "Brody flipped out about the Jake thing, and we fought...like, seriously fought."

I touch my swollen tender eye, just to check and make sure it's not bleeding again. "Anyway, I thought things were okay, but he left me this letter this morning." I grab the note out of my pocket and hand it to her. Having her read it is easier than explaining it.

"Shiiiiit, Finley. What the hell?"

I nod, "I know. It's bad."

"So, what are you going to do?"

"I'm sure as shit not going to make this easy on Brody. I'm not just going to lie back and let him just fizzle out of my life. Space is the last thing I want. But you know, I'm actually glad that Jake said all the crazy things he said to me. Because, the beautiful thing is, A, I didn't care! Like, not at all! I didn't even need to hear what he said to me. I mean, I'm not going to lie, it's a little nice knowing that he really is just a douche." Angela huffs a knowing laugh. "But even if I never would have known why Jake wasn't into me, it wouldn't matter. Brody completely and utterly eclipses Jake. There's no comparison!"

Angela smiles. "So you just have to tell Brody that!"

I nod, "I think I need to do more than just tell him that, though. I need to make him feel the way he made me feel when we first met." I pull my lower lip into my mouth, deep in thought. "When I think back to our first date…he made me feel like, like…*everything*. I have to do that for him."

Angela squeals and lies down next to me.

"So, you have a plan then?"

"I think so. But I'm going to give him a couple days. I can't show up looking like this anyway. He wants time, so I'm going to try to give it to him."

"I'm here to help anyway you need it."

"Thanks, A. Hey, how was the rest of your night? Did Mark drive you crazy?"

She looks at me with a naughty smirk.

"Why are you giving me that look?" I laugh softly and shove her. Damn, it feels good to laugh. It hurts, but it feels good at the same time.

"I feel dumb talking about this after all the craziness that happened to you today."

"Oh, please, I need some lightness. Seriously. I'm so freaking depressed. Give me something else to focus on besides myself."

"Okay, okay," she says, sitting up and looking at me with an adorable brightness in her eyes. "He's so weird, but shit…I think I actually like him!"

"Give me details!" I say, excitedly. "What changed your mind?"

"Oh my gosh, how did it even start? So, he was kind of sticking close to me a lot when we were walking around on the strip." Angela continues, "He was being weird…like he always is…he kept doing that asking-then-answering-his-own-questions thing that he does. But after last night, I now think it's flipping adorable."

"Why? What happened?"

"I was standing in that alley area by The Tank, fixing the strap on my purse that broke. Anyway, he came over to help me, which was nice. And while we're both staring down at it, he goes, *Question: Can I kiss you? Answer: Hell yes.* And he just laid one on me. Like…smoking hot, scorching kiss, Finley."

My jaw drops and my eyes go wide. Or, at least, one of my eyes.

"It was like…I wasn't really seeing him sexually before then. But once he kissed me and…just like…took the kiss like a man. Shit, I see him in a whole new light now!"

"So, what happened after that?"

"Well, I mean, not a ton. We went to that afterhours party where you ran into Jake. Thanks for bailing on me, whore—you're lucky I had Mark with me."

I cringe at my rude behavior and she rolls her eyes, clearly letting me off the hook.

"I didn't really want to go back to our place 'cause I figured you and Brody were getting it on or fighting. So I went back to Mark's and spent the night there."

"You did?" She nods, enthusiastically. I nod back at her like I'm waiting for her to finish. She doesn't say anything. "Come on! Then what?" I squeal out in frustration.

"I didn't sleep with him if that's what you're asking!" She looks at me with outrage. "We just cuddled all night." She shrugs her shoulders and laughs, appearing to remember something funny but she doesn't share it. I grin at her beaming smile, feeling happy for her.

"We may have hooked up a little this morning, but there was this crazy girl screaming at a basketball player in the Wildwood parking lot that totally interrupted our moment."

I groan. "You could hear me from Brody and Mark's place?"

"Yeah, dude. You were loud as hell."

I shake my head, "Wait, was Brody there with you? Did you see him then?"

She looks down, uncomfortably. "What, A? Tell me!"

"I promised I wouldn't."

"Wouldn't what?" I ask, leaning toward her, preparing myself to physically force it out of her.

"Argh. I knew when he asked me that I would tell you. Why would he think I wouldn't? Girl-code before bro-code any day." She pauses and looks at me, thoughtfully.

"He left his apartment really early. It was still dark out even. I think he was surprised and taken off guard to see me there, in Mark's clothes, no less." She sneers. "I was just coming out of the bathroom and saw he had a bag with him. I asked him where he was going and he refused to tell me, at first. He only told me after I promised I wouldn't tell you." She looks down, avoiding my eye contact.

"Angela, tell me!" I say urgently.

"He said he needed time away from Wildwood…from everything. He's skipping classes this week, I guess."

"Where'd he go?"

"His parents' house…in Topeka."

My heart drops. Topeka? To his parents? I don't even know the address there. We've not yet come to the *meeting the family* portion of our relationship. I know he has two teenage sisters he's very protective of. He even admitted to being a bit of a momma's boy. Mostly, I remember him telling me how much he admires his parents relationship. He said he rarely ever saw his parent's watch TV. They'd always sit in their sunroom and visit every evening. He speaks fondly of his family. We'd been planning on going back for a weekend soon. Honestly, we've been too wrapped up in each other to make time for family meetings.

Him being gone for a whole week is definitely not what I anticipated when I was dreaming up a way to get him back. My heart clenches. Jesus. If he had to skip classes for a whole week, he must be really serious about this break. What if I can't get him back? What if this is final?

"I have to go there, A. I have to see him. I need to do something big to make up for everything. I can't let him be gone for a whole week figuring out ways to end us permanently!"

"Yeah, okay. What can I do?"

"Jeez, I feel like such an ass. I don't even know his parents' address. Their names are Anne and Mike."

She smiles, saucily. "Mark and Brody grew up together, he'll help us."

***

The next day, Angela and I go over to see Mark. Jake looks horrified by my injuries in class, but thankfully doesn't ask me anything about them. He instead eavesdrops on my whole conversation with Jen about my car wreck. I don't want to say a word to Jen about the whole ordeal, but if I don't tell people the truth, rumors will circulate. If a rumor gets started about Brody giving me these injuries, I'll never forgive myself. Parni was the real shock. She seemed genuinely concerned and even went out and bought me lunch today. It was really sweet.

Before Mark even allows me to ask about Brody's parents' house, he starts firing off medical questions. After asking me exactly 37 questions about my injuries, he concedes that I'm not suffering a concussion or bleeding internally. Finally, he listens to Angela requesting information about where Brody's at.

"Your request is blasphemy. Brody made it very clear that we weren't supposed to say anything. While your injuries are tragic, they aren't life threatening...so nothing changes." He glowers down at Angela accusingly. "So no, I will not tell you where his parents live."

Angela turns her back on Mark. "It's fine, we can find it on the internet."

Mark looks wounded at her blatant shift in body language. When we came over, he hugged her tightly and rubbed his thumbs on her earlobes. I was stunned to see Angela appearing to love the gesture. She's normally so tough. Mark is bringing out a whole new side of her.

"My pet, he didn't want to be disturbed. I will admit that I think he may want to know about Finley's accident, but that's not our place to say anything," he says, placing a hand on her hip.

"Mark, remove your hand right now. You are now the enemy."

"The enemy?" he asks with wide, horrified eyes. "I'm not the enemy. I'm your snuggle-snatcher!"

I laugh loudly at Angela's horrified expression. She turns and cuts him a mean look. "Mark, I like you. That's established. We had some fun the other night. But Finley needs me right now and you're only making our mission more difficult." She crosses her arms over her small chest and narrows her eyes on him. "So, Question: Will you help us? Answer: Hell yes you will...or my ass won't step another foot into that room." She points at Mark's room and his brows knit together.

"This is snuggle manipulation. I do not approve." He appears to be warring with himself but then relaxes. "Very well. I'll help you. But don't ever threaten to deny me my one true beauty again." He strokes her long black hair adoringly, and kisses the top of her head.

Her face softens at his touch and I find myself grinning at the blatant chemistry between them. Mark jots the address down and explains that Brody's mom stays at home, so she should be home all day with Brody, unless Brody is fishing at his uncle's creek. The creek is apparently where Brody spent a lot of his time growing up. I remember him mentioning it to me before.

The paper feels heavy in my hand. Going to Topeka and marching into the house that hosts his whole family, a family I haven't even met yet, is going to be horribly uncomfortable. And with my messed up face, this could all go really bad.

"I'll drive you," Angela offers as we walk back to our apartment.

"Actually, I'm going to ask Cadence." Angela looks wounded. "I'm sorry, A. Normally I'd have you be right there beside me. But the fact that we haven't met each other's families yet feels like just another barrier. I'm thinking if I bring Cadence, and maybe my nieces, it might help move us over this bad patch. I know it's a lot to throw at him right after a breakup, but I just want to do something big. Something more. I'm ready to take the next step. I have to show him I'm serious."

She nods thoughtfully, seemingly understanding my plan. "When are you going to go?"

"Hopefully tomorrow, we'll see what works with Cade. She's going to grumble about taking the girls out of school, but I know she'll do it." Cadence is just one of those sisters. She acts tough but she would do anything for me. And I'm the same for her and her two girls…they are a part of me. Having them with me tomorrow will help me no matter what happens.

CHAPTER THIRTY-TWO

"Parni, can I talk to you for a second?" I ask from behind my computer lab desk. She looks up at me, confused.

"Sure," she says, looking back at her computer, obviously engrossed with her work.

"I was wondering if maybe we could step out into the hallway?" I look around at the other students stationed throughout the lab. Brody was right—you can hear a pin drop in this place.

She sighs and follows me out the door. I lead the way over to a more private area down the hallway.

"Hey, so, I wondered if I could ask a favor of you?"

"Me?" she does nothing to hide the surprised expression.

"Yeah, I need to go do something. I have to head to Topeka to see Brody. We had a big stupid ordeal this past week and he sort of...I'm sorry, you probably don't even care about this stuff."

"What is it you need?"

"I'm wondering if you can monitor the lab for me tomorrow.

It's just for a couple hours. Normally I can have another tech fill in from a different lab, but on such late notice, they can't find me anybody. I really need to leave town tomorrow."

"I don't know, Finley." She looks torn.

"Parni, all you have to do is sit there. You don't even have to tell anyone you're the monitor. Just sit at your regular place and if they ask where I am, just tell them I went to the bathroom or got food or something. I'd call in sick but I've already called in too many days this year."

"I guess, maybe…"

"I wouldn't ask you if I wasn't desperate. And since you're in the lab all day on Wednesdays anyway, it would be the perfect solution! I'll pay you!"

She scowls even further. "I don't want your money. That's offensive."

I raise my eyebrows. "So, you'll do it?" I ask, feeling desperate. If I can't do this tomorrow, it will kill me. The longer I stay away from Brody, the more I obsess over what this break is doing to us. We don't need a break. We need to be together. He's had enough time.

"Yes," she clips out. I squeal and hug her. She instantly stiffens and I release her, feeling like I overstepped a major boundary.

She gives me the tiniest of smiles and then puts on her *all business* face. "I'm not sitting in your desk. I like my desk."

"Whatever you're comfortable with," I nod, eagerly.

"Okay, tell me what I need to know."

I relay the very minimal information Parni needs to know in the event that she has to actually do something. I then give her the lab keys to open up tomorrow. I could get in so much trouble for this, but I just feel like I can count on Parni. We exchange cell numbers so she can call if she needs to, but I'm certain she'll be fine.

***

I toss and turn all night, feeling gutted that I've not heard a word from Brody in three days. My injuries look better in only a few days. However, while all the obvious injuries look better, more black and blue bruises pop up throughout my body in areas I didn't even realize suffered trauma. The E.R. nurse followed up with me the day after I left and said that the bruising was normal and to be expected after suffering the crash I did.

My right eye looks considerably better though. Today was the first day I was able to apply makeup onto it without cringing. It has a red patch that looks like a big curling iron burn up near the temple, but the swelling is a lot better. I'm starting to look like myself again. Hopefully my injuries aren't the first thing Brody notices when he sees me tomorrow.

It's killing me not to call or text him. I don't know how it's so easy for him to take this break from me. Considering a life without Brody, pains me beyond comprehension. My eyes well with tears any time I picture our lives with anyone else. I don't want anyone else. I want Brody. That night on the floor in my room, when I said I loved us, meant more to me than any other moment in my entire life. When I said those words, I never imagined a barrier like stupidity and jealousy breaking us. We need to become more than our flaws. We need to become us again. I need to show him how we can do that together.

***

Cadence and the girls show up at Wildwood the next day, just after lunchtime to pick me up. I'm already waiting on them outside, feeling too nervous and claustrophobic in my own apartment.

"Finley!" McKinley yells my name and comes rushing up to me, wrapping her arms around my hips.

"MK! You look so pretty!" I smile, astonished. Damn, my sister pulled out all the stops. McKinley's wearing a bright yellow sundress with pink converse sneakers. The sneakers make me smile. They are *so* McKinley.

"Hey, Fin," Megan comes walking up to me, looking way taller than the last time I saw her. If I end up leaving today without Brody, I at least got to see my beautiful nieces.

"Your hair is getting long!" I tug a strand of her nearly white blonde hair and she smiles shyly. "And you're so tall!" I pull her into my side and rub McKinley's back at the same time.

"Mommy said you crashed," McKinley says, grabbing my wrist brace curiously. The constant aching has finally stopped but I'm still treating it carefully.

I squat down to look her in the eyes. "I did crash. I crashed hard. But I learned a really, really good lesson. I need to be much more careful whenever I drive. I need to put all of my focus on the road and nothing else. Not even cute little nieces like you!" I finish, and pinch her nose.

She smiles but then turns serious. "My bus driver yells at us on the bus sometimes. I'm going to tell him that he shouldn't do that anymore. He needs to focus."

"Well, that's not your place, MK. A bus driver is a really good driver. You let him do what he thinks is right, okay?"

She scowls at me, clearly not convinced. Oh Lord, she is so her mother's daughter.

"You guys want to meet my boyfriend's family?" I ask, attempting to change the subject.

"I thought he dumped you?" Megan blurts out.

"Megan!" Cadence scolds as she walks up to us stuffing her keys inside her purse.

"What? I thought you said Finley was trying to win her boyfriend back. Doesn't that mean he dumped her?"

I turn wide eyes to Cadence.

"You don't need to know the details, just smile and look cute, okay?" Cadence ruffles Megan's hair and Megan groans and heads over to the side mirror of their vehicle to inspect the damage.

"I want to meet your boyfriend, Finley," McKinley says, wrapping her small hand around mine.

"I want you to meet him too!" I reply, smiling, but I'm suddenly sick with nerves. God, this could go so bad. I should have thought this plan through more. What if his parents don't let me in the house for hurting their precious son?

***

I've never actually done anything in Topeka, except get gas on my way to Kansas City. It's an hour drive from Manhattan, so my nerves are bubbling the entire way with anticipation. I'm scared out of my mind that I'm pushing Brody too hard. Showing up at his parents' house is a lot. I could very well be in for an awkward pat-on-the-back dismissal. Not to mention this is the worst kind of first impression to a family. What do I even say to them? *Hi there, I'm Finley. I got in a rip-roaring fight with your son Saturday night and I'm here to beg and grovel.* I cringe at the audacity of my actions right now, but I don't care. I have to try. That's why I called in some reinforcements.

Cadence complained for a good five minutes about having to drive herself and her two young girls across the state of Kansas. But I knew she'd do it. She is dying to meet Brody, and if this helps me win him back, she wants to be a part of it.

Having her here will be good for either outcome. First of all, my two beautiful blonde nieces can win over any family. So, if showing up on the doorstep of Brody's parents after a terrible fight is a bad first impression, I'll have two cuties with me to soften the blow. And if things go bad—if Brody laughs in my face and sends me packing, at least I'll have Cadence and the girls there to comfort me.

"So, what's your plan here?" Cadence asks, interrupting my silent contemplation.

"Well, I figured we'd go to the door together. You, me, and the girls, I guess. I'm just assuming someone will be home. Brody's mom doesn't work, so I imagine she's home…and Brody, I hope. His sisters will still be in school and his dad will be working, I'm sure."

"So, your big grand plan is to use my beautiful babies as leverage to make you not look criminally insane?"

"Yeah, pretty much."

"Perfection. You owe me big for this one, sister. I pulled the girls out of school for this."

"I know, I know. I owe you big. You didn't tell Mom, did you? She will think I'm crazy."

"I may have mentioned it. But don't worry, I sold the story well. She said that you must really love this guy to go to such extremes."

I smile at that. "I do. I love *us*, Cade. I have to get him back."

"It'll be okay, Finley. With all of us there, the situation will feel very light and proper. Stop worrying!"

The directions my phone is giving me take us into a beautiful residential neighborhood with newer looking large family homes. Not mansions by any means, but nice, well-kept houses. The neighborhood looks like it should be featured in the Topeka Visitor Guide. Huge orange fall leaves are scattered all over the streets and the weather is unseasonably warm for Kansas this time of year.

"Okay, it's right up here. Park on the road." I say, fidgeting in my seat.

Cadence parks up along the curb in front of Brody's house. I hop out of the car and smooth down my teal colored sundress. I never wear this dress, but anticipating that this will be the first time I meet Brody's parents, I knew I had to ditch the hoodie. I'm hoping no one notices the black bruises on my two kneecaps from hitting the dash.

"Let's do this before I lose my nerve."

Cadence straightens the girls' clothes and we walk across the street toward a two story Colonial-style brick house with a deep red painted door. My curiosity peaks, wondering what Brody was like growing up here. I take a deep breath and ring the bell. I glance nervously at Cadence. She smiles at me, reassuringly. A moment later, a beautiful, short, curvy woman answers the door.

"Hello there," she says, opening the door wider.

"Hi, I'm, uhh, I'm Finley. This is my sister Cadence and her two daughters, Megan and McKinley."

"You're Finley, Finley?" the woman asks, repeating my name twice, looking shocked and awed.

"Yeah, you're Brody's Mom, right?" I ask nervously, touching my right eye, hoping my makeup is still concealing the scab.

"Yes, I'm Anne!" she says brightly.

"Hello, um…is Brody home?" I ask, not sure what else to say.

She shakes her head quickly, "I'm sorry…he's not…he's fishing, I believe. I'm so sorry! Did he know you were coming?"

"I uhhh, umm…" I trail off.

"Finley wanted to surprise Brody. My daughters and I happened to be in Topeka today. She mentioned Brody was home this week and I begged her to introduce us. She speaks so highly of him. You're his mom?"

"Yes, I am. How nice of you to stop! Please, please come in!"

Anne steps back and we walk into a beautiful foyer with knotty wood flooring and a large, traditional staircase. This house is so warm and inviting. Gorgeous, but lived in. Comfortable.

"Um, let's go out back. We have a patio area and the weather is so nice. I can grab some drinks!" She leads us out through a three season porch and onto the back patio with a large backyard. The girls light up when they eye a swing set.

"Can we go on that, Finley?" McKinley asks, tugging on my dress.

"Yes, of course!" Anne interjects. "It hasn't been played on in years. Our girls are too old to use it. Please, go have some fun!"

Megan gives a sideways smile like she's too cool for swing sets, but follows McKinley out anyway.

McKinley stops halfway and turns around suddenly, "Oh! Thank you, Anne!" She turns and takes off again. I can visibly see Anne's heart melting already. This is why I brought the girls. I hope Brody's mom can see what a close family we are.

I love my nieces so much. I love the fact that McKinley asked me, instead of her mom, if she could go on the swing set. I love that they look at me as someone who can answer things for them. I hope to never lose that. Having that car accident was a wakeup call for me in more ways than one.

"Okay! I'll go make some lemonade or something. Does that sound good?" Anne asks, standing by the doorway.

"Sounds great. Thank you!" Cadence replies, sitting down on a cushioned patio chair as she puts her sunglasses on.

"Do you need any help?" I ask, feeling nervous but trying to make a good impression.

"I'd love that, Finley," she smiles warmly.

I follow her back into a big beautiful kitchen. It's messy with lot of cooking gadgets all over the countertop and some dirty dishes in the sink. It's perfect.

"Sorry to just barge in on you like this," I say, placing my hands on the counter and feeling horribly awkward.

"Honey, there is nothing to be sorry for! I'm so glad to see you. To meet you, I mean!" she laughs lightly. She has a great laugh, it's natural and deep. Her hair is medium length, dark brown and curly— just like Brody's. My heart aches at the familiarity of his mother's features. I need to see Brody so badly.

"I'm glad to meet you, too," I say.

"Kaylee and Haddie will be home from school soon. They will be so happy to meet you, too! You have no idea." She chuckles, as if enjoying a private joke.

"Really?" I say.

"Of course, Finley, why wouldn't they? Brody says the most wonderful things. His sisters just torture him for information about you. He doesn't have a chance at any privacy." She chuckles again. "But he doesn't fight them off very hard. He likes talking about you. I feel as though I know you already."

I frown, trying to comprehend everything. If he tells them a lot about me, then does that mean he's told them about our fight? Surely, it's not common for Brody to come home for a visit during the week. They had to connect the dots.

"Do you know when he'll be back?" I ask, not knowing if I can sit here another second longer without him.

She shakes her head. "He might be a while."

I nod, feeling sad, like I'm getting the brush off.

"I think it might be a good idea for you to go find him. He has a favorite fishing spot that he usually goes to. It's a small creek. I could give you directions if you like." She turns her deep blue eyes on me and they look like they are saying so much more than her words are.

I smile sadly and nod. She grabs a notebook out of the drawer next to me and rubs my back encouragingly before writing down directions. My eyes sting with the understanding touch of her hand on my back.

"Go on, honey. I'll take care of your family. I'm sure we'll get along wonderfully. Bring our boy back in a better mood, please?"

I nod and smile and she opens her arms for a hug. Her embrace is soft and comforting, everything a great mom's hug should be. It makes me ache for my own.

CHAPTER **THIRTY-THREE**

I ask Cadence for her keys and she makes a serious comment about driving safely. I stop myself from rolling my eyes because I know deep down she's right. I take off out the front door and punch in the address Anne gave me into my phone for directions. Originally, I brought Cadence and the girls with me to help me win Brody back. But now that I'm here, I realize the real benefit to them being here is to help me win over Brody's family. I need Anne to know I'm so much more than Brody's drama-filled girlfriend from college.

Anne's subtle hints aren't lost on me. She probably knows pretty much everything. So leaving Cadence and the girls to entertain her and show her a glimpse of my family, which I am incredibly proud of, should hopefully help. Who knows, Cadence and Anne might even have a good laugh at the excitement of young love. But Brody and I are more than young love. He's everything to me. I have to fix this. I have to make him understand.

I pull up under a huge weeping willow tree next to Brody's black car. I feel a ping of nervousness and fear, wondering how he'll react. I unbuckle and remove my wrist brace. I don't want the first thing he notices to be my injury. I open and squeeze my fist and feel the tenderness in my wrist, but it's miles better than it was a couple days ago. I then reach around to the backseat and grab the brand new black trash bag I snatched from the box Angela and I keep beneath our kitchen sink.

I walk down the trail Anne described and see Brody squatting and messing with the lure on his fishing pole. The creek is green and surrounded by huge golden-leafed trees. The varying fall colors are simply breathtaking, but I can't tear my eyes off of Brody. He looks gorgeous, as always, his curly hair perfectly rumpled, his jeans torn and distressed, and his biceps bulging on the tight sleeves of a gray *K-State* t-shirt.

He hears my approach and glances in my direction, then looks back down to his lure, only to snap his eyes back up to me.

"Finley?" he asks, standing with his fishing line in hand.

I continue walking until I'm no more than twenty feet away from him. The golden sunlight behind him makes him the picture of beauty. I clear my throat.

"Do you know where there's a dumpster around here?" I ask, shaking my still perfectly pressed trash bag.

He looks nervous and awkward, shaking his head like he's not interested in my song and dance. "What are you doing here?"

"Something big," I say, and shrug my shoulders.

"How did you know where I was?" His eyes look around the area like he'll find his answer in the woods.

"Your mom," I say, and his eyes widen. "She's cool. It was nice to put a face with the stories you've told me. My nieces already won her over, I think."

"Your nieces are with my mom?"

"Mmmhmm…and Cadence."

"Why?" He looks down with a sad expression.

"I wanted you to meet my family," I shrug my shoulders.

"I don't get it."

"Just hear me out, okay?" I go to stand just a few feet away from him.

"What happened to your eye, Finley?" he asks, stepping toward me to touch it. I grab his hand and hold it off. Feeling his hand in mine, feels like ecstasy. I never want to let go of this hand. *Ever.*

"Please, Brody. Just hear me out first and I'll explain later."

"Did someone…Finley, did you get…" His chest puffs up as he pulls his hand out of mine, attempting to gain control of his impeding outburst.

"No! God, no, Brody! I was in a car accident, that's all."

"A car accident? When?" Astonishment and sympathy spread across his face.

I shake my head. I didn't want to discuss this first, I wanted to give him my speech and then tell him later. "Brody, please. Will you just hear me out first?"

"Finley," he says, sounding sad and broken.

My pulse is pounding in my veins and my nerves are blasting wildly all over me. I hate his pained face. I want to see his smiling, loving face. I have to say this. I have to do this. I hold up my black trash bag and shake it, showing him that it's completely empty. "I have no baggage, Brody. None. And whatever baggage you think exists, simply doesn't." I drop the empty sack to the ground.

He frowns, seemingly unimpressed and looks out toward the creek. He looks like he's about to say something but I cut him off, determined to say my piece.

"You came to me with a half-empty bag of trash. That's all. Not very much. Not even enough to throw in the dumpster that day, if you recall. You put it back inside your apartment when you went in to find some shoes." I smile back at the simplicity and honesty of our first meeting.

His brow furrows and he looks up at me, his jaw ticking. "Seeing you Saturday night like that. It just brought it all back for me, Fin. So much has changed since that first day I spoke to you."

"I don't care! I want you to throw whatever trash you're still holding onto away, Brody. I want you to toss it." He turns away and I reach out to stop him from walking away from me. I'm overwhelmed by the intense urge I have to kiss him. But I need him to hear me first. Saturday night we skipped over the talking and went right to making up—look where that left us.

"It's not that easy, Finley. That shit with Jake killed me. Seeing you with him…" He cocks his jaw off to the side and looks away like he can't stand the sight of me.

I swallow hard. "I'm sorry. I shouldn't have even let him get that close to me. But none of this matters. I don't need you to be perfect. I just need you to be mine. It's okay for us not to be perfect." I grab his face and force him to look at me. His eyes focus on the spot above my right eye and I see a fleeting emotion of sadness ripple over his features.

"Listen, Brody. I threw out my bag…I need you to throw out yours. This is my way of showing you that everything is in the past. *Everything*, Brody."

He shakes his head, looking down at me.

"You are my everything, Brody. You…forever…I want *you* to be my everything." I reach into my bra and pull out the napkin from our first date. I unfold it and show him the thick bold letters.

EVERYTHING

He looks at the napkin in amazement, his eyes glittering with emotion. "You've kept that all this time?" His expression is awestruck.

"Yes, Brody. I hold it close to my heart…because you're everything to me."

His features soften and I see his last bits of reserve crumble. "Do you mean that, Finley? Because I need you to mean that. I don't think I can handle a life without you in it."

"I mean it! Jesus!" I drop my hands to my hips in frustration.

"No…I mean…don't. Don't get mad. I'm sorry. I believe you. It just still stings. My shit…it haunts me." His eyes glaze over and my heart breaks at the blatant sight of his torment.

I reach out and grab his two wrists in my hands. "This is going to sound crazy, but hear me out." He nods. "In a way, I'm glad Saturday night happened."

I feel his body stiffen. I turn my round eyes on him and pierce him with all the sincerity I can muster. "Jake was a weird, dumb, stupid crush I had. But he never liked me like that, so I left him with all the power. And that sucked. It was an uncomfortable place to be in for those few weeks we hung out. But having him admit he had feelings for me was sort of awesome because it gave me all the power back." Brody eyes me uncomfortably, clearly not impressed with this line of thinking.

Wanting to make myself clearer, I pull his wrists toward me and he stumbles in closer to me. "The beauty of everything Jake said to me was that it made me realize I didn't, period, give, period, a *shit*...period!" I pull his large hand up to my mouth and kiss his palm, letting my lips linger on the pad of his thumb. He closes his eyes, his reserve beginning to break. "I mean it, Brody. You gave that confidence to me. You made me feel like someone again. I didn't even realize it until Jake started trying to explain himself. But seriously, since meeting you, Jake isn't even a blip on my radar anymore. You are everything I need."

"I hope you mean all that, Finley, because you're all I see anymore. I wouldn't have been able to stay away from you for long."

"Likewise, stud." I giggle, feeling my heart soar at his admission. Finally. He sighs and pulls me in for a hug, his big arms wrapping around me tightly. I relish in the familiar smell and comfort of his embrace. This man is everything I never even knew I was looking for or needing. I can't imagine being without him—and I don't want to. There isn't a doubt in my mind I want a forever with him.

He brings his hands up to cup my face, stroking his thumbs on my cheekbones. "I'm sorry," he rasps out, his eyes red around the rims. "I'm sorry I left you in bed that morning. Dumbest fucking idea ever."

"Yes. Dumbest. Don't ever do that again," I pout. I bring the napkin up and he glances over at it. I hold it tightly to my chest and return it to the inside of my bra.

"It's so fucking hot you kept that all this time." He shakes his head in amazement, then leans in and connects our lips in a smooth, soft reunion. When he inserts his tongue, settling in for an unforgettable, all consuming Brody kiss, I pull away and murmur against his mouth. "Your hands stink like worm guts."

His chest vibrates with a warm chuckle. "Damn, my girlfriend has such a sexy-ass mouth." I exhale a laugh on his face. "I love us, baby," he adds, his eyes looking seriously into mine.

"I love us more."

"Not possible." And he kisses me again, making my toes curl.

***

"Babe, you have to tell me what happened to you," he says, pausing our make-out session to touch my face.

I tell him all the details. He grimaces when I mention how emotional I was during the drive to KC. I can see him blaming himself and I tell him what I've been telling everyone else that wants to shoulder some of the fault. This was me, my fault, my issues, my lesson. And it's one I'm never forgetting.

"So I'm curious then," I look up at him as we walk back to our cars. "What was your plan? You said you wouldn't have been able to stay away long. What does that mean?"

He half smirks, looking down as he rubs hand sanitizer all over his hands. "I was miserable here. I knew as soon as I drove out of Wildwood I was being an idiot."

"So why didn't you turn around?"

He shakes his head and wipes the excess on his jeans. "I needed to talk to my mom. She's pretty amazing to talk to."

I silently groan. "She knows everything that happened, doesn't she?" I'm suddenly crippled with the fear of having to face her again.

Becoming US

"No, not at all."

I sigh in relief.

"She just knows my issues, my insecurities because of my past. She's a Finley fan, actually." He raises his eyebrows and nods confidently at me.

"A Finley fan? She just met me!"

"She can tell. She knows you're something special, just based on stuff I've told her."

"So, what have you told her?" I ask, poking his ribs playfully.

He shakes his head. "I'm keeping that to myself."

"Well, jeez! I wouldn't have had to call in the big guns if I'd have known your mother was already a Finley fan!"

"What's *the big guns?*" he asks, looking confused.

"My nieces! Cadence! Don't you dare tell Cade that your mom already likes me. She'll kill me for making her drive for nothing."

"It wasn't for nothing. I can't believe they are actually here. That's fricken' cool as hell. And I get to meet them finally."

I laugh, "They were my plan to make me look a little less crazy to your mom."

"My mom loves you already. She would have never thought you were crazy."

"Yeah, well, you've never mentioned that before." I nudge my hip into his and he stumbles off the walking path slightly. "You talk about me to her a lot, huh?" I bite my lip, coyly.

"Not a lot a lot. Not like a creepy amount. My sisters just won't shut up about you. They are relentless."

"I can't wait to meet them," I smile.

"Likewise," he stops near the front of his car and pulls me in for another kiss. I savor the taste of him. Seriously, I could kiss this man all day.

"Hey, I wanna do something," I say, running over to my car and grabbing my cellphone. I flip it into selfie mode and hold it out and snap a photo while kissing Brody's cheek.

"Where are you posting that?" he asks, clearly confused.

"Nowhere, I'm texting it to Parni."

"You and Parni text? I didn't even know you had her number."

"Oh, yeah, we're tight, remember? You were the one who told her that I like her so much!"

The corners of his mouth pull down like he's trying to conceal a smirk. Dammit, he looks sexy as hell when he does that.

"She covered for me today at the lab and I think she might appreciate this," I add, clicking send on our kiss pic to her.

"Don't take any selfies right now," he says, shoving me backwards onto the hood of his car and spreading my legs so he can fashion himself between them.

I raise my eyebrows, feeling suddenly nervous. "Brody, someone could see."

"Nah, it's a private creek. My uncle's. No one's coming down here." His hand strokes up my calf, then up my thigh. He pauses briefly, noticing the bruises on my kneecaps.

"It kills me I wasn't there for you," he says, kissing above my eye and then bending over and kissing the spots on my knees gently.

"It kills me what an idiot I was," I grumble and oh holy shit, his hand is between my legs. I squirm at his erotic touch over top of my underwear.

"I'm so hard right now thinking of taking you right here where I grew up."

My back arches into his touch, involuntarily. In a not very convincing tone, I say, "We should get back to our families." I gasp as his finger slips around the strip of my panties.

He rubs his five o'clock shadow against my cheek and whispers, "I used to come out here and fantasize about girls just like you, Finley. You're my own fucking fantasy come to life. And you in this dress." He exhales a growl and kisses me hard.

He suddenly breaks the kiss and mutters, "You're wet as hell. Damn, I missed you, babe. It feels like we've been apart so much longer than just a few days. I'm sorry as hell."

I groan, relishing the feel of his fingers moving inside of me. "We can't leave your family back there waiting, Brody." God, who the hell am I fooling?

He stops and looks at me seriously. "There is always time for makeup sex. You make time for makeup sex. It says so in the title." He smirks saucily at me. "Don't worry, I'll be quick. We have a lifetime to make up for it."

He kisses my nose and I smile at his sweet words. A lifetime sounds pretty freaking great to me.

CHAPTER **THIRTY-FOUR**

We arrive back at Brody's parents' house to see his sisters have come home from school. Kaylee and Haddie are 14 and 17—and super sweet. They are continually beaming at their big brother. I feel happy that they seem to approve so easily. I even get a glimpse of his protective big brother side when Kaylee begins to tease Haddie about a boy at school. Brody instantly puffs his chest out and demands answers to ridiculous questions about who the boy is. I save Haddie by discreetly putting my panties in Brody's pocket. Suddenly, Haddie's boy troubles are the last thing on his mind.

My heart swells with pride when I see Kaylee and Megan swinging and chatting easily. They seem to have really hit it off despite their small age difference. Bringing my sister and nieces may not have been completely necessary, but having Brody and his family meet them seems to take us to the next level in our relationship. We were ready for this. We needed this.

Brody's dad, Mike, is big and tall and has a huge head of thick dark hair, just like Brody's, but cut much shorter. Brody is the spitting image of his father, aside from his eyes—those beauties are courtesy of Anne, who hasn't stopped smiling at me since I came back with her very smug-looking son. Brody's satisfied appearance may have something to do with him bending me over the hood of his car moments earlier, but we obviously won't be getting into that.

Cadence and Brody seem to have an instant, and fun, witty banter. It seems natural. I can tell from her eyes alone that she most definitely approves. Mike and Anne invite us all to stay for supper, but Cadence declines because she needs to get the girls home for school the next day. Brody tells Cadence that he'll be taking me back to campus and that he's really grateful she came today.

Brody and I stay for supper and fall into an easy rhythm with his family. They all said they hope to meet my parents someday soon. I mention something about graduation day and Brody's eyes positively twinkle at my mentioning our future together.

"You ready?" Brody asks, pulling me down the sidewalk in front of his parents' house. "I can't wait to get you in bed."

I smirk. "Are we upgrading from car hoods when we get back to Wildwood?"

"Car hoods and showers are excellent places for makeup sex. Who knew?"

"You did, apparently," I laugh and bite my lip.

"Today was awesome, babe. I'm so glad you came. Meeting your sister and nieces…" he pauses, and I can tell what he's thinking.

Meeting the family has catapulted our already fast moving relationship to a whole new level. Seeing this part of his life only makes me want to keep him in my life even more.

"I'm glad too." I pull him toward me by his belt buckle after he tosses his bag into the backseat of his car.

"Your sister and nieces are everything you've described them as. Jesus. I think my mom might actually have withdrawals from McKinley."

"I know the feeling." I purse my lips together thoughtfully.

"Well, you pretty much have that Kansas City job already, so you'll be a lot closer to them again."

"Yes, that will be nice," I reply, feeling slightly edgy about where our future will take us after graduation. He has his internship in Kansas City next semester and I hate the idea of being away from him again. We've spoken about graduation in grand ideas, but nothing specific yet. My hope is we'll be moving in together somewhere, but I know it's still way too early to push it. We just went through a huge rough patch. We need time to reconnect.

Brody leans down and kisses my lower lip that I'm chewing on nervously. "Love us."

"Love us, too," I say, and get into his car to head back to reality.

CHAPTER THIRTY-FIVE

"Yay! The lovebirds are together again!" Angela sings as Brody and I walk in the door. She and Mark are cozied up on our couch with a movie and popcorn, looking perfectly at ease with each other.

"Ha ha," I say, dropping my stuff by the door and perching on one of the red barstools. Brody heads to the fridge, pops the lid off a couple of beers, and hands one to me.

"You guys look comfy," I say, looking down at the pair of them lying on the couch. Mark is spooning Angela, who looks smug as hell.

Mark pulls her in closer, "My own personal snuggle snatch."

We all burst out laughing and Mark looks confused. "You can't say it like that!" Angela exclaims in response to his confused expression.

"Why the hell not?" he asks, looking truly offended that we are shutting down his playful endearment for her.

"Because it sounds like you are talking about my vagina!"

"I think we should be talking about your vagina a lot more, as it is. So again, I don't see the quandary."

"Mark, buddy," Brody laughs, taking a swig of his beer.

"What? If we are to be intimate someday, I should be allowed whatever endearments feel appropriate. Question: Do you want to have sex with me someday? Answer: Hell yes! I know you do. I can tell."

"Mark!" Angela cries as he shoves his scowling face into her neck and starts nuzzling. She giggles loudly, halfheartedly attempting to fight him off.

My phone blasts with the *Dynamite* song again, indicating a text message.

Leslie: How'd it go? Did you win him back with your sexual prowess? I don't want to hear from sad panda Finley any more. No one likes a sad panda.

"That song on your phone is really freaking annoying," Angela says, tearing her face away from Mark's.

"What? I like it! I think it's funny. Leslie installed it."

"You two are funny," Brody says, pulling me toward my bedroom door. "When I listen to you two on the phone together, I swear you're speaking a completely different language."

"Don't knock Leslie! She's the shit!" Angela bellows defensively.

"I'm not knocking her! I think it's cute." He tweaks my nose. "We'll see you two later," Brody says to Angela and Mark, pulls me into my room, and shuts the door.

I smile, affectionately. "Hang on, it's Leslie. I need to text her back real quick. She's going back to London soon, so I'm trying to get phone time in with her as much as possible."

He slowly starts dragging down the zipper on the back of my dress, his fingers grazing my bare skin as he does.

"You…are making texting very difficult," I say, looking at him with hooded eyes.

"I'm not butting in on your friend time. Please continue. I'll just help myself here." He pulls the straps down on my dress and it falls easily to the floor, displaying my nude strapless bra and black thong. "I take that back. I'm going to butt in on your friend time, real soon."

"Just wait! Seriously, hang on a sec," I say, pulling back from him. "Leslie wants to meet you before she goes back to London."

"So let's meet," he says, tugging on the thin strap of thong on my hip.

"Tomorrow, okay?" I ask. He looks up, like he's mentally checking his calendar.

"Yep," he quips and nuzzles his face into my neck, dragging his tongue slowly up toward my ear. I shiver in response and type back a quick, *mostly* legible response that tomorrow works great.

***

Waking up with Brody the next morning is incredible. He more than made up for leaving me high and dry a couple days ago. Gosh, that morning feels like a lifetime ago.

I stare at him well and good, crossing the creepy threshold. Unable to stop myself, I kiss the freckle below his eye that's been taunting me all morning. He stirs as I crawl on top of him and straddle his boxer-brief covered crotch. Brody in black boxer briefs is about as sexy as my heart can take. Any more, and it would simply burst into a million oversexed pieces.

I feel him already growing beneath me. "Oh, no, we have to get going. We're meeting Leslie for brunch," I tease, wiggling slightly.

"What kind of college student does brunch?" Brody asks, bucking his hips into me playfully.

I bat at his chest in response. "Lez loves brunch. I don't know. Maybe it's a British thing. Either way, you have some brownie points to earn with her. She's just as important as my family."

"I'm great with best friends. Best friends and mothers. They all love me." He starts stroking my hips and squints at me as the early morning sunlight streams in.

I smile down at him, feeling overwhelmed at the fact that he is mine. "I'm not worried. Lez will love you because you're charming and sweet and sexy."

He sits up quickly, and rolls me onto my back, smirking. "You can't say nice words like that and get away. I'll be quick. I promise." He pecks my nose and I relent. Who was I kidding—I wasn't going to put up a fight.

Brunch turns into supper because Leslie gets tied up at home. I offer to meet her in KC so she doesn't have so far to drive, but she said she wants to spend the night with me before she flies out. Both of us know it could be a long time before we see each other again. London isn't exactly a hop, skip, and a jump away. I would do the same thing if the roles were reversed. She's still the most amazing friend.

Brody and I situate ourselves on one side of the booth at the cool, 50s style diner in Manhattan. It's a ways off campus, but since we're skipping classes today, we don't mind.

I hear Lez before I see her.

"FINNY?" she screeches. I twirl around and see her bounding toward me in a vintage 50s style camel-colored dress, her dark auburn hair flowing thickly around her shoulders.

"Lezzy!" I screech right back, and all but shove Brody out of the booth so I can get out and hug her.

She pulls me in for a tight embrace then looks my outfit up and down. "Are those vintage *Guess* jeans?" she shoves me to the side so she can look at my rear end.

"EBay!" I offer brightly.

She gives me a proud mother look and smacks my ass. "I've taught you so well."

She turns her attention to Brody, standing and enjoying the display between the two of us. "And this dashing young lad must be the lil whipper-snapper that stole your precious heart?" She opens her arms and pulls Brody into a big hug.

"I'm Brody," he says, looking slightly bashful and even more adorable than usual in his cute gray button-down and jeans.

"Bam!" She purses her lips and shakes her head. "My Finny has good taste in men."

We all laugh and settle in the booth. I opt to sit next to Leslie. Brody doesn't seem the least bit surprised, and I love him even more for it.

After we make small talk about Topeka and order our food, Leslie turns her serious green eyes on Brody.

"Brodster. We need to sincerely talk."

"Shoot," Brody says, eyeing her acutely.

"Finny is my best friend. Like. Best. Friend. I need to know you're a good enough guy for her. I'm leaving again for London and I can't leave without knowing you're going to live up to the hype."

He nods and his eyes glance to me. I squirm, feeling a bit guilty about Leslie's difficult question, but not surprised by it.

"Honestly?" he starts and pauses. She nods for him to continue. "I'm probably not." I frown and he continues looking straight into Leslie's eyes. "I'm probably not good enough for Fin. I'm not going to lie. I have my issues. I'm working on them. But I can promise you that I know what an extraordinary person your best friend is. And I'm going to spend as long as it takes to become good enough for her."

I stare at him in wonder and Leslie's big, goofy grin breaks my trance. "That's cheesy as hell. But, honesty will always get you biscuit points in my book. You'll do." She takes a drink of her tea, and I relax and allow her words to lighten the mood.

The three of us head back to Wildwood and opt to stay in for the night instead of going out. I'm happy for that because I don't want to share any of my time with Leslie at a crowded bar. She's got an early flight the next day, so laying low sounded perfect to her. Angela orders several crates of Chinese food and Brody and Mark join us to eat. We laugh like crazy all night long at the insane competition Mark and Leslie have going for who can say the most ridiculous things.

Brody wins Leslie over completely when Mark tells us all about Brody's impression of the old York Peppermint Patty commercial. Apparently, growing up, Brody used to perform that commercial at family gatherings by jumping up on the coffee table and everything. Just when we all give up begging Brody to do it, he leaps up out of his seat and onto the coffee table in the blink of an eye.

Leslie and I are crying, we're laughing so hard as he recites the entire commercial verbatim. My heart about bursts when Leslie laughs loudly, and exclaims, "Finny! He's one of us! He's perfect!" I just smiled proudly at my unassuming man. He's not perfect, but he is everything…and that's more than perfect for me.

At the end of the night, Brody doesn't even ask to spend the night. He just asks me to walk him out the door so he can kiss me goodnight without everyone watching. I love that he knows Leslie will be sleeping in my bed with me. He gets us, and that makes me feel giddy with excitement. Brody charmed Leslie all night and I know that when we go to bed tonight, she'll tell me all the nitty-gritty tiny things she likes about him. And I can't wait.

***

CHAPTER **THIRTY-SIX**

The next few weeks leading up to the holidays are a blur of blissful busyness. Midterms hit hard and Brody and I agree to separate a couple nights a week so we can focus on our studies. These are the last classes Brody has before graduation because next semester he's doing a fulltime internship in Kansas City, working for the city. It's a crazy awesome internship that's very hard to get in to. I'm not the least bit surprised they picked Brody out of several applicants.

We still haven't discussed our exact living situation after graduation. And the reality of him being gone for a whole semester is looming over both of us. It's all we talk about. There's no question we're going to do the long-term thing, but not knowing where each other will end up after graduation kills me. I know for certain, that I'm heading to Kansas City to work for Val, so it goes without question I want Brody to find a job there too. But it might not be that easy. Brody seems nervous enough about his internship. I'm not going to start pressing him about plans after graduation yet. I'm doing my best to live in the now with him and enjoy the time we have together before he leaves.

***

For Christmas break, Brody comes back home with me for a whole week. He's nervous and excited to meet the rest of my family. I tell him to relax because he's already won over Cadence and she's the tough one. I sort of love his nervousness over meeting everyone else, though—it's adorable.

My mom gives Brody a big hug and he charms her instantly by complimenting all the food she's stuffing into him. Dad is brooding and intimidating, as he so often has been for all my past boyfriends, but still polite, overall. They both know how important Brody is, so I know deep down, they are happy for us.

My sister's husband, George, is even worse than Dad. He scares the crap out of Brody by acting like a huge, royal asshole to him the whole first day we are home.

"Jesus, your sister's husband is scaring the shit out of me!" Brody says as we dig into our suitcases for pajamas. Mom put us up in the spare bedroom with a queen-sized bed. My parents never have been very conservative, so when I told them how serious Brody and I are, they said if I felt that way, I'm old enough to sleep in the same bed.

"What? Why is he scaring you?" I ask, looking innocent and confused.

"He just keeps glaring at me. I asked him to pass the milk this morning and he told me I better learn how to get my own damn milk if I knew what was good for me. I don't even know what the hell that means, but I'm seriously uncomfortable!"

I do my best to conceal a smirk. George texted me before we arrived, telling me I had to go along with whatever he said or did, and to not ask questions or give him away.

"Yeah, that's so weird. George is usually a big teddy bear. I don't understand why he's being like that with you." And George truly is a big teddy. He's big and stocky, but has a bit of a menacing look to him when he makes the right expression. He's been the big brother I never had, and he does a great job of tolerating me being at their house all the time.

"Frick, do you think it's something I did?" Brody asks, looking concerned and depressed. "I must have made a bad impression somehow, but I don't know how."

"Maybe it's because I told him you fucked me in the parking lot at that restaurant last week," I say, looking deadly serious.

"FINLEY! You better be fucking kidding!" I widen my eyes and suddenly the door to our bedroom flies open and crashes against the wall.

"You fucked Finley in a parking lot!" George booms, and comes thundering toward Brody like a mad man.

Brody crumples into a ball on the bed, his hands raised to cover himself from George's attack. I burst out laughing and Cadence comes in and joins me. Brody looks up at us in confusion as George's murderous gaze eventually morphs into a large grin. His grin then turns into a huge belly laugh while looking at Brody's confused face.

"Oh, my God, Brody! Your face!" Cadence squeals, pointing and laughing. "You look like you're about to puke!"

That comment just makes George and I laugh harder, crumpling into each other and wiping tears out of our eyes. Earlier, George pulled me aside and said he needed some juicy tidbit of info for the grand finale, so we hatched a plan for him to listen outside the door after Brody and I went to bed. I can't believe we actually pulled it off!

Brody stands up off the bed and puts his hands on his hips, glaring at the three of us laughing like immature teenagers. I don't think I've ever laughed this hard in my entire life.

"You've been messing with me the whole day?" Brody asks. George can't even answer him because he's laughing too hard.

"What going on?" Mom yells from downstairs. We all just laugh even louder.

Cadence is the only one able to compose herself enough to answer. "Yes! He has!" She starts laughing again, holding her rapidly growing pregnant belly. "You should have seen your face all day, Brody. I don't know how we all held it together! Even Mom and Dad knew!"

George straightens, finally composing himself enough to speak. "You handled it well, dude. Welcome to the family." He offers his hand, and Brody purses his lips off to the side and glares, but takes his hand anyway, eventually laughing along with all of us.

The rest of the week goes very similarly, with a lot of laughing and a lot of bonding. Mom and Dad got a good kick out of Brody being let in on the joke, and we all get really comfortable with each other. Brody and George form an bond over the whole trick and I can easily see them being very close throughout our life together.

***

CHAPTER THIRTY-SEVEN

The entire final semester of my senior year is miserable. Brody and I spend every night talking on the phone and face-timing to try and pass the time. He comes back on weekends, and I go visit him in Kansas City. It's hard, but we're dealing with it.

All the phone time has been furthering our relationship and figuring out what we want out of life. Neither Brody, nor I, care much about getting married after graduation. We both agree we have a really great thing going and feel like just staying in a fully committed relationship feels more right than getting married.

We are one-hundred percent on the same page with wanting children someday, though. Whether we're married or not, we want a family. I love the concept of being a young mom, like Cadence. The idea of having a baby that is all Brody and me—*us*—makes me excited beyond comprehension.

If we have children together, I assume we'll need to live together, but Brody still hasn't asked me to move in. And I'll be damned if I'm going to ask him. It would feel similar to me proposing, and there are just some things guys should do.

Knowing I need to figure out living arrangements, because Val wants me to start working for her right away, I decide to make plans with Angela. Despite her reservations, she's headed to KC to work in the same building as her father. Following in his political footsteps, it would seem. Her parents already have a couple great places for us to look at over spring break.

Because I have no grand plans for Spring Break, and Brody has to work, I volunteer to cover the computer lab for the diehards, like Parni—who has somehow morphed into one of my favorite people on campus. She'll be there all week to keep me company, so it won't be all bad.

***

"No big plans for spring break with Brody?" Parni asks, walking in her familiar shuffle into the computer lab. She is damn near pleasant to me these days. Gone is that solemn, Grumpy Gus she used to be. Granted, she hasn't morphed into Susie Sunshine, but I get a lot less glares from her these days. She's the only one that's come in all day so far.

"'Fraid not," I say, looking and feeling glum. "Brody's working in Kansas City, and I need the extra money for a car." Mom and Dad gave me one of their older cars to take back to college with me after Christmas, but they told me it was only temporary and I need to start saving to buy my own.

Not to mention, going to KC and staying with Brody just doesn't feel right. First of all, he didn't invite me. He's felt quiet and stand-offish lately. It's killing me to be this far away from him and not able to see him whenever I want. Graduation is just around the corner, and I want us to both be in the same place, more than I want to breathe right now.

"You okay?" Parni asks, eyeing me thoughtfully.

I nod quickly, trying to brush off her concern. She smirks in response, and I frown at her in confusion. Parni never smiles. She silently points to the large bank of windows. I look over, and my heart explodes at the sight of Brody standing there with a stack of white papers in his hand.

Tears instantly fill my eyes at the overwhelming joy of seeing Brody again. I haven't seen him for three weeks. He's been under so much stress with his internship, so I've been giving him space to focus. I run to the window and place my hands on it, my eyes dancing around his sweet face. It's wonderful laying eyes on him again.

He offers me a lopsided smile, looking totally at ease with himself out there. He holds his finger up and grabs the first sheet. My heart patters rapidly inside my chest at the excitement of what this special message will be.

He presses the sheet against the glass. His familiar thick black scroll makes me beam.

GUESS WHAT?

I touch my fingers to the letters and shake my head in question. He grabs another sheet.

I GOT THE JOB.

My eyes turn wide. I clap and jump up and down in excitement. He throws up a new message.

WHICH JOB, YOU ASK?

I shake my head because I'm assuming he's referring to the job working for the city in construction management. We've only been talking about it since he started his internship! I squint to read the message on the next sheet.

THE ONE WITH THE CITY....DUH.

I cross my arms over my chest and frown at him. He chuckles, apparently pleased with my reaction. He looks so delicious right now, I could jump through this window to hug him, but I want to see what all his other signs say, so I refrain.

GO ON SPRING BREAK WITH ME?

This sheet stuns me. My eyes turn wide and I bring my hands to cover my wide-open mouth. I nod, eagerly and enthusiastically. Hell yes I'll take a whole week with this man. Screw saving money for a car. The computer lab can go to hell for all I care. I glance back at Parni to share my excitement. She's full on smiling!

I look back and see Brody's face fall slightly when he looks down at his next sheet. He hesitantly grabs it and shoves it against the window, looking away.

MOVE IN WITH ME.

My eyes turn wide and instantly burn with the presence of new tears. As the request permeates in my brain, I shake my head in disbelief and glance back at Parni again. She covers her smiling mouth with her hand, unsuccessfully attempting to conceal her happiness.

I look back at Brody's beautiful boyish smile. His eyes turn wide and he flips the same sheet over.

TOO SOON?

He's cringing and his lips purse together, sneering in disgust. I shake my head furiously, feeling frustrated that I missed my big chance to say yes to the last sign. He quickly shoves another sheet of paper up to the window.

TERRIBLE IDEA. FORGET IT.

I feel my emotions plummet to my feet. No! This isn't how this moment is going to end. I step up closer to the window and urgently point down at his stack of papers indicating I want him to bring the last one up.

He looks at me seriously and rustles into his pile and holds up the *guess what* sheet to me again—I scowl at him furiously in frustration. He then grabs the *spring break* sheet and I slam my fist against the window. Suddenly, he's smiling cockily, and presses the most beautiful sign in the world up against the glass.

MOVE IN WITH ME.

"Yes," I say, in a normal voice. He holds his hand up to his ear and I repeat louder. "Yes!" He again gives me a look, like he can't hear me, and I cup my hands to my mouth and yell as loud as I can. "I SAID YES, I'LL MOVE IN WITH YOU!"

He chuckles and digs deep into his huge stack of papers. Jeez, what do all those sheets say?

NO NEED TO SHOUT.

I'm not even feigning anger at this point. I just beam at him, tears flowing freely down my cheeks. He grabs one more sheet.

I LOVE US.

"I love us, too," I mouth back to him. He crooks his finger, beckoning me out to him. I turn and run down the hall. "Cover me, Parn!"

"Got it, Fin," she croaks as I blast past her.

I hurry down the hall, out the side door, and around the side of the building to where Brody is standing. He grins at me when I don't slow down my approach. I run full bore into his wide-open arms. He strokes his hand down the back of my long hair, and his vibrating chest is the best feeling in the world.

"So, was that a yes? It was kind of hard to tell."

I pull back and grab his smirking face in my hands, and unceremoniously kiss that look right off his damn face. My punishing kiss turns to insane passion the minute his arms tighten around my waist. Brody's lips have never tasted better, and I've never felt so completely consumed by anything in my entire existence.

Wanting to say the words, I break our incredible kiss. "Yes, Brody. I'll move in with you. And I love us. I love us, like, you have no idea."

"I'm glad, because I really didn't make signs for every scenario." He laughs and I kiss him deeply again. "I love us, Fin," he murmurs against my mouth. "I waited a whole damn year to ask you out. I'm not waiting anymore. I love us, and I want us to be each other's everything. Will you be my everything?" His eyes are serious and sincere.

I reach into my pocket and pull out the tattered *everything* napkin and hold it up to him. "Yes," I say, simply, and kiss him fiercely, feeling elated for what's to come in our life. I'm so ready to start a forever with this man. I'm so ready to give him a life that is uniquely and perfectly *us*.

***

CHAPTER THIRTY-EIGHT

3 Years Later

"We're really doing this?" Brody asks, walking in the door on a Monday night after work.

I laugh gaily at him. "No *hi, honey, how was your day?*"

"Hi babe, how was your day?" He rushes over to me and pulls my hips into his, walking us backwards into the dining room table. My butt perches on the edge as he begins to unbutton my white blouse.

"Mine was good," I say, with a smirk. "Val was a tyrant as usual, but I still love her like crazy."

"Good. My day was awesome," he says, slowly shoving my now open blouse off of my shoulders. He gently kisses my shoulder and pulls the straps down, exposing more of my breast. "I was driving around to all these building sites in a big daze 'cause I got this awesome text from my woman that said we can start trying what I've been begging her to try for two years."

I roll my eyes. He's right, though. Brody has been begging me for two years to have a baby with him and I kept pushing him off, telling him we were still young and had time. I want a baby with him—so, so bad. I just wasn't prepared to share Brody just then. But the truth was, we both had great jobs. Our house was in a great neighborhood on the outskirts of KC. We had life by the balls. Nothing was stopping us anymore.

Oh, except that pesky little thing about us not being married. I internally groan every time I think about it. Both Brody's and my parents have been hounding us forever about getting married. Neither Brody, nor I, are too concerned about it. We already feel married in every sense that matters. We just don't have the legal document to prove it.

Deep down, I was scared that if we got married, we would lose the passion. And damn, do Brody and I have passion, in spades. Him coming home right now and jumping my bones before even asking how my day was is not something I am prepared to give up.

I look at Brody seriously in his eyes. "I want to have your baby, Brody. I want to give you the *us* baby we've been talking about and dreaming about since we graduated. I love us and I want to continue that love."

Brody's face turns serene, like he could implode from the emotions inside of him. He pulls my face to his and kisses me deeply—oh, so deep. My hips instinctively push into his groin as the hotness of his kiss awakens my already very active libido.

"Babe. Would it be the worst thing in the world to make a baby on the dining room table? 'Cause I don't think I can wait another second."

"Make-up sex on top of cars and in showers—baby sex on a table sounds like our style."

He smiles proudly, and crushes his lips to mine in a hungry, frantic kiss. It takes my body mere seconds to catch up to his excitement. I quickly help him wiggle me out of my pencil skirt and underwear. He unclasps my bra and pushes me back onto the table. He steps back and begins slowly undressing himself. His eyes are hooded and screaming *sex*.

"God, I hope our baby has your eyes. Those eyes are the most gorgeous things I've ever seen."

I bite my lip, watching his striptease. Needing some type of pleasure, I begin playing with my breast. "Your eyes are sexier," I say, in a raspy voice.

"Babe. What have I told you about doing that?"

"Huh?" I say, looking up from his exquisite erection.

"You can't touch yourself in front of me like that, unless you want me to come like a damn teenager." He half-smiles and I mimic the expression. He fashions himself between my legs, and says, "You ready?" I nod, silently. He pauses, bends slightly, and sucks my nipple deeply into his mouth.

I cry out at the pleasure, and he releases. His head comes up, his breath warm on my face. I stare at his lips, in awe. Before, it was only a dream to kiss a man like Brody. Now, it's my reality. It's my daily reality and I claim his lips as mine just as he enters me, in one fail swoop. He stills, waiting for my wet center to adjust around his girth.

"I love us, Finley. I can't wait to have a family with you. I can't wait for our future together," he says, while slowly and rhythmically thrusting in and out of me. I groan at the pleasure of his movements.

"I love us more, Brody. I love us more."

He continues whispering sweet nothings in my ear as he rides me to a state of delirious happiness at the potential of creating new life between us.

THE EPILOGUE

Another Year Later

I knew instantly that I was about to receive the kiss of death when the nurse escorted me into the doctor's personal office and not a sterile exam room. Blood pounded in my ears as I attempted to comprehend the news the doctor just delivered.

"I'm sorry, Finley. I've run all the tests I can. This is just one of those tricky diagnoses that we can't treat."

"Can you tell me that percentage again?" I croak, feeling my eyes well with tears.

He looks at me sadly, and his eyes glance downward as he says, "Less than one percent. And even then I would not recommend it. In fact, I'd like to recommend a procedure to ensure there are no surprises. The last thing we want to do is complicate matters with your condition even further."

I nod, and a sob breaks free from my mouth. Grief and humiliation blanket me, as the only sound in the way-too-quiet doctor's office is my rapid, uneven breath. This is my worst nightmare coming true. *My worst possible nightmare.*

He looks uneasily at me and reaches into his top desk drawer and offers a pamphlet. I glance down at the thick bold letters and the smiling happy faces on it. I stare at it in his hands for a beat before accepting his offering. The paper feels cold, stiff, and ugly.

"You should go over all of this with your...well, boyfriend. He can help you cope. You need support to go through this journey. There are support groups that can help you come to terms with it, too."

My boyfriend. It sounded like a swear word coming from this doctor's mouth. This is the first time in my life I've ever cared that Brody and I aren't married. I know nothing about the pamphlet he just handed me, but it doesn't take a genius to know that a married couple is going to be able to handle it better than a non-married, non-traditional couple. I'm basically still considered single in this doctor's eyes. How pathetic.

One Percent. The number keeps reverberating in my head as my mind reels with the finality of everything. I can't believe this is happening to me. I'm relieved I did all this testing by myself.

Five years with someone, you'd think there would be no secrets, no mystery, no stone unturned. That was part of the reason Brody and I never wanted to get married. We looked at our relationship, and ourselves, as the lucky ones. We still had the passion. We still had the heat, the fire—the spark. We were still that special *us* that we fell in love with in college. We hadn't morphed into a complacent, boring couple.

This exact moment is why I did this testing alone. Picturing Brody here next to me, holding my hand, and being the perfect, wonderful, supportive boyfriend would have killed me. I would have to watch his normally lustful gaze turn into one of *pity*—sadness.

About three months ago, I felt like something was wrong.

Something in my body just felt off—different—broken. I called the specialist that I found on *Google* and the receptionist said it was going to be a three-month wait to talk to a doctor. I almost hung up immediately, feeling silly for even considering this appointment. But then she said there'd been a cancellation for that day. I took it as a sign and immediately accepted.

The doctor was warm and friendly and ordered a slew of tests. It felt very matter of fact and par for the course. When I left the clinic that day, I felt hopeful. Sure, I'd been poked, prodded, and spoken to about things I had never even heard of, but I felt like whatever was wrong with me was something that could be fixed with a simple medication, or a specific plan of action. That's usually how doctor's offices seem to work. All that mattered was that I was taking an important step in figuring out what the issue was, so I could fix it. I'd wait and tell Brody once the doctor called with my test results. When the doctor called with a course of treatment, I'd tell him everything. That's what I kept telling myself.

Then the doctor asked me to come in so he could do a minor procedure to rule something out. The way he explained it seemed pretty minimal. But laying on this exam table in a sterile operating room, while a nurse wiped the tears dropping down my temples, felt anything but minor. The longer I waited to tell Brody what I was doing, the harder it got, and the more I began pulling away from him.

After two months of testing and blood draws, I knew before I even came into the clinic today, the issue was much worse than I ever expected. This isn't the life I signed up for with Brody. I'm certain it isn't the life Brody signed up for with me.

The nurse comes in to confirm everything the doctor shared with me, and I can't take any more. The room was too small. The nurse was too ugly. Her smell was too rancid. I have to get out. I have to leave this place. This office. This clinic. This city.

As I hastily exit the office, my stomach twists into a million tiny knots, envisioning a sad forever with Brody. He is everything a man ought to be. He deserves everything he wants in life. Will he stand by me through it? Do I want him to? Does he deserve to give up on his dreams because he decided in college that I was pretty? *Beautiful* was the word he used back then. I am anything but that now. I am damaged. *I am broken.*

I can't stand the thought of watching him fall out of love with me. Out of love with us. This magical us that we created in our own little bubble. It's more than I can bear. I know in this instant what I have to do.

I have to break us.

I have to leave us.

And I know just where I will go...

THE END

Read on for a look at, A Broken Us,

the continuation of Brody and Finley's story.

**If you enjoyed this book,
please consider taking the time to post a review.
Reviews are extremely helpful to authors
and there is no better way to thank them for their hard work.**

THE ACKNOWLEDGEMENTS

What a trip this book journey I've been on is. I've learned so much and had such overwhelming support from people that I have to take a moment to say thanks.

First, to my sister, Abby. Creative partner? Creative cheerleader? What do I call you? What's the official title? You're awesome. Thank you for reading every single one of my chapters as I sent them to you chunk by chunk, without fail. You always came through for me and I owe you some Zimas.

To my husband, Kevin. I know this book world is a stressful one for our family. And I know you're carrying the burden of a lot of things at home when I'm in the thick of it. But I love it, babe. Thank you for continuing to soldier through the extra work so I can keep chasing this dream.

To the rest of my family. Thanks for allowing me to write some sexy books without disowning me.

My editor, Heather Banta...this one hurt a lot less! I think I'm improving! Thanks for making a Kill Word list for me and for speaking my language in your comments. #fuckyouverymuch Mwah!

Beta readers! This book was a tricky one for me and I couldn't have developed it into more without all your incredibly insightful feedbacks! Mama Bear, Twinsie, Belinda, Venture. Thank you ladies for donating your very valuable time to help a newbie figure things out. It's just crazy how much you gals give and give and give.

And I love me some proofers. My final sets of eyes. Faith, Abby, Mercedes, Patricia, and Angela: Thank you all for taking the time to read and re-read my manu to catch any last minute errors. It looks awesome!

Bloggers! I love you guys. The majority of you do this for nothing but the sheer love of reading. Your value is something to be cherished.

To the Book Industry and fellow authors. Thank you all for being so generous with your time, your ideas, and your resources. We're all a part of this crazy, awesome pay-it-forward thing and I fully intend to do my part the minute someone stops looking at me like I don't know anything.

To my six angels in the sky. Thank you for being the hope and encouragement and light I need to follow my dreams. One day I'll read your story to you…but not this one. You need to be way older. Keep inspiring your sister, Lorelei. She's our miracle and we know you guys had something to do with her being here with us.

And of course, love to my Lolo! My sassy miracle that keeps me on my toes. Keep calling zebras—horses, and lions—tigers, baby. It makes you *you* and reminds me just how much you were worth the wait.

FOR MORE ABOUT THE AUTHOR

www.amydawsauthor.com

www.facebook.com/amydawsauthor

www.twitter.com/amydawsauthor

Check out more novels in the London Lovers Series, available at all major retailers!

#1 Becoming Us

#2 A Broken Us

#3 London Bound

#4 Not The One coming soon

Also, a Memoir by Amy Daws:

Chasing Hope

A mother's story of loss, heartbreak, and the miracle of hope.

Sign up for the Amy Daws newsletter to stay informed of official release date announcements!

www.amydawsauthor.com/news

AND NOW, A LOOK AT, A BROKEN US:

A BROKEN US

The London Lovers Series

A Novel

AMY DAWS

CHAPTER ONE

Brody aggressively paces the hallway of our tiny split-foyer house. I cringe as he rakes his hands through his curly brown hair and lets out a frustrated sigh. Anger and tension are radiating off his body like blurry lines surrounding a campfire.

I turn away from him because I can't stand seeing him like this. So hurt. So broken. A sadness creeps over me as I look around our home we built together. I painfully take in my last moments here. I can't believe this is the last time I'll be sitting on this very couch. Four years ago, we picked it up off the side of a curb. Sure, we may have been one step away from being labeled dumpster divers, but we knew it was nothing a $40 carpet shampooer couldn't fix. We were senseless like that together, and it was great.

Every flat surface in our house is littered with picture frames. Brody didn't mind my obsession. I'm infatuated with finding the wackiest frames I can. I frequently receive them as gifts from friends, family, and even coworkers. I love putting unconventional pictures in frames. There's a photo of Brody sleeping on the couch, and one of me with my three nieces, eating mashed potatoes. My favorite is a mustard-colored pleather frame with tiny black seahorses glued around the edges. Inside the frame is a picture of Brody and me on a four-wheeler. I'm facing backward, straddling him while his arms grip the handles. He's biting my neck as I laugh. We were so happy. So innocent. So perfect.

Candid photos show more about one's life and personality than posed pictures. My heart sinks as I realize none of these pictures will be going with me.

"How can you do this, Fin?" he barks, spinning back on his heels to stride down the hallway again.

Still sitting on the couch, I stare at my hands in stony silence, swallowing big gulps of air while he adjusts to the news I just dealt him.

"How can you need time?" he throws at me in a mocking tone. "Away from me?" He trudges swiftly across the living room. In only four paces, he's on his knees, directly in front of my face, gripping my cheeks between his soft, large hands.

"You can't mean this, Fin. You can't!" his voice cracks as he says my name and his expression melts from anger to desperation.

"Brody, don't." I state, pragmatically. "I have to. I told you I can't do this anymore."

"THIS IS US!" he booms, loudly, while turning my face back to look into his eyes. "You can't do *us?* That kills me, Fin—it kills me!"

"This is what I need, Brody. I've explained everything. There's nothing more to say. I told you this isn't up for discussion."

I've been practicing these very words in the mirror for the past week, fixing my expression to look strong, and not insecure. The last thing he needs is to receive mixed signals from me.

Brody looks down and appears to be collecting his thoughts. As his gaze comes back up, his eyes rove quickly over my whole face. I know he's searching for any glimpse of reservation in my decision to leave.

"Please, Finley," he says, with shaky breath. "You love *us*, you can't do this to *us*."

I knew he'd use *us* against me. I knew he'd say this, and I'm prepared for it. *Us* has the potential to be my kryptonite. But I can't let it get to me.

When Brody and I first started dating, we were incredible together—like two peas in a pod. We were goofy, stupid, funny, and playful. We were all the things that made a person laugh a lot in life. We both lit up inside when we made our relationship official.

One night, back in college, after a rousing and playful wrestling match in my apartment, we'd been laughing so hard we had tears in our eyes. In that moment, I let out a large exhale and said, without thinking, "I love us."

Brody froze and looked at me in shock. My eyes widened as I realized the intensity of the proclamation I'd just made to him. I'd known I loved him for nearly a month, but we'd only been together for two, and I sure as hell didn't want to be the first one to say *the L-word*. But my big, fat mouth blurted it out like it was just a normal Tuesday!

As I realized he wasn't responding, I awkwardly tried to get up off the floor and think of a quick excuse to get him the hell out of my room. I silently chastised myself for scaring the crap out of him, and therefore ruining the best thing that had ever happened to me. He grabbed my wrist before I stood all the way up, and unceremoniously pulled me down on top of him. He sweetly said, "I love us, too."

The only emotion I remember feeling in that moment, was giddiness. I felt giddy! As my heart pounded happily beneath my chest, Brody appeared to be contemplating something. He had just reciprocated my feelings, so I couldn't fathom what he could have been pondering.

As he tucked my hair behind my ears, he spoke softly, "Actually, I think I love *us* more than I love—you—does that make any sense at all?"

It made perfect sense. Brody and I fit together so naturally, in a way I didn't even know was possible. It was like I'd evolved into a better version of myself I didn't even know was inside of me. I'd never met anyone I could laugh with so often and be my complete self with. It was Brody who brought that out in me. And I did the same for him. It was *us*. Ever since the day we first declared our love, we never said, *I love you*, we always said, *I love us*. I was so excited in our early days of love. I'd been transformed into a hormonal teenybopper. I was like a 14-year-old girl talking with my bestie about my first kiss with a boy, squealing the last word of my sentences because I couldn't contain my excitement. *Good Lord, I was a goner.*

Brody and I made it five years and still said, *I love us*. It was strange to others, and probably sounded a bit egocentric, like we were announcing to the world that we thought we were this hot power-couple everyone should strive to be, but that couldn't be further from the truth. We were simply in our own bubble, playing by our own set of rules. It was *us*, and it was perfect.

"It's *us*, Fin! I love *us!*" Brody repeats, snapping me out of my memories of a much sweeter time. Our love was so much easier when we were in college.

As I look into Brody's deep, navy-blue eyes, my heart begins to break and bleed inside of me. Brody and I had so many dreams together. But they were made when life was so much easier. I squeeze my eyes closed, trying to erase the beauty of his face and our love. Tears quickly escape down my cheeks. As I attempt to turn my head away from his grasp, he grips my face harder between his two hands, forcing me to face him. I feel his warm, soothing breath on my lips, panting with desperation. My lips betray me and part ever so slightly; with that, he attacks my lips with fervor.

Brody works passionately on my firmly closed mouth—begging, pleading for a return in gesture. I sniff back a gasp of air through my nose as his hands drop from my face and wrap around my lower back, binding my arms against my sides.

I have to hold out, I can't give in. I can't show him I still love *us*. He won't want me when he learns the truth. This is the best way— the easiest way.

But deep down, I know that this is Brody. I love him. I don't just love him; I love *us*, which means more in our weird, remote world. He's kissing me and begging me to stay. *Why the hell am I doing this to us?* I want to give in and let us be us, in whatever capacity that may be. *No, no!* I've thought this through; I can't let him sway my decision. He might not love us if he learns the truth, and I can't stomach that. In the long run, he will be much happier without me. He'll find someone new and she can receive his passion—*his kiss*.

And Brody doesn't just kiss, he *commands*. The man has a technique I have never experienced, and I have kissed my fair share of guys in my wild college-girl phase. His hands touch my cheek in a way that makes me feel cherished and consumed with one simple touch. I swear I've come close to orgasm multiple times from Brody's incredible kisses.

I contemplate one last kiss, one last goodbye to take in, so I'll never forget—*us*.

I slowly turn my palms out to feel the sides of his denim clad thighs, so muscular and familiar. I move my head slightly, giving him better purchase of my mouth. As my lips begin to move against his, Brody's hands move up my back, releasing my arms to roam. His right hand reaches the nape of my neck and threads through my long brown hair. He gently pulls my hair tightly, just how I like. I know exactly what he's doing.

This is a reminder kiss. This is Brody's way of making me remember how great we are and how hot we make each other.

My reserve breaks as I feel gentle flutters in my lower belly. I'm past the point of no return. I can't help it. I'm needy for Brody. I always have been. His total package is completely irresistible.

Brody has gorgeously thick and curly brown hair. He cuts it short, leaving just enough length for me to comb my fingers through. His navy-blue eyes contrast perfectly with his creamy complexion. Brody has an unexplainable look about him that feels comfortable and undeniably sexy. It's not only his appearance that draws me to him, it's the comfort I feel with him. Brody feels like home to me. When we made love for the first time, he commanded my body with the deeply intense emotions he had for me—it was simply profound.

It's amazing how hot finding your soulmate can be; to find someone who truly gets you, and encourages you to be yourself by just being who he is. When the physical aspect of our relationship took off, it was everything I could do to keep my hands off of him for any extended period of time. We were always touching each other and being complete goofs at the same time. It worked for us.

Some of our hottest sex sessions escalated when we talked in ridiculously stupid voices, laughing obnoxiously. We relentlessly made fun of each other and called each other out on the stupid stuff we did. It made us feel connected and safe. We understood each other. We'd be laughing at something ridiculous, then with one glance, we were all over each other. It was as though our happiness and sex drive combined tracks on a railway and ignited us into a frenzy.

I feel that frenzy now as my fingertips brush the side of his bare skin peeking out of his soft, fitted t-shirt. The skin-to-skin contact zaps Brody into action. He quickly breaks away from my lips and pulls my t-shirt up over my head.

As he begins to come back for my lips he pauses and looks down at my breasts. I'm ashamed to see I am wearing his favorite bra—a sheer, teal brassiere that covers nothing. My nipples harden under his hot perusal.

I don't know why I wore this set of underwear today. I wasn't planning on things escalating like this, but my mind betrayed me when I got dressed for work that morning.

A frustrated grumble rises out of Brody's chest and he commands my mouth again. His hands run down the backs of my thighs and lift me up. My legs wrap around his waist in response. Brody is strong. He's not what I would call bulky but he's tall, lean, and toned.

I'm nearly six-foot tall myself, so he towers a good four inches over me, giving him the caper for these types of antics. I'm not blessed with the willowy runway model frame. I have an hourglass figure with a plump behind that Brody seems compelled to touch every time I pass him in a room. It doesn't matter if we are in a crowded restaurant or at a family function. He has no shame. He doesn't like being referred to as an Ass Man though; he says my eyes are his favorite feature. My eyes are blue, according to my driver's license. The blue is so light that my surroundings are reflected in them and they change from blue to grey, and sometimes green. I'm told aqua is the best color description.

Brody's one free hand begins roaming over the top of my full B-cup breast as he carries me down the hallway into our bedroom.

He lays me down on our familiar and comfortable bed we've slept in together for the past three years. I feel an ache in my heart, knowing I'll never be back in this bed. I thoughtfully watch him as he undresses me—and then himself. He kisses me tenderly up my leg. When he reaches my belly with his lips, I close my eyes and will the pain in my heart to stop. *Not there, don't kiss me there.*

I quickly roll him onto his back and take control of the situation. I don't want to have that conversation, so before he sees the pain in my eyes, I connect our bodies and we begin moving together in perfect synch.

Brody strokes my hips and thighs, and my hands wrap into my hair as I ride him into a state of oblivion. Brody loves me on top. *This is a good farewell position. He deserves this—it's the least I can give him.*

As if sensing something in my demeanor, he sits up. While still inside me, he places his ear against my chest. His hands caress my back while we continue gyrating against each other. I'm desperate to focus on our bodies and not what this means. He pulls back to look into my eyes and I quickly look away.

"Look at me, baby. I need to see us," he says, in a raspy, aroused voice.

My eyes instantly crash into his and we stare deeply at each other until our bodies can't hold out any longer. I cry out loudly and Brody kisses me passionately, swallowing the pleasure coming out of my mouth. As we come crashing back down together, he pulls me down on top of him and turns us on our sides, tucking me into him.

When my body settles back down, I can't stop the tears from pouring out of my eyes. We didn't use protection and it doesn't even matter. We haven't used protection for nearly two years...and it doesn't freaking matter. Sex with Brody is always incredible, but the sick, doomful feeling afterward is more than I can bare. It is utterly painful to feel so incredibly amazing one minute, and be slammed with crippling depression the next. I can't give *us* what we want. My body is broken. Barren. *Us* is broken.

This is why I have to leave.

How can I force Brody to be stuck with someone like me? Someone who can't give him all he deserves in life? Am I expected to get over the idea of never being able to see a tiny, pink, cuddly bundle of *us?* As narcissistic as it might sound, not making a mini-us is not what I signed up for. I'm in love with *us* and loved the idea of seeing a tiny person who had a little bit of me and a little bit of Brody.

And what if Brody decides he doesn't want me? How can I possibly live with the horror of being dumped for not being able to do the most important thing a woman's body is designed to do? I am in baby-making hell with a man who gets me so innately well that it physically hurts to continue being with him. Brody and I have had an incredible connection for years, but this feels like the *one thing* that he just might not be okay with.

We never married, so there's no fuss to it other than moving my stuff. Brody and I never wanted to get married. We were so confident and content with *us*, that marriage seemed irrelevant. To us, it felt like an archaic thing to do to make other people happy. We knew we had something above the normalcies of other couples; getting married and putting rings on our fingers would sully the commitment we had to each other.

Our families were uneasy with our arrangement. We both come from traditional families in the Midwest. *Get married, have children— blah, blah, blah.* We assured them we were just as committed to each other as any legally-married couple—even more so. They gave up arguing about it so fervently, but still made small, snide comments here and there.

When we finally revealed we were going to try to have a baby, they were excited. I think they thought if we had a baby together, we'd eventually decide marriage would make things easier as parents because then we'd all have the same last name. And maybe they were right, but Brody and I didn't feel that way, so we were just taking things in stride. I guess they'll all have a good laugh when they hear about this.

I turn over and hug Brody as tightly as I can. Burying my face in the crook of his neck, I breathe in his musky bar-soap scent.

"That wasn't goodbye," he softly whispers into my hair.

I pull away and look into his eyes, and I finally see it. *Defeat.*

"It was, Brody," I whisper back, my eyes welling with tears.

"I don't understand. Why won't you at least tell me where you're going?" he croaks as his eyes become red around the edges.

I rub the pad of my thumb along his cheekbone and thread my fingers into his hair. "You don't have to understand. Just know it's what I need."

I kiss him one last time with all the passion I can muster and he doesn't even respond. His lips form a hard line against mine and I know it's over.

I creep out of the bed and quickly grab my clothes before dashing into the bathroom to clean up. I'm quiet as I step out, nervous Brody will be waiting for me in the hallway, attempting to prevent me from leaving. When he's nowhere to be seen, I tiptoe down the hallway then step outside into a blast of unseasonably warm air. The last days of summer don't appear to be leaving Kansas anytime soon.

As I settle into the driver's seat and glance at the suitcases in the backseat, I breathe a sigh of relief. He's letting me go; this is what I want. To reassure myself, I reach into my purse and pull out my boarding pass, passport, and the British pounds I had transferred from American dollars. I glance at the time on my boarding pass and check the clock on my dash.

In four more hours, I'll be on a plane to London. Well, New York first for a layover, then on to London. I take one last look at the place Brody and I have called home for three years. This place used to be full of happy, magical memories—now it stares back at me with an ominous threat of disappointment. I can't stay here and live this life. Not like this. London can be my new lover.

CHAPTER TWO

My best friend Leslie gave me the courage and motivation to make the big trip over the pond. Leslie lives in London, in a flat with two or three other roommates. I can never keep track because it always changes.

I'm sure Leslie fits right in in a big city like London. When we were kids, I always felt she was destined for something bigger than our small hometown of Marshall, Missouri, just two hours east of Kansas City. Leslie lived on a big family-run dairy farm and I lived on a small acreage, so we had a lot in common growing up around livestock and farmers. Together, we would get into all sorts of mischief, but we always managed to stay out of any serious trouble. Sometimes we would hang out in my parents' cozy basement watching movies, eating junk food, and being ridiculous together. I remember one time Leslie and I laughed for hours about how her nostrils flared when she talked. She had the wackiest sense of humor and I was always along for the ride.

In fact, I never laughed as hard with anybody as I did with Leslie, until I met Brody. That was one of the first things I told Leslie about the new, hot guy I met at college. I said, "Leslie! You won't believe it! He's one of us!"

She understood exactly what I meant and was genuinely happy for me. So a few weeks ago, when I called her crying on the phone about another negative pregnancy test, it was her idea I come to London to get away for a while. She didn't want me to break up with Brody, she just wanted me to relax and get my mind off things for a bit. But Leslie didn't know all the facts. I was too scared to tell her I'd actually broken it off with him and planned to move to London indefinitely. I'd be damned if I let her change my mind. If there wasn't room for me to live with her, I'd find a place on my own. She did it; so could I.

Leslie moved overseas on her own and was a legitimate, proper, freelance designer. She is currently working on a big project for *Nikon* designing a camera-bag line. She's been living in London for a year now, traveling back and forth between London and China, teaching factory workers how to create her designs. What an amazing life. She was seeing the world and thriving, she wasn't worried about babies and fertility cycles.

I'm full of nervous energy as I board my international flight at JFK. I find my seat and recline. There's no turning back now. I try to convince myself I've ruined Brody's sweet and perfect idea of me, and even if I wanted to go back, I'm certain he wouldn't accept me.

I can do this, I can be alone. I can be without us. Brody is the love of my life, I know and feel it in my core, but I will find happiness elsewhere. Maybe even with another guy. At the very least, I can find someone to have a fling with—someone to take my mind off *us*. Maybe I'll find a nice Brit to settle down with who doesn't want children. But first I want to be wild and crazy and forget about getting serious with anyone for quite some time. London can be my lover.

I've dreamed about living in London ever since I developed a huge love for British Chick-Lit novels. I never used to be a big reader but my sister, Cadence, handed me a book and said, "Just try it, you'll like it! When you finish, you can watch *Debra Messing* in the movie version!"

I immediately asked her the name of the movie, because I was an avid movie watcher and I loved *Debra Messing*. When she said *Wedding Date*, I couldn't believe it. One of my all-time favorites! *How could the book ever compare?*

It didn't compare. Not at all. It was a thousand times better! It gave me so many more details about a story I'd already loved. The book was called *Asking for Trouble* by *Elizabeth Young*. Her funny, quirky British sense of humor and writing style resonated so strongly with me, I immediately purchased paperbacks of all of her novels. They were all wonderfully fun and romantic; they are now my most prized possessions in my book collection. They are books I frequently reread; it's like visiting an old friend each and every time. I know I love a book if the moment I read the final page, I quickly turn back to reread all my favorite parts again—which are almost always the romantic scenes. My novels are an escape for me when I need it most; a great distraction to ease the fear of being barren; and so began—and continues—my love affair with British Chick-Lit. For years, I've been reading *Elizabeth Young, Sophie Kinsella, Jill Mansell, Marianne Keyes,* and *Samantha Young*. It's all so interesting to me, being from the boring old United States. Anything across the ocean is a place I have never seen. The UK is a country with fascinating history and vibrant fictional characters I instantly fell in love with. What better place to run and hide from a life I'm scared to live?

I can be a new version of *us* with my pal, Leslie. She doesn't want to make a baby with me! Thank God, because that'd be an awkward conversation to have.

I know she can show me a world that will make me forget all about babies, marriage, and *us*.

CHAPTER THREE

I feel butterflies in my belly as the plane finally hits the tarmac at Heathrow Airport. I nervously tuck away *A Girl's Best Friend*, my favorite *Elizabeth Young* book, into my oversized carry-on. The flight has been long and arduous, with a three-hour layover in New York. I have been traveling for fourteen hours and I feel like crap. I want to brush my teeth and change my clothes. But holy shitballs, I'm in London!

Just hearing the different dialects of British accents on the plane gets my blood pumping. The flight attendant is giving her final directions to us in this gorgeously posh tone that simply melts in my ears like butter.

As I make my way over to luggage claim, I turn my phone on and a slew of texts begin popping up on the screen.

Leslie: What gate are you at?

Mom: Did you land safely?

Cadence: George and I picked up your car. I can't believe you are flying to London right now! Call me and tell me everything when you get settled.

The last one from my sister makes me smile. I'm really going to miss her. She's married with three daughters and a baby boy on the way. She's totally living vicariously through my adventures. She is settled down now with kids; she knows this is an adventure she could never take.

Not to mention, she is one-hundred percent *Team Brody*. Regardless, she's happy for this big change in my life and feels a large sense of pride being the one to spark my love affair with London by giving me that book so many years ago.

My heart drops in my chest as I see Brody's name pop up.

Brody: Not that I give a fuck, but I hope you're alive and shit. I have no clue where you are or who you are staying with. Hope you're having a ball. I'm in hell.

A lump forms in my throat as his obvious pain and anger exudes through the text. That does not sound like my Brody. Yes, he is candid and curses frequently, but he's always treated me like a prized possession he would forever love, adore, and protect. *I did this to him. I brought out this ugliness.*

I quickly open Leslie's message and text her my gate number. After what feels like an hour, my four gigantic luggage bags come rolling toward me. I struggle to grab them, then realize I'll need a cart to carry everything. After some finagling, I'm able to roll all four pieces of luggage at once with my carry-on purse draped over my shoulder. *I'm a big girl, I can handle these without a man.*

I slowly and carefully make my way outside, searching the crowds of people, taxis, and buses, looking for my long-lost childhood friend. I swear the people here even *look* different. They all have a different style of dress than I'm used to seeing in the Midwest. In Kansas, you see plenty of people with cute style and clothes, but it's not common. The majority stick to classic jeans and tee shirts.

Here, nearly everyone is wearing different colored pants, leggings, or slacks. Even the facial features here seem different than the people I grew up around.

A loud, obnoxiously long whistle overpowers the noise of the traffic and people. I scrunch my brow and look over to see a flamboyantly dressed redhead sauntering toward me.

"Leeeeez?" I screech, hardly able to contain my excitement. "Leslie!" I finish loudly before I let go of my four suitcase handles. She bounds into my arms animatedly. I am so freaking excited I lift her off the ground.

"Fin-fin!" she declares fondly, smiling at me with tears in her eyes. "You made it, you lil' world-traveling-whipper-snapper, you!"

"Me? A world traveler? Schyeah, right—Miss Big-important-worldly-designer, dashing between London and China to big important meetings," I goad, in a smug British accent.

"'Tis true! 'Tis I! I am designer extraordinaire, straight outta' London, love! Why, I oughta…aww, crap! I think I went Australian there. My roommates would kill me if they heard me talking like this!" she laughs at her own feeble attempt at a British accent.

As I take Leslie in, I see that while her clothes, style, and hair have changed dramatically, she is still the same old Lez that used to pedal her bicycle down the gravel roads to meet me in my sister's car. I was easily a good year younger than legal driving age, so I'd make her ride her bike; I was too chicken to cross the highway and pick her up. We never did anything particularly bad. We would stuff her bike in the trunk—make a failed attempt to close it—then cruise the gravel roads with the windows down and our hair blowing wildly. We just savored in the rebellious act of driving without a license.

Back then, our clothes were pretty standard: jeans, flip-flops, and t-shirts. But standing before me now is a stylish, artistic creator.

Leslie's thick, auburn hair is chopped short into a bob with short pixie bangs. The Brits call it fringe. She's wearing loud-print leggings with multi-colored swirls all over and a deco-checkered sleeveless blouse with a collar. It doesn't match by any standard, but she's rocking it with ferocity.

I feel rather plain in comparison in my black leggings with my loose, cream-colored, off-the-shoulder top.

"Oooo, God, that's ceeeeuuute!" Leslie drawls as she gently touches the Native American-style statement necklace around my neck.

"Oh, thanks," I reply, my hands touching the same place, "I bought it at the airport in Kansas before I left. I knew I'd need to dress this outfit up somehow with you coming to pick me up at the airport. I feel like Humpty Dumpty next to you right now!" I tease, while playfully smacking her ass.

"Don't be ridiculous, Fin!" she states, with a huge wave of her hand. "You couldn't be more fabulous if you were carrying *eight* suitcases. Speaking of which, what the bloody hell are you thinking, bringing four ginormous suitcases for a one-week vacay? I told you to pack light!"

Her eyes bore into me with indignation. I know she's not really pissed, but I also know I need to explain my plan for staying here longer. I decide to avoid the question; telling her at the airport is not ideal.

"What can I say? I have to have options to keep up with you!" she laughs and reaches around me to drag two of the suitcases behind me.

"This is so unlike you, we'll have to take a cab now, you know. We can't bring this kind of luggage on the tube. We'll get mugged, raped, and sold into international sex-trafficking," Leslie says, deadpan.

My eyes bug out of my head as I take in what she just said.

"Kidding, Fin! Good Lord, you better brush up on your British dry sense of humor or you'll never have any fun here!" she laughs as we make our way over to the next available cab driver waiting at the curb.

The driver stows away three suitcases in the trunk and sets one in the passenger seat next to him. Before I know it, Leslie and I are out on the streets of London in a proper, historical-looking, black, English taxicab.

CHAPTER FOUR

After I get over the initial odd feeling of the driver being on the opposite side of the car, and driving on the wrong side of the road, I take in the scenery. I'm even checking out the small pubs located on every other block, daydreaming about what those people do for a living that allows them to be in an old English pub at this time of day. It's all enthralling to me! Sure, there are bars in Kansas and Missouri, but they are more extravagant here—more excitement, more hustle and bustle—there's an overall charm to everything.

Leslie turns to me in the back of the cab, "So, my neighborhood isn't real posh or exciting, but it's cool. It's located in Brixton, which I suppose you would say is like South Central London. It's a pretty diverse community. There are definitely some sketchy areas but the house we live in is cool. It's a large Victorian townhouse. It reminds me of the brownstones you'd see in, like, Brooklyn or something—but older."

I have no idea what brownstones in Brooklyn look like, but I can imagine. I've watched *Sex in the City* for Christ's sake! I'm not a complete loser. Or should I be saying wanker now? Tosser?

"We could never afford it on our own," Leslie continues, "One of my flatmate's parents own it, but they never stay there anymore. They live in some villa in Italy almost year-round. Occasionally, they come back to the city, but thankfully, they get a hotel so there's enough room for all of us!"

I'm floored. Villas in Italy, Victorian mansions in South London, I have no clue where the hell we're going; I don't care. It's new and different. *Exactly what I need.*

The cab driver pulls up alongside a big beautiful brick house on the corner of a busy narrow street. Traffic whizzes by as I take in the Rapunzel-type tower on the corner of the block. "Is this it?" I ask Leslie as we clamor out of the cab.

"You bet yer ass it is! We're gonna rock this house the whole week you're here! Get ready, sista', I'm getting you naked-wasted tonight!"

Leslie heads to the back of the cab to grab the rest of the bags while I take in the grandeur of the home. Even the door handle looks exquisite. I can't help but notice the entry; the door is painted a bright purple with ivy vines growing all around it onto the beautifully shaded patio area to the right. The rest of the house looks old and important—maybe a little ominous, but this vibrant-colored door practically screams, *WELCOME!*

I help Leslie with my bags as we make our way up the steps into the old house. It even smells British. What the hell does British smell like? Like I have any freaking clue. Jesus, I better not say that crap out loud or people will think I'm mentally deranged. But if I had to guess what *British* smells like, I'd bet it would smell just like this house—old and interesting.

I glance up the staircase just past the foyer, and see what looks like three stories. The main floor consists of a tiny living room on the left with a neat fireplace. Connected off of that room is a long hallway leading toward the back of the house. There's a big dining room to the right of the foyer, with ten plush chairs seated all around it. The greatness of the large expensive-looking table is a bit lost amongst the clutter scattered all over it. Covering almost every surface are various books, papers, pens, CDs, and mail, right next to two large packing boxes with packing peanuts spilling out of them.

"Gotta run to the loo. Sit tight, Fin!" Leslie squeals as she dashes past me to the hallway off of the living room.

"Fucking magazines. Magazines! Can you fucking believe it?"

A tall and uncomfortably skinny redhead ambles into the dining room from the kitchen and looks at me pointedly.

"The cow sends me boxes of fucking magazines when all I bloody-well want are my damn clothes!" he barks and gives a box a shove across the table.

"Are you talking to me?" I ask, confused.

"I don't see anyone else in the room, so yeah, you'll do." He roughly tousles his bright orange hair. I'd never seen hair like his. It was cut short along the sides and sat high on top of his head with a natural frizz, seeming to help it stay afloat without product. Almost like...a rooster. I conceal my smirk as a side-by-side comparison pops into my head.

"Oi, Frank! Stop being a bitch to Finley!" Leslie shouts, coming into the foyer again. "For Christ's Sake, she just got off an incredibly long flight. She doesn't give a fuck about your ex-whore's magazines."

"He *was* a whore. The bitch. Probably wiped his arse with these magazines, too. I can't imagine what it cost to post these bastards. What a bloody waste of money. Money that could have been better spent on booze! Speaking of which, who's up for a drink? I've about had it with this bollocks all day," Frank looks at us expectantly with his hands on his tiny hips.

"Sounds great to me," Leslie replies. "You're up for it, aren't ya, Fin? Only way to beat the jet-lag!"

"Um, okay!" I answer, excitedly. Was this really how my first night in London was going to be? Leslie's roommate, Frank, seems a bit out there, but I have a feeling I'm going to have a lot of laughs with him.

"Fuck your kit and let's roll," Frank says, coming out of the dining room and into the foyer. "Christ! How many bloody bags did you pack? Are you moving the fuck in?"

"I know!" Leslie adds, "I still can't get over it, Fin. What the hell? It's so unlike you. I've traveled with you before and you've never even needed to check a bag!"

I know I can't let this question slide again, so I decide to get it over with and see what happens. "Actually, yeah," I say.

"Yeah, what?" Leslie replies, curiously.

"I'd like to…um…move the fuck in, if that's okay." I query, self-consciously, adjusting my necklace and looking around the house to see if any of the other roommates are around to hear this request.

"Blimey," Frank replies, "I thought you were trying to get up the duff with your bloke back in Chicago."

"Chicago? What?" I question.

"FRANK!" Leslie bites, "Shut the fuck up, you loud cow! Sorry, Fin. Frank knows everything…he's my gay boyfriend. We talk—it can't be helped."

"What does he know, exactly?" I question, still totally confused.

"He knows you're trying to have a baby with Brody," she says, glaring at Frank. "Back in Kansas—*not* Chicago, Frank!" Leslie finishes, looking at me, apologetically.

It's like a cold bucket of ice-water has been dumped on top of my head. I'm not prepared for this conversation. I knew I'd have to have it eventually, but I feel sideswiped. I'm still trying to decipher the odd jumble of words that came out of Frank's mouth. Even if he is Leslie's gay boyfriend, a little word of warning would have been nice.

Frank interrupts my shock and says the only logical thing anyone could in this moment, "This seems like a chat best had over drinkies. Come along, loves!"

Frank grabs my arm and pulls me out the door and down the concrete steps. I follow them around the corner to a pub just two blocks away. The pub is dark, with old wood and hunter-green carpet all over. It smells like musty beers have been spilled on it for centuries and never been properly cleaned.

"Zoey, three pints of our usual, please. On the double—we got trouble over here!" Frank states, grandly, to the room full of strangers. No one appears to give a damn what this lanky redhead is talking about, so I don't lose much thought over it.

"Spill, Fin. Now!" Leslie demands, looking at me with earnest eyes.

"Christ, Lezzie, at least let the bitch have a drink first," Frank replies.

Frank is like no one I've met before. His sharp tongue and dry wit are extremely appealing to me. I find people with no filters refreshing; I always know where I stand with them. I think I've heard him say more curse words than anything else so far, and I've only known him five minutes, but he has a way about him that makes me feel comfortable.

The waitress brings over three large glasses of dark beer; I grab mine, nervously. *Do I like dark beer?* I'm not sure I've ever tried it.

I sip it gingerly at first and immediately taste the chocolaty-coffee richness to it. *Yes. Yes, I like dark beer.* I take three large gulps, wincing slightly at the lack of coldness as it travels down my throat. Beer in America is ice cold, which makes it so easy to drink. Maybe dark beer isn't served cold?

Leslie and Frank's eyes are glaring at me with anticipation.

I can already feel the effects of the beer in my head, so I know it's time to spill.

"I've left Brody," I say, before losing my nerve.

"What. The. Fuck?" Leslie asks, slowly, her auburn bob framing her face closely as her jaw drops.

"It's over, we're done. I'm done. I can't do *us* anymore," I reply, taking three more large gulps of my beer as Leslie and Frank gape at me.

"Wait, you dumped him, or he dumped you?" she asks.

"I don't know why that matters," I reply.

"Just fucking tell me, Fin!" she throws at me, angrily.

"I ended it, okay? But it doesn't matter; it would have ended anyway. There's no point in continuing things," I say, as I take another gulp.

Frank clears his throat, "So you're moving here—to London? You want to live with us?"

"I mean, yeah, if you'll have me. Er, I mean, if there's room. But if not, I'll find another place if I need to."

"What about your job, Fin? You love your job." Leslie asks, with a hint of alarm in her voice.

"Well, technically, I'm just taking a leave of absence right now. I have four weeks of paid vacation banked, and then I'm on my own. Val's company has a sister agency here I'd like to get involved with, but I don't really know anything about them yet, and I really don't want to bring it up to her. She'll probably lose it on me."

I work as a creative director's assistant for an advertising agency. They do TV, radio, web, and literary marketing for high-profile clients. I was in the process of being primed to be creative director and take over for my boss, Val, so she can fill the shoes of the vice president who is looking to retire in a few years. It's an incredible opportunity, and I've networked my ass off to get it.

"Well, no shit she'll lose it on you, Finley! You're blowing the opportunity of a lifetime by leaving! You're lucky she hasn't fired you!" Leslie spits out.

"Val's fine with it. She understands." I reply back, "She hired two interns for the fall and is demoting one of the sales executives to help her out for the next couple months. She said I can do copy editing and write from here, and she'll pay me as a freelancer until I come back." I pause, "She still thinks I'm coming back. I didn't have the balls to tell her I'm not."

Frank looks to Leslie, gauging her reaction. Leslie's face is covered in disappointment. *I can't stand it.*

"You're a fool for leaving that job, Finley," she says, shaking her head.

"I can't fucking stay there, Lez!" I croak, a sudden onset of tears filling my eyes. "I can't be *that girl* for him anymore. It was killing me, Leslie! *Killing me.* I can't walk around anywhere back in Kansas or Missouri without a baby. You know what it's like there!"

Leslie makes a motion like she's going to interrupt me, but I don't give her the chance, "I can't give him what he wants, and he won't want me without it. I know him, Lez, I know *us*. It won't be *us* anymore without creating a mini-us. We are wrecked. I refuse to sit there waiting for Brody to wise up and leave me for somebody more…more…fertile." I turn my face away and wipe the tears off my cheeks, quickly. "It was only a matter of time, I'm just beating him to the punch. I'm not sure it's even the life I want anyway."

"Fuck me. Don't let the old blokes at the bar see you blubbering, they'll get all awkward and call a doctor. Brits don't like emotions," Frank says, trying to lighten the mood.

I look back at Leslie and see her eyes welling with mine.

"Fucking Americans," Frank whispers under his breath, looking at the two of us.

Leslie sniffs and reaches her hand across the table, "I wish I knew how to fix this, Fin. I'm ill-equipped!" she says, her voice trembling. "This is a lot different from our problems as kids."

"I know," I groan, tipping back the remainder of my beer, savoring the feeling of numbness crawling over my skin.

"Well, fuck it! The flat is yours if you want it," says Frank. "You'll get the shit room because it's all that's bloody left. But who knows, you're American, you might think it's quaint."

I look at Frank, wide-eyed, as realization sets in that he's offering a room to me, indefinitely. *Thank God.* This is a huge load off my mind, knowing I at least have an affordable place to live while I figure my damn life out.

Suddenly Frank stands up on his seat and shouts, "Zoey, another round! We've got a new roommate to toast."

"Get the fuck off that chair er I'll rip your bloody arse off there myself!" Zoey shouts back at him with a thick dialect I barely understand. Maybe Irish?

"My arse hasn't bled in years, you wench!" Frank shouts back.

Leslie and I burst into a fit of laughter at Frank's announcement in a room full of strangers.

I think I'm going to like it here. I think I'm going to like it a lot.

***

**A Broken Us is available at all major retailers.
For Order Links, visit:**
www.amydawsauthor.com

Made in the USA
Monee, IL
18 December 2022

22485009R00184